SHATTERED BLISS

SHATTERED SURVIVAL BOOK ONE

S.J. BRADEN

Abby Moss Publishing

I dedicate this book to my son Bradley. He has endured all my crazy endeavors on the road to finding my true passion — writing.

Love,
Mom

ACKNOWLEDGMENTS

To Donna B. McNicol, the best fairy godmother ever, and a superb coach.

To Elizabeth Mackey for the cover design.

CHAPTER 1

*I*T WAS A DARK AND stormy night. No, not the weather. Inside her mind and her heart, a fatal storm brewed. The realization that she was at a breaking point. She had to go, had to end the misery, the fear, the conflict, the daily battles, the feeling of never being enough, or doing enough, of being inconsequential. The feeling of being the piece of detritus you can't seem to part with, but you constantly move from place to place because it is always in the way.

Abby was tired and weary, at the point of giving up. She wished she could fade away. But try as she might, it simply hadn't happened. She didn't know where to go, or how to go, she only knew she must. So Abby began doing what she did best, making a list and researching.

The first list was of all the medications available in the house. If they were combined, would they be enough to end the suffering, the pain of a broken heart, the feeling of hopelessness, and a life without promise or hope? First the list, including dosages and quantities. Then the research including interactions and fatal dosages. It quickly became clear that she didn't have enough in the house for that particular option. It was a bad solution, to boot.

As far as Abby could see, her only remaining possibility was to get in the tired old truck and go as far as it would take her. She made a new list — what she had to have and what couldn't be left behind. The must-haves included the dog and a week's worth of clothes for each of the two southern seasons. The pictures depicting the happy times with her precious son Kendall. Personal care items such as a brush and comb, toothbrush and paste, fingernail clippers. Just the basics. Important papers like birth certificates, social security cards, and medical records. The laptop. Must have the laptop. And the power converter. A pillow and blanket.

That summed up the absolute necessities. Yes, it would all fit in the truck with enough room to sleep. Now to plan the escape.

She couldn't tell her son. He had a wife, a job, a life, and didn't need Mom hanging around, but he would never have allowed her to live in her truck. She couldn't even tell her own mother. Mom would argue that she couldn't do this and insist Abby come to her place. She already felt as though she was a failure at life. Bunking with your mother at the age of fifty — who did that?

Two women in one small apartment with two female dogs would be entirely too much estrogen under one roof. No, this had to be the one thing Abby did on her own. Her own choices, decisions, and actions had put her in this situation, and she alone had to suffer the consequences. Okay, the decisions were made, and she was feeling a measure of relief knowing what she must do, but she never had felt such deep desolation.

Damn it, I give my all to my family. How is it I have such poor judgment and am such a loser that I have two failed marriages? Well, one thing's for certain. I know it isn't all my fault things fell apart, but I also know I apparently have terrible judgment. Why else would I find myself in this place again? No More Men is my new mantra. Not because all men are bad, but because I obviously can't tell the difference between the good ones and the bad ones.

Once daylight broke, the raging storm subsided, sliding into a dark, gray, drizzly kind of mood. The mood that came with the realization it was all over, all but the logistics. It was two weeks until payday. She had two weeks to explore her options, prepare, finalize her plans, and make it happen. She had a plan and would work it. But as her husband began to stir in the bed, she made her most fatal error to date.

"Wha's wrong?" he asked, his voice still groggy from too little sleep, his words slurred from too much alcohol still in his system.

"I can't do this anymore." She blurted in frustration.

"What do ya mean? Can't do what?" he asked confused.

"This. Us. Our life."

"What more do you want from me? I've provided a nice house for you. I go to work. I bring home a paycheck. Is there never enough for you?" he yelled. He was sitting up in the bed now, and his body swayed from time to time. Abby hoped he wouldn't try to get out of bed. She knew this routine. When he tried to walk his knees would turn to jello from the mix of Tequila, vodka, and beer he'd sat up all night drinking.

"I need two weeks. In two weeks I'll be gone. I won't be here to make any demands on you. You can do whatever you want," she responded. She loathed that his words no matter how untrue scorched her and burned her very soul.

She didn't take into account the fact that he only had been asleep a couple of hours and was still quite drunk before she spoke her words. Until he pointed to the AK-47 leaning against the wall next to the head of the bed and told her ever so calmly, "I know how to put you out of your misery." The cold, shocking chill ran up her spine. She was certain she misunderstood or hadn't heard him correctly.

As she left the room, trying to get some distance from him, she was sure he didn't mean it. And although only a few hours ago she had contemplated ending her life, if it wasn't her choice to do so or God's choice, she for sure wasn't going to let it be his choice. Not if she could help it. *Work the plan*, she told herself.

She muttered a silent prayer as she walked through what was once her dream home and now felt like her prison. A pray that he would pass out again and forget the conversation had ever happened. She needed that prayer answered now more than any she had ever prayed.

~

She had not always been broken. Starting life as the adored first child, the first grandchild, first niece, Abby had a joyful personality and was precocious, as well. During her school years, she was always part of the in-crowd. People told her she was pretty, although she didn't see it in the mirror; she was considered popular, but always felt as though she was a little on the outside edge. Not really low self-esteem or anything, just a little shy.

No one else ever thought of her as shy. She seemed to be every-one's best friend. The one person they all felt comfortable telling their deepest secrets, fears, and desires — because they knew it would go no further, and she never judged. College was the same way.

Then she married. Married poorly, she supposed, when it hadn't worked out after a few years. By then, she was a mom. And for her, that was her identity. Mom. A divorcée, she became a devoted mom and career woman. She was respected and liked everywhere she went, whatever she was involved in. Despite feeling shy, others perceived her as outgoing, joyful, and full of life.

Three years into her relationship with Cole, everything changed. She became clinically depressed, a bundle of anxious nerves. Every-one, from her family to her doctors, to Abby herself, thought it was her job. Cole and her doctors convinced her it was best to get out of the rat race and focus on taking care of herself and the family. But she didn't get any better. In fact, as time wore on, day after day, month after month, year after year, she became more withdrawn, almost a recluse. She seldom left home.

Cole facilitated her reclusive tendencies to the point that he even did the grocery shopping. At the time, she didn't think of him as controlling; she thought he was trying to be helpful. When her truck broke down, he told her he would get it fixed. However, five years later, it still sat in the driveway. He told her it wasn't safe to drive, so she was even more trapped. Abby told herself repeatedly it was okay; there really wasn't anything she wanted or needed to do. All of which furthered her reclusive state. Abby didn't comprehend that her years-long lack of an operating vehicle was just another way Cole controlled her.

The therapist told her it was time to break free from who she had been, who she was now, and decide who she wanted to be. She was free to become whoever she wanted to be. As Abby thought about the prospect, she was overwhelmed and devastated. It was too hard and she was too tired to start over and recreate herself. So she stopped the therapy sessions and withdrew even more.

Then the gaslighting increased, although at the time she didn't know what it was called, or that it even had a name. She knew nothing about gaslighting, indeed had never heard of it before. But Cole sure knew about it and was a master.

Following her diagnosis of PTSD, Cole used every opportunity to belittle and confuse Abby. He told her she didn't remember correctly, that things she thought she remembered clearly had not happened, and that she had said things she could not recall. Cole also reminded her of conversations that Abby was certain had never occurred. It worked well for Cole.

Abby was pretty well convinced that her memory had suffered from all the medications the doctors had prescribed following her PTSD diagnosis. She knew she pretty much had been a zombie that first year — from all the prescriptions. Luckily, over the next several years, doctors adjusted her medications until she almost could function.

Her decision to leave made, she felt stronger, had more energy. Abby spent the morning hours of every day going through the house, packing up important papers, mementos, and anything small enough to go into large plastic totes that she maybe could sell to raise some cash. She cleaned out and reorganized the detached garage. She was there working when Cole came home from early and caught her.

"What are you doing out here?" he asked, startling her.

"Cole, I wasn't expecting you, what are you doing home?"

"I called you like I do every day at lunchtime. You didn't answer. I waited five minutes and called again and you still didn't answer. I thought something was wrong. So I came home. What are you doing out here?"

"Oh, I'm sorry. I guess I left my phone in the house when I went in for a cold drink. I can't believe it's lunchtime. Where does the time go? Kendall called and said he was going to come home as soon as his classes are finished for the semester and he wants to go through all his stuff stored out here. You know, all the stuff from his childhood and high school. It'll be nice to get it out of here, won't it? Then there might even be room in the garage to park the cars," she explained hoping he would believe her and just go back to work. "I thought I would do a little each day separating his boxes so he can go through them. I'm sorry you had to drive all this way and use up your lunch hour. Do you want me to fix you something to take back with you?"

"No, I'm not going back to work. You scared me to death, I can't focus on work now," he said popping the top on a can a beer that magically appeared out of nowhere.

She knew that was the real reason he wasn't going back to work. He already had the beer in his hand when he walked into the garage and found her.

Abby also knew if Cole actually started taking an interest in what she was doing, it would be all over with, and not in a good way. So she made sure to play it down and not mention her actions any more than was necessary. With any luck, he would continue to be lazy about the house and not start looking for tools in the shed. She made lists on the computer, now password-protected, after she had caught him snooping through her Facebook chats and emails.

Abby worked hard at minding her p's and q's. She hoped if she could manage to avoid any confrontations, if everything appeared as normal as possible, she would fare much better. If Cole's suspicions were aroused, it could be disastrous for her. She never forgot the threat he made about putting her out of her misery, and for those two weeks, she never slept when he was home. She truly didn't trust him any longer; she couldn't afford the luxury. Fortunately, it seemed he thought her outburst and talk of leaving to be simply "one of her hissy fits." For him to continue thinking that way, while frustrating and demeaning, was definitely in her best interest.

She found an apartment she could afford, scheduled a rental truck, rented a storage building, and arranged for some family members to come for a visit. Those visitors, unbeknown to Cole, would be the muscle to get her stuff moved. Gone from her mind was the initial plan of leaving with nothing. She would be damned before she left all her worldly possessions for him to trash, burn, or shoot up with one of his many guns. And she knew that's what he would do — she had seen Cole do it before. He hated Christmas, so one year he found all the garlands and Christmas lights and burned them in his Saturday evening bonfire. When she discovered they were missing, and asked if he knew where they were, she was shocked by his carefree response.

"I thought they were garage and I threw them into the fire. By the time I realized what it was it was too late. Sorry, Baby."

Another time he decided he hated a painting she'd bought for the living room. She came home from the grocery store to find him and his buddies using it for target practice in the backyard. Before they were done, laughing and drinking and shooting at the piece of original artwork, there was nothing left of the canvas and frame was a pile of splinters. The perfect site for a new bonfire.

Since the doctors told her she could no longer work, her only income now was the long-term disability insurance that paid a fraction of her previous salary. She knew she would have to be frugal, and she wasn't at all convinced she could survive on the small monthly payments. But she was determined to try. She began training her body to eat only once a day and to eat less. She mentally prepared herself to need only the essentials. Abby realized her freedom was her most important possession, and she needed little else.

Still, in her mind, she thought Cole's drinking was the root of their problems, and if she actually left, maybe it would be the impetus he needed to stop. Abby never thought the separation was going to be final. She frankly thought this was a hiccup, and in the end, everything would all work out. Otherwise, she would have been too frightened to take the necessary steps, and wouldn't have been strong enough to walk away.

She found a small apartment in town, in a secure gated community so she would feel safe, yet wasn't too far away, in case things did work out with Cole. Two days before her family was to arrive, Cole surprised her.

"Abby, I've been thinking. I want a divorce," he said as casually as if he was saying he wanted ice cream for dessert.

Oh praise God, Abby thought.

"Okay, Cole. I understand and I don't blame you," she said taking the blame for their now unhappy home.

He seemed a little taken aback, probably from the lack of emotion his declaration had evoked and the resolution with which she responded.

"Damn! I thought you'd put up a fuss about it. Cry. Beg me not to go. Ask me how you're supposed to take care of yourself."

"Cole, I've always said I don't want to be with someone who doesn't want to be with me. We've talked about this every time our friends go through breakups and divorces. I don't understand begging someone not to leave. If they want to go, they should go. And you should too."

"Oh, I'm not going anywhere. This is my home. I want a divorce and I want you out of here. You can't afford to stay here anyway."

"You're right. I can't afford it. I'll have to find someplace else to go," she said thoughtfully.

Even in a depressed state, Abby swore she wouldn't be reduced to begging for affection. She absolutely couldn't imagine living with someone who you knew wished you weren't there. Apparently, Cole had not believed her.

"I'll make arrangements to go as soon as the family leaves from their visit next week."

"Great! Time to celebrate," he said as he poured an iced tea sized glass of tequila.

She never let him know that she had been planning to move in two days, with or without his declaration. The bonus for her was since he had made his wishes known, she would be able to take with her half the property and everything that had been hers before the marriage. She would have what she needed to set up a household and possibly have some things she could sell to raise some much-needed cash. She altered her rental truck reservation, feeling he wouldn't be overly suspicious over her few preparations if he even noticed.

After dinner the following evening, Cole seemed more relaxed than he'd been in months. She decided it was safe to talk to him and tell him plans.

"The family is all coming in later tonight. Tomorrow they're going to help me move out." She expected him to be pleased about it. She did not expect what happened next.

"What? How in the hell did you work that all out so fast? Where are you going?" he asked with a raised voice and clearly agitated.

"You said you wanted a divorce. I have help while they're here I won't have after they go home. I just thought it made sense," she said trying to reason with him and remind him it was his idea that she should go. With that, he seemed to remember he should try to appear to be indifferent. Abby watched as, almost visibly, he threw a mental switch.

"No problem. You're right it makes perfect sense. Let's go through the house and plan what you're taking with you. I'll be here to help and to send you off. Bon Voyage or whatever."

That shook her up, as her plan always had been to escape while he was at work. Abby collected her nerves, told herself she could do this and pressed forward. She arranged for plenty of family members to be there, to hopefully prevent anything too dastardly from happening. She also made sure she had a few friends who would *not* be there, who knew what was going to transpire, in case something untoward were to happen.

The next morning, she and Kendall said they were going to get breakfast for everyone. When they returned they arrived at the house with a small rental truck for things going to her new apartment and a large truck for her half of their life together that was headed to storage. Her mom, her son Kendall, and her nephew Rusty were all there to help her get it done as quickly as possible. It was a beautiful day, not too hot, but sunny. Abby knew, had Cole not been there, she would've loved this day. It would've been a beautiful day to start a new life.

WHOA! It IS a beautiful day to start a new life. My family, my real family, is here by my side. We are making this happen. My heart has been forged like steel. I am not hurting, I am a survivor, I can do this, I will do this, and it is a beautiful day! She reminded herself.

But Cole was there, and his son, daughter-in-law, and their three small children were all there, and that contributed to it being a supertense day. Besides having to work around that many people in the way, Abby was dismayed to see that Cole was throwing all kinds of stuff into the truck she didn't want. She didn't want the gifts he had given her. She mostly only wanted what was hers before their marriage, gifts from her other family members, and all the things from Kendall's childhood. Because of all the extra people, and the small children underfoot, it took all day to load the trucks instead of the few hours she had anticipated.

By the time they pulled the trucks out in the late afternoon, Abby was an emotional wreck. Unwanted tears were pouring down her face, her hands were shaking, and she had chest pains. She was determined to make it through this, and she certainly didn't want Cole to see the tears. She just desperately wanted to leave that place. It was supposed to have been their dream home, and she had loved the house, but now she thought of it as the *Nightmare Palace*.

~

Abby had no way of knowing that the simple act of her leaving so soon after he asked for a divorce, and so quickly showing up with two moving trucks, would be the catalyst for literally years of anger from Cole. She thought she gave him what he wanted. After all, it was what he *said* he wanted.

She now was aware that there were devious people and manipulative people — then there was her husband. In her now semi-rehabilitated thinking, she knew he was devious with a generous dollop of manipulative thrown on top. She thought of it as topping on an ice cream sundae for the demented. Add to that a drinking problem, and well, that was the proverbial cherry on top.

Cole would've been a psychological study's cream-of-the-crop specimen if you actually could dissect a working brain. However, his complex personality seemed to fool even the most noted authorities on personality disorders. He had them in spades. She was his victim, his project, his entertainment. She was his experiment.

The week after she moved out, she realized somehow, when she was at her breaking point, when he had almost succeeded in obliterating her soul, that she had found the strength to run, and run hard. But the harder and farther she ran, the longer his grasp seemed to be. She couldn't sleep, waking with a racing heart and a definite flight response, and she constantly was looking over her shoulder. Abby wasn't only running from him physically. The way his devious manipulation had interwoven itself through her psyche was like the tentacles of an octopus and simply couldn't be outrun. At least not yet, but she was proud of herself for physically getting out — and getting out alive.

Exactly at this moment of realization and frustration, she received a text message from Lizzy that sent chills down her spine.

"Abby, he's crazy again. Get out of town. He says he knows where you are, and it's time to teach you no one runs from him." Now haunted and hunted, with the knowledge only she possessed — he's killed before, and she believed he aimed to kill again.

She was stuck. There wasn't much she could do. Her truck wasn't running, and she didn't have the money to rent a car to leave town. So, she and her faithful, furry-white companion Prissy hunkered down for the weekend. She kept the blinds closed, and they only went outside for walks through the rear of her apartment, which couldn't be seen from any road. She jumped at every sound, and it felt like the longest weekend of her life. But she discovered binge-watching TV shows on Netflix on her computer. Who knew?

She spent the weekend in her pajamas, eating pretzels, drinking diet sodas, and watching television shows she had missed while she was married to Cole. All of their TV time had been watching the History Channel or the Discovery Channel. She spent the entire weekend watching six seasons of the latest medical drama.

On Monday, once she was able to confirm Cole was at work, she slept. Not a peaceful sleep, but some sleep nevertheless, knowing as long as he was at work, she was probably safe.

CHAPTER 2

*I*F ABBY THOUGHT SHE WAS *going to play him, she had another think coming.* Cole had assumed that telling her he wanted a divorce would devastate and frighten Abby to the point she would stop this silly nonsense. He expected her to whine and cry and ask what he wanted her to do, what she was supposed to do, beg him to let her stay, and promise to get off his back. Instead, she refused to answer his phone calls most of the time. Her responses to his emails were usually single-word responses.

I don't understand the change in Abby. What is going on? Threats are no longer scaring her. She seems stronger.

He decided early in their relationship that he would make sure she never felt she was strong enough to leave him. He learned if he made a targeted comment, in the right tone of voice, it would make her question herself. Sometimes, she was adamant things were not like he said they were, and that is when he would pull out his ace.

"Now Abby, you know you can't remember things. It's all the drugs you were prescribed when you were so sick."

That little trick had been working for years now. He had her convinced there were two whole years she didn't remember at all.

13

Lately, she seemed to be rejecting that story. So he was forced to find a new weapon. His newest tactic was to tell people she was doped up all the time. At one point, she was on fourteen different prescriptions for depression, anxiety, and all the physical complications that resulted from either the stress conditions or side effects from all the medications. Now, she was only on one prescription at night to help her sleep, but he would tell people not to worry about Abby because "She's doped up all the time." And he did it when and where she would overhear him. He knew it irritated her, so he used that phrase every chance he could.

It might have worked better, except unknown to Cole, she had stopped taking the sleep medication, as well. So when he would say that or use it as an excuse why she was wrong, it alerted her to the fact that a lot of things he was telling her were outright lies.

It appeared the tricky little bitch had been planning to leave all along. He knew she thought she was clever, that he wouldn't notice all the cleaning out, rearranging, and the sudden order to the garage. He knew she thought he was unaware she password-protected her computer. The truth was, he couldn't care less. Let her play out all her little scenarios; let her spin her wheels. It wouldn't change anything. She would never leave him. She had no job, no money, and no future. He made sure of that. She had no friends or family in this town. She didn't even have an operating vehicle, for crying out loud. Yes, her truck would start, he felt she probably knew that, but he had told her for months it was not safe to drive.

So how in the hell did she think she was going to leave me? Where in the world did she think she would go?

He was confident in the knowledge she wouldn't go to her mom's or Kendall's. He was certain he knew her well enough to know those wouldn't be an option for her, in her mind.

For the first forty-eight hours after she was gone, he felt free and unburdened. He could do whatever he wanted, whenever he wanted. Payday hit and he suddenly had plenty of money to buy the booze he wanted to buy. But as the laundry and dishes started to pile up, as he was expected to babysit the grandkids like she always had, as he had to deal with his less-than-bright daughter-in-law and immature son, he started to get even angrier. He began drinking at the bars, not concerned with the double and triple-digit bar tabs because there was money in the bank. And then all the past-due notices started arriving in the mail because Abby wasn't there to pay the bills.

Cole was furious she left so quickly. He refused to accept she outsmarted him, called his bluff. Abby wasn't smart enough to outmaneuver him. He didn't know where she went, but he didn't care because he knew she couldn't survive on her own and would come crawling back. He was determined to make it hard for her. He still talked to her on the phone occasionally, when she would answer. But the conversation seemed to repeat each time.

"Baby, I really would like to take you out to dinner. How about steaks. I know you love steaks."

"Cole, I don't think I'm ready for that. Maybe after some time has gone by, we can be friends. But not yet."

"Okay, whatever. Did I tell you I talked to an attorney?"

"Yes, you did."

"Since we don't have children together, and you can't afford the house, he said the divorce would be simple and fast. You've already taken everything you want out of the house, right?"

"And then some," she responded remembering all the crap he kept throwing into the truck.

"If you agree we can use the same attorney. No fighting. Just plain and simple, boom. Divorced. Just like you wanted. Then, maybe we can start over. Maybe it can be better next time."

"Cole, you said you wanted a divorce. If you want to work things out, maybe we should try that before we get a divorce instead of after," she answered him logically.

"No, no. I think it's better this way. We get a divorce, and then we can start dating again. Start over fresh. Leave all the baggage behind us. Just a boy and a girl."

"I don't think it works that way. Cole, I have to go. It's time to take Prissy for her walk. We'll talk again later."

"I love you, Baby," he always ended every call, every email with the proclamation.

The call dropped.

She never tells me she loves me anymore. It's a game she's playing. But I'm smarter than that. I know she does. She has to love me. She's got nothing and no one else. I can't wait til she's hungry enough to come crawling back to me. Next time, I'll keep her on a much shorter leash.

After Abby left, Cole took off from work the whole first week. He drank and drank and drank. He drank until he passed out, and when he woke up, he drank some more. He tried contacting all his old friends from back home and discovered he no longer had phone numbers for most of them. He then called a couple of the single girls from work, cried on their shoulders, and invited them out for drinks. After several $200 to $300 bar tabs, he drank at home. When friends would drop by, he would repeat the same mantra for as long as they would listen.

"You know Abby left. She is one screwed up bitch. You know, she has some mental issues. I'm pretty sure she's off her meds, and without them, she's not even reasonable."

"I know she'll be back. Where the hell do you think she'll go? She's got no job, she's driving around in that SUV with plastic where the tailgate window should be. Bald tires. No air conditioning. I'm guessing she's living in it somewhere."

"She'll be back. I know she will. And yeah, I'll take her back. It's the right thing to do, right? I'm not gonna make it easy on her though, that's for sure. I mean if I don't teach her some kind of lesson, she'll pull this crap again and I just don't have time for that."

And then, as the level of his intoxication increased, the dialog would change.

"I don't need that crazy bitch in my life. Look at me. I can do whatever the hell I want now. She was always bitchin we didn't have money for this or money for that. But now, I've got plenty of money. I paid for the lawyer. I told him she was cheatin on me. He says I probably won't have to pay any alimony. Screw her, I don't want her back. She just better answer my phone call tomorrow. I'm tired of her not answering my phone calls. Hell, I think I'm still paying for her phone. Maybe I'll turn the son bitch off. If she won't talk to me, she won't talk to anyone. I bet she hooked up with one of the guys from that stupid online game she plays...." On and on it went.

His few friends got tired of hearing it. They got tired of the drunkenness, got tired of the moaning and complaining, and got tired of listening to him threaten her. So they stopped coming around. Forest was the only friend who still came around.

"Cole, maybe you should stop drinking for a while. You know they say alcohol makes you depressed. Maybe you'll feel better. Clean yourself up. Go out and find yourself a pretty young thing without all the issues. Be happy, man."

"Yeah, yeah, I know you're right. I'm just drinkin right now because I can. She's not here to look at me with those disapproving eyes. To go to our bedroom, *our* bedroom, do you hear me and shut the door. Ignore me. Like I'm a child. I'm tired of being treated like a child. She said I disappoint her. Can you believe that shit? And dude, it feels like I have so much more money now. I think she was hoarding money. Or spending my hard-earned dollars on that damn game she played all day."

I drink because I can because it makes the loneliness go away. Because I forget she's gone and it's like she's just gone to see her mom. She'll be back. I know she will. But this here bottle makes it seem like she hasn't been gone so long. When she comes back, I'll stop drinking. It's just to tide me over while she's gone. The inner dialog he had every day with himself, only furthered his delusions.

At times, it saddened him to think about where they were. In the beginning, they'd been a beautiful couple — the envy of many. Then that inner dialog would turn darker.

Where did it all go wrong? What is she thinking? She can't leave me and the family. Nobody leaves me. Does she really think I'm going to let her leave? I'll find her. Does she think I'm stupid? Our vows were until death do us part, and by damn, that's the only way she will ever leave me.

Two weeks after her escape, Abby received an instant message, a text message, and an email from Lizzy Grant, all within seconds of each other. Lizzy was the wife of Cole's best friend, Forest. All the messages said the same thing.

"Forest wanted me to call you because he just came from your old house. He said to let you know not to go to the house for any reason, and if it's at all possible, you need to get out of town. Forest said guns are lying around everywhere. Cole is drunk and calling you every-thing but a nice girl. He's furious, and Forest says it's not safe for you here. He says if you can't leave town, don't go outside, hide your truck if you can, keep your doors locked, and be very aware."

Abby called her new best friend.

"I understand. I can't go anywhere anyway. I think I need a starter in the truck. Prissy and I will hunker down for the weekend and binge-watch old tv shows again. I guess I'll just be a prisoner in my home whenever he isn't working. It's not a bad thing. I spend all weekend in my PJs eating junk food and watching tv I actually like. It's way better than living with Cole."

"I hear that. I don't know how you stayed there as long as you did, girl. That man is a monster. I do wish you could leave town."

"I know. I do too. But I can't. Where would I go? Kendall's at college. I can't afford to move around whenever he does. And honestly, I'm not sure this old truck would make it to the interstate if I even trusted it to drive out of town."

"Couldn't you go to your mom's?"

"Yeah, no. I love her. She means well. But the last thread of my sanity would be gone before breakfast. I'm okay. We're okay. You know, Prissy doesn't even act like she misses him. I guess she thought it was time to go too. Don't worry about me. But I do appreciate the heads up."

"Oh, Forest just said he's threatening to turn off your phone too."

"It's okay. He can't. I took my phone off his plan the day before I moved out. I don't trust him. And the sooner I cut ties with him the better. I'm doing everything I can to ensure he has no control over me anymore. Y'all have a good weekend, okay."

Meanwhile, at the family house, a new storm was brewing. Cole's son, daughter-in-law, and three children moved in with him. He absolutely couldn't face coming home to the empty house. It felt like a yawning, cavernous void without Abby there. The added benefit of having his daughter-in-law there to cook and clean seemed appealing until he found out she didn't do it the way Abby did. The only cooking she did was warming frozen food in the microwave or oven or boxed macaroni and cheese. He absolutely couldn't and wouldn't eat boxed anything. So most days, he purely drank his dinner. He told that line to everyone who would listen because he thought it was so funny.

Cole would come home from work and find the kid's breakfast and lunch dishes still on the table, toys everywhere, and laundry in various stages of being folded on every piece of furniture. It took hours of planning for him to wash his clothes for work, as he had to wait for Jenny to vacate the washer and dryer.

He had been trying to coax Abby back through emails because this past week, she had changed her cell phone number, and email was now his only method of communicating with her.

I guess you changed your phone number. So email is my only way to communicate with you now.

Baby, I know you were mad. Though I don't know what you were so mad about. But look, the family needs you. Jeremy, Jenny, and the kids moved in. This girl needs to be taught how to cook like you do. And someone needs to teach her how to clean up after these kids.

And the poor kids. They need love, discipline, attention, and guidance they aren't getting from their mother. They need you, Abby.

I don't want to do it. But the lawyer wants me to charge you with abandoning the family. That won't end well for you. So, come on back. I won't even ask where you've been.

I love you, Baby.

He checked the email constantly waiting for her to reply. He wasn't expecting the reply that he got.

Cole,

I understand that it sounds like things are pretty bad over there. What I don't understand is why you think I'd want to come back to that. Even if I did want to come back to you.

I raised my child. This is your child and his dependents. They aren't related to me. And they aren't my responsibility. Your son is grown. He has a mother and a father. Your grandchildren have parents too.

I'm sorry this lawyer is trying to get you more riled up, but there is no court anywhere that will charge me with abandoning a family that isn't mine.

Just let me know when the court date is.

That stupid bitch! Since when did Abby think clearly enough to formulate that kind of comeback? Since when did she have the nerve to stand up to me that way?

Have it your way, Abby. But if you don't come back, I'll call that disability insurance company and tell them you've been making jewelry and selling it under the table. Then you'll come crawling back when your checks stop and they threaten to charge you with fraud.

. . .

Abby waited until later in the evening to respond. She hoped he was getting as drunk as usual and would fall for his trap.

Cole, that's an outright lie and you know it. Making jewelry was part of my therapy. And if you are callous enough to report to the insurance company, the doctor who encouraged me to do it, will tell them so.

It will never work, your threats don't scare me. You said you wanted a divorce. You don't have any control over me anymore. Move on with your life.

She didn't have to wait long to know if it worked. The response was almost immediate.

You stupid bitch. Of course, it's a lie. But won't you have fun trying to prove it? They'll stop your checks while they investigate. And you'll be up shit creek. Or will your new boyfriend take care of you? Is he controlling you now? For all I know he's the one writing these emails because you're not sharp enough to think this out with all the drugs you're taking.

Just you wait. I have lots of tricks up my sleeve. You'll pay for leaving this family. Watch your back, bitch.

Abby read the email. She laughed. The biggest heartiest laugh she'd had in months, maybe years. "Gotcha!" she said aloud and took Prissy out for the nightly walk. The next email she received made her wonder. Like he had accused her, of someone else answering her emails, she thought it was likely someone else wrote this one.

. . .

Here's my final offer, Abby. If you agree to the following terms I will pay you $200 a month alimony for two years for your half of the equity in the house.

You agree to use my attorney and not contest the divorce.

You will sign a quitclaim deed for the house.

You agree that you already have half of the household contents.

You need to get your own phone plan.

You can keep your truck.

I'll be responsible for our credit cards and taxes due.

Let me know if you agree and I'll have the attorney draw up the papers.

At that moment, Abby's phone rang. For a moment her heart stopped like every time it rang. Afraid it was Cole calling. And then she would remember he didn't have her new number. She looked at the caller ID and saw it was her son, Kendall.

"Hi kiddo, how's it going?"

"Everything is fine here. I just wanted to call and check on you. Are you doing okay?"

"Yeah, I just got an email from Cole. His terms for the divorce. He offered me $200 a month for two years for my half of the house."

"That's great, Mom. That will help out."

"No, it isn't. That's $4800. There is at least $20,000 equity right now in the house. Unless Jenny, Jeremy, and the kids have totally destroyed it already. I made those house payments every month. It took my whole insurance check, but I made them. It's not fair or good at all. And besides that, I bet you a dollar to doughnuts he doesn't pay the alimony either."

"Mom, just a few weeks ago you were willing to walk out of that house with Prissy and the clothes on your back. You just wanted out. You're out, you're safe. I think you should let it go."

"Yeah, you're right. He also offered to let me keep my truck. Like he's being so freaking generous. I bought and paid for that truck. He didn't. But. I don't have a choice. I can't afford to hire an attorney and fight this."

"Take the deal, Mom. Close this chapter and start your new story."

"How did I end up with such a wise son?" she asked, fighting the tears of pride that always threatened when Kendall was being Kendall.

"I had a great mom, blame it on her." And they both laughed because everyone knew everything was the parent's fault.

After the phone call with Kendall, Abby replied to Cole's email.

Agreed

It was a holiday weekend, and Cole had been trying to sort out in his mind his course of action. He had to find the right button to push to bring her back. He was finding it impossible to concentrate, with two small children running through the house as if they were on fire, screeching at the top of their lungs, while their mother sat watching television and ignoring them. Jeremy still was sleeping, despite it being one o'clock in the afternoon.

"Would everyone please shut the hell up. I can't hear myself think! Jenny, would it be too much to ask you to get off your ass and take care of your kids?" Cole yelled.

Those same children, in addition to the baby, immediately started crying — all three of them — causing Jenny to yell back.

"They're fine. They're purely being kids. What do you want me to do, lock them in a closet? Anyway, they weren't crying until you started screaming." All the ruckus brought Jeremy out to see what was happening.

Cole told Jeremy, "I need you to drive me somewhere. I probably shouldn't be driving since I've been drinking waiting for you to get up, and there's somewhere I need to go."

"Yeah, where's that?" Jeremy was unaffected and unwilling to accept blame for his father's drinking that morning. He knew full well, even if he had gotten out of bed before his father, Cole would've been drinking by noon.

"I need you to take me to Abby's. I know you know where she's living now. I don't have her phone number anymore. She changed her damn number so I can't call her. I think it's high time I remind her what her vows are and let her know her behavior is unacceptable, and it's time for her to come home."

Jeremy fixed himself a cup of coffee and called Jenny to fix him something to eat, before responding. "Dad, you should think about this. I don't think it's such a good idea."

"I don't remember asking what you thought. Just drive me!" Cole blustered and popped the top of another beer.

"No, Dad, I won't. Not today. And probably not any day. This is a really bad idea. Besides, you said you would watch the kids for Jenny and me so we could go fishing. But I want to go for a run first." Jeremy eyed his wife fixing his breakfast.

Cole's thoughts and temper escalated at Mach speed. *Why, this ungrateful brat. After all, I have done for him, he dares to tell me no about anything? I guess he needs a lesson, too.*

He took a swing at his only living son and missed, but his second attempt connected square in Jeremy's gut. The only problem was, Jeremy's gut was rock hard, and when Cole's punch hit, it sent Cole, who was inebriated and unsteady, reeling backward and made Jeremy as mad as a hornet. That was the last thing Cole remembered.

Then, all hell broke loose. Jeremy unleashed a rapid-fire fury of punches that all connected. Cole hit the hard floor and passed out. Jenny tried to wake him up, while Jeremy went outside to walk off his anger. After about ten minutes, Jeremy returned to the house and finding his father still crumpled on the kitchen floor, tried to revive him. When he couldn't rouse the older man, he panicked and called 911. When the ambulance arrived, he explained what had happened, his father was drunk, he threw a punch, and Jeremy instinctively hit back. His father hit the floor, and they called 911.

The paramedics were not fooled. By the time they arrived, Cole had started bruising. Both sides of his face were bruised, his neck was bruised, and his hands and arms were bruised. They called the sheriff's department, and Jeremy was arrested for assault of a household member.

When Cole awoke three days later in the hospital, his face black and blue and bruises on his neck, he was told that Jeremy assaulted him, he was unconscious, an ambulance was called, and Jeremy was in jail. The hospital doctor also explained to Cole that his test results showed he had suffered a stroke in the last thirty days, and they needed him to stay for further tests. Cole reacted in true Cole fashion where his children were concerned. He checked himself out of the hospital against medical advice, hired an attorney, and bailed his son out of jail. Telling everyone who would listen it was all his fault, he had gotten in an argument with his son over "something stupid," and passed out and hit the floor. The overworked small-town sheriff's department dropped all charges.

As soon as they got home, the two men drank a beer. Of course, it didn't stop there for Cole. By that evening, it was all Abby's fault. Everything was Abby's fault. If Abby was still there, the kids wouldn't be living there, he wouldn't have asked Jeremy to drive him to Abby's, there wouldn't have been a fight, a hospital stay, or an arrest. Now he had to pay for an attorney for Jeremy, hospital bills, and suffer the resulting time off work. Tomorrow, he was going to find her and bring her ass back where it belonged, no matter what it took.

Til death do us part.

CHAPTER 3

THE LONGER ABBY WAS AWAY from Cole, the better she felt. She got out and walked, she visited with her new neighbors, and she began to take an interest in the community around her. Every day, she got up, got dressed, and walked Prissy. It was a new experience for her since they had always had a yard. But she found the fresh air, the exercise, and the periods of being out in the sun made a huge difference in how she felt. She went to the pool, cautious not to stay too long and get sunburned. But in the small adult-only community, very few people used the pool, and she usually had it all to herself. She discovered it was peaceful and helped her to relax, as well as allowing her to get some exercise. She generally swam some laps and then reclined on a float, enjoying the peaceful surroundings and the sunshine.

Abby began making friends, although tentatively at first, and always without ever letting anyone know what she had been through. If she were asked, she simply would say she was going through a divorce. Prissy began making friends, too. Both the human and canine varieties. Abby began to blossom in her new community and was liked by everyone.

Her natural caretaker instincts served her well, and she became the go-to girl for all her neighbors' needs. That was fine with Abby; it gave her a purpose. She was well aware of her inherent need to take care of others, usually to the detriment of herself. She helped with flowerbeds, ran errands, determined where to hang pictures, and whenever someone needed an extra pair of hands or opinion on where to place furniture, or a recommendation of who to call for this or that, she was there to help. And unlike her previous situation, she found her neighbors were appreciative of her efforts to help them, much more than Cole had ever been.

She didn't have the money to have much social life, and she certainly didn't want anything to do with men at this point, but she did develop cordial relations with her neighbors. They began to plan get-togethers for holidays, community yard sales, and occasional coffee and dessert events. She hosted a *Birthday Pawty* for Prissy and all her neighborhood canine friends. They decorated the picnic area with balloons, served puppy ice cream with bone-shaped dog-friendly cakes for the pups, and she made bandannas for all the fur babies. Everyone had a great time among tangled up leashes and lots of wagging tails.

Abby also discovered she enjoyed having a reason to get dressed once or twice a month in something other than pajamas or sweats, a reason to get in the kitchen and cook, or a reason to craft little home-made gifts or decorations for her new friends. They all told her she should open a restaurant, or sell her crafts, and she would wrinkle her nose and tell them, "Then it would be work, and it wouldn't be fun anymore." The truth was, her self-confidence wasn't to the point yet where she could imagine anyone paying for her items.

While perusing local Facebook pages one day, she discovered a new shop looking for volunteers. It turned out there was a woman's shelter in town dedicated to getting abused women and children out of their current situation and into a new life. One of the ways they raised their funds was to operate a thrift shop, totally manned by volunteers.

Abby signed up. She met some wonderful ladies there, and a few became friends. It also provided her an inexpensive place to buy quality clothes. She had not had any reason to get dressed for so many years, but with some weight loss from her new exercise routine with Prissy, she found she was enjoying buying clothes again and putting together outfits. Even if she were only going to the grocery or running typical errands, she discovered she felt so much better with hair and makeup done and a cute outfit. It didn't matter that the clothes weren't new; they were new to her.

She had never thought of herself as abused. Not mentally, physically, or in any way. Abby determined in the months since her escape, though, that she had been in a toxic relationship. That was the most she would ever admit, to herself or anyone else. But Abby had a real passion for her work at this organization devoted to helping the abuse victims. It never occurred to her the possible reason for her passion was that she had suffered abuse and identified with the victims she was trying to help. She just knew it made her happy to feel she was helping in some small way, no matter how far she was removed from the situation, or the women she was helping. Through the process, though, she did learn a lot about mental and emotional abuse and started realizing that most of the problems she faced were directly the result of how Cole had treated her, and it was not okay. It was not normal. And she felt even more like a fool for having allowed it to happen.

Abby often considered how much she loved her new little life. The friends she had, the activities she was involved in, the volunteer work she did, were all her very own. They had nothing to do with Cole, and no one in her new life knew Cole or anything about him. That was her secret. She was not comfortable with anyone knowing about her past, and she kept it to herself. Abby's friends all knew she was going through a divorce, but she didn't talk about it, and they didn't ask.

Yes, she would have days where her mind reminded her she was going through a divorce and was a participant in a failed marriage. Some days Abby was frightened of her future, and some days she was sad she might go through the rest of her life by herself. But the fears and self-pity never lasted long, because she realized she was so much happier, so much more at peace than when she was a wife, a fifty-percent shareholder in a failed marriage. She made up her mind that being alone wasn't so bad. She had family, and she had friends, and that would be enough.

But each time she felt she was starting to heal, starting to put things behind her, she would get another warning message from Lizzy. It always started with "be careful," the middle part of the message would contain whatever new escapades Cole was up to or threats he was making, and the ending was always, "lay low, and is there any way you can get out of town?"

Although she felt she was getting better, she still was subject to anxiety attacks and depression. Her episodes were getting further apart and, most of the time they were less severe, but she still had nightmares, she still awoke in a cold sweat, heart racing, and a rapid, painful pounding in her chest, and her hands shaking. Most times when that would happen, it would take her hours to get back to sleep, if she even could go back to sleep.

But time heals all wounds, right? How much time? I'm so tired of feeling broken. I want to feel like myself again, I want to be myself again. Her mind processed this refrain time and time again. Her family told her it was nice to have the old Abby back, but she didn't feel like the old Abby, the strong, confident, capable woman she used to be. She did keep trying, though. She remembered all the people and family along the way who had told her, "pull yourself up," "buck up," "put your big girl panties on," and all the other cliché phrases that meant, in her opinion, "Quit your whining, girl, and get on with life. We all have problems."

Abby wanted to, had always wanted to, but when you're stuck in the mire of that kind of situation, you absolutely cannot see the way out. The proverbial forest-for-the-trees dilemma. It is always so easy for others to take what little bit they know about a person's situation and quickly see a perfect way out or the best way to overcome it. But it usually didn't work that way. Until now.

Now that she was on her own, she could see more clearly — and how bad things were.

She was beginning to realize exactly how much trauma she had endured. Abby thought she and Cole were happy until he started drinking again. But as she started to find peace, she began believing her PTSD had less to do with her work situation and more to do with her home life. She battled the effects of PTSD for years and was truly frustrated that she never seemed to get any better.

After trying medications, therapy, herbals, any remedy she could find, now that she was away from Cole, she seemed to be finding her way out of the darkness. She was smiling more and laughing more. She was determined to continue to try to break free of the hold of her past life and start a new one, free from strife, drama, and turmoil. Abby vowed she never would succumb to any type of abuse ever again. Her eyes were open now — she knew and admitted what the past years of her life had been all about. Of course, now it would be much easier to make sure she never found herself in that place again since she was firmly committed to her mantra: *No More Men!*

Through Facebook, she got in touch with some old friends from college and high school. Abby had started her account when her son went off to college because she found it was the best way to keep up with what was going on in his world. After, she found it was a great way to reconnect with people who had been important to her in a better time, but because of distance, work, and family, had simply drifted apart and lost touch. She decided Facebook was a great invention, and she was thankful young people had it to keep in touch, wherever their new lives took them.

During one conversation while catching up with an old friend, she discovered the friend now lived in Ecuador.

"How and why in the world did you end up in Ecuador?" Abby asked.

"My husband and I owned a restaurant. He's diabetic and he got sick. He had neuropathy so bad, he couldn't walk anymore. He finally had to take disability. There was no way I could care for him and run the business by myself. We had two teenage daughters. So I started searching for someplace a family of four could survive on his disability and had great medical care. I found it in Ecuador, so we moved here three years ago."

"Wow, that's fascinating. I admit I don't know much about South America and nothing at all about Ecuador...except the Galapagos. I'm so sorry for your troubles and his failing health. How is he doing now?"

"Ha, he's walking again. He's healthier than he's ever been. The weather, the abundance of inexpensive fresh fruits and veggies year run, the lack of processed foods have all helped. And walking is a way of life here. He walks all over town now."

"Isn't it hot there?" Abby asked. She loathed the heat and humidity of the south, but she always imagined South America would be even hotter.

"No, it's like perpetual spring."

"Hold on, I'm on my way, what time's dinner?" Abby teased.

Abby's main problem was a lack of funds — that and the seeming decline in Cole's sanity. If she could avoid his messages, she could be much happier. If she could move away from this place and go where Cole couldn't find her, she would feel more secure. Additionally, she felt her sanity and well-being would profit. But it was the lack of funds that hampered just picking up and moving somewhere. Abby talked to her doctors, and they felt she was not well enough to return to regular work yet. She still suffered many physical effects of PTSD, and those were going to take a while to heal if they ever would.

Abby started wondering why, exactly, she felt better. Was it simply being away from Cole? Was it learning about and recognizing the meaning of *gaslighting* and that she was a victim of this syndrome, and now she could begin trying to counter that thinking? Was it the people she was around, a more active lifestyle, a more involved life-style? She decided, however, that the most important part of the equation was getting away from Cole, followed closely by the friendship of the people who were now an almost daily part of her life. She enjoyed talking with them, even hearing their problems and complaints, because they were so different from her own. Sometimes they seemed much worse, other times they seemed silly to her, but she was able to recognize that to the person affected, they were a big deal.

She lost weight and started taking even more of an interest in her appearance and her clothes than she had in a long while. She never thought of herself as beautiful, but at least she started to feel cute again. She began wearing makeup, dressing casually, but better, and wearing jewelry she hadn't worn in years. And with that, came the return of her sense of humor, the joking and kidding, and being silly.

The realization she was happy was profound. Yes, her life sometimes was limited. At first, Abby made a conscious effort to avoid places where she might run into Cole. After a while, it was unconscious, but it was her practice. So it became a normal part of life, instead of something she had to dwell on. Subconsciously, she most always was in an alert state, planning her days around his work schedule, literally watching over her shoulder. Nevertheless, she truly was becoming a happy person from the inside out. In many ways, she just wanted to kick up her heels, sing, and dance a little jig.

CHAPTER 4

COLE WAS HIS MOM'S FAVORITE. He was the youngest and always would be her baby. Therefore, no matter what he did, she would defend him to anyone, anytime, anywhere. Abby had tried telling her mother-in-law that Cole was in danger. Danger from his drinking. It was getting worse, she said and told her mother-in-law she was fearful for Cole's health, his job, and their marriage.

Alice Grey was a beautiful woman. She was finely petite, was always perfectly coiffed, and she loved her clothes almost as much as her shoes — and her shoes followed closely behind her jewelry. She always presented herself in a coordinated fashion, generally in high heels, even with ironed jeans.

Alice was in her seventies, yet could run circles around her grown grandchildren and even found it easy to keep up with the great-grandchildren. Most of the time, she exhibited more energy than their parents. Alice was super high energy, as physically fit as a woman half her age, and didn't let anything slow her down or stop her from doing what she wanted.

She was active with the church, community, and her family. Alice also had a collection of friends, and in her retirement, needed a calendar to keep track of her full schedule. Her youngest son was the one thing that could cause her to cancel a social commitment. All Cole had to do was call. She didn't butt into her children's lives, but if they asked for advice, she gave it. Otherwise, she kept her opinions to herself.

She was no-nonsense and fairly philosophical in her thinking. For her age, Alice was pretty open-minded, and her grandchildren thought she was cool — they could talk to her about anything. She, of course, was always on their side. When her children or her grandchildren found themselves in a tight spot because of bad choices, she would say that either it wasn't their fault, or that we all make mistakes and everything would be okay.

Cole called his mother after Abby left. Since he needed Alice to be as mad at Abby as he was, he knew he had to embellish the truth a bit. Fortunately, he had been telling her things about Abby for quite some time, sort of half-truths about her condition and even downright lies about her actions, which would make this thread of the story seem all the more plausible.

Alice's phone rang. It was Cole, her baby.

"Well, hello Son. How are you?" He could hear her smile through the phone line.

"I'm not good Mom. Abby left." Cole insinuated as much grief as he could into his voice.

"Where did she go? To see her mom or Kendall?" Alice was not alarmed. Abby had visited family from time to time, and it always devastated Cole. He didn't like to be alone, or left behind, even if she was going somewhere he didn't want to go. Alice knew in her heart that Cole was the weakest of her sons and couldn't survive on his own.

"No. She pulled in two moving trucks, loaded out half the house, and left. It's over," he said, feigning mock shock.

"Cole, what in the world happened? What did you do? Did you have a fight?" Alice knew something wasn't right. This was the last thing she expected. Every time the couple had a spat, Cole would call his mother and say, "Are you behind me, Mom?" When he got to that point she knew he was drinking. She constantly told Abby the way to deal with it was to get in the car and go somewhere. To a bookstore, to McDonald's, wherever, to chill for a while before returning.

As recently as last month, Cole had called her. He began with the familiar refrain, "Will you support me if I divorce Abby?" Come to find out, the girl had driven down to the corner to cool off after dealing with his three-day bender. Cole went ballistic. Abby returned while they were on the phone as Alice was telling Cole she had done the very same thing with his daddy. Alice thought the situation was diffused, but maybe not.

"I didn't do anything Mom. She just snapped. I have no idea what came over her, where she's gone, or how she thinks she's going to live."

"I knew she wasn't doing well," Alice said softly. "She's seemed more and more withdrawn lately, but I never thought she would leave." She remembered Abby pleading for help and telling her things were bad. She had not worried, because she thought Cole and Abby were so steadfast. While they had problems from time to time, they always seemed to work things out.

"I'm pretty sure she was seeing someone else," Cole said. "It's the only thing that makes any sense. I honestly can't believe she left the kids, the grandkids, and me. She hasn't called you, has she?" Cole was beginning to feel the anger bubbling up inside. If this call were to sway her permanently to his side, he knew he had to keep it under control and not let his mom hear his anger.

"No, she hasn't. I can't believe she walked away like that. It sure doesn't sound like the Abby we knew and loved. Is she still taking her medications?"

She knew Abby had issues with depression and anxiety. Hell, didn't everyone these days? From others in the family who wrestled with mental issues, Alice knew how different someone could be without their medication — how they could be a totally different personality altogether. She also knew, when people went back on their meds, things usually got better and worked out.

"I'm pretty sure she has been. But she stayed confused all the time. Recently, she accused the kids and me of stealing her prescription medications. I told her she had taken them and simply didn't remember, but she was convinced she had not. Abby was adamant that someone stole them. She's flipped out." Hearing this, Alice became increasingly sympathetic as the call progressed.

"I am so sorry to hear that. You know she promised your daddy, on his deathbed, she would take care of you. She's been so helpful and supportive of me since he died. I thought she was doing better. Until the last couple of months. Then when I talked to her, she seemed more distant, withdrawn, and strained. I should have picked up something was wrong." Alice was sincerely concerned for him. She knew Cole didn't do well on his own, and this was going to be a very trying time for her sweet, sensitive, son. He needed someone to keep him rooted and grounded.

"Hell, I lived with her. She was leaving the house less often and was interested in even less. But I didn't realize she had grown so distant, either. I have no idea what is going through her head, but I know Jeremy, Jenny, and the girls are devastated. They feel she abandoned them. They say she didn't tell them anything about her plans. All of a sudden, one day she was here, and the next she was gone. It's ripping my heart out. I don't know how I'm supposed to live without her or what I'm supposed to do." Cole began to sound more choked up.

"Cole, I assume you've tried talking to her." As always, Alice was the voice of reason. She still wasn't convinced Abby's move was permanent, but she was beginning to see this was going to drive her son deeper into the bottle. For that, she would never be able to forgive Abby.

"Of course, I call her fifteen to twenty times a day. But she doesn't answer my calls. I email her but she doesn't respond to them." Cole was almost whining.

"That doesn't sound like our Abby. What are you going to do next?" Alice knew the best way to help her son was to keep him focused on a task.

"I'm going to talk to an attorney. I'm going to file for divorce. Since I don't know what she's doing, or what her plan is, I have to protect my bank accounts, the house, and anything else she might be planning to attack. I need to get the jump on this. If she finds her mind somewhere and comes back, we can deal with it then, but for now, I don't know who she might be involved with, or who might be calling the shots."

Alice could hear he was getting pretty wound up.

"I'm afraid in her current state of mind she could be coerced into doing things she might not ordinarily do. You know she was on the computer all the time, and she had a lot of friends on there. Whatever that stupid Facebook thing is. There are so many stories about online predators, and she was so screwed up in the head. I have to protect myself if someone got to her."

Cole knew if his mother thought Abby might put him in some kind of peril, she would become his mama bear, and Abby would be doomed. If Abby were to contact Alice now, she wouldn't give Abby the time of day. Or as Alice liked to say, she wouldn't pee on her if she were on fire.

"Okay, son, you know I'm behind you 100 percent. If there is anything I can do to help, let me know."

"Could you notify the rest of the family? I want to call Bruce, but can you call everyone else? After the loss of Dustin and Dad, I can't keep making these depressing calls. I don't know what I've done that's so bad that I keep losing all the important people in my life. I don't know how much more I'm supposed to take. I can't keep talking about this. It hurts so much." He broke down in tears and sobs because he knew that would seal Abby's fate with his mother.

"Of course, dear. I'll call you tomorrow and see how things are going. Keep your chin up. You're going to be fine. I'll come down in a week or two, and we can spend some time together. Or if you want to come here and relax, you know my door is always open."

Alice Grey had been married to an alcoholic. It was the better part of thirty years before he began his recovery. She had tried to tell Abby that it would get better one day. She counseled that Abby should try and stay out of Cole's way — not make the situation worse. And she had believed Abby would stick by her son, no matter what. Alice thought she had impressed upon the girl that, in their family, marriage was forever. For better or worse. She knew living with an alcoholic fell into the "worse" category, but she kept telling Abby that when Cole was ready, he would stop. Then, it would be better. But she knew more than anyone that Cole wouldn't stop until he decided to. Nothing anyone said to him would matter or make any difference.

She hated that things had gone south because she liked the girl. They all did. Her late husband had adored Abby. He had told their son on multiple occasions that Abby was the best thing ever to happen to him, and that he shouldn't screw it up. Before he died, he believed that they had made it through the worst of times and even made Abby promise to take care of Cole. He knew his death was going to affect Cole in a bad way and wanted Abby's assurance she would be there for him when it happened. Abby had promised with tear-filled eyes.

Alice knew Abby was as attached to her husband as he was to her — it was a true father-daughter relationship. She couldn't have imagined what was so bad for Abby to break that promise. Alice also couldn't imagine Abby would walk away from Jeremy's children. She adored them so much — as if they were her flesh and blood.

Cole must have been right. The girl was seriously mentally ill, or maybe she had become involved with a con artist among those online friends of hers. Well, if this was the case, they were all better off without her. Cole was right to do whatever he needed to do to protect himself. Alice hoped whatever attorney he went to would be able to encourage him to change bank accounts and to protect all his other financial matters so Abby couldn't access them. She didn't think Abby would do something like that, but none of this sounded like the Abby she knew. Cole might be right; there may be someone else involved.

Alice made the phone calls, to tell the rest of the family what poor Cole, Jeremy, Jenny, and their girls were going through. Everyone was shocked. They all liked Abby and couldn't imagine how things had gone so wrong. Everyone agreed that this seemed sudden and out of left field.

Cole got off the phone, knowing he had done the job well. The more his mom retold the story, the madder she would get. Especially with all the questions that people were bound to ask because he knew everyone was going to be more shocked than he was. She had given him a warning, but he never believed Abby actually would leave.

He started thinking he should have taken care of her the day she told him she was leaving — muted her permanently. He should have made sure she wouldn't be out talking to others about their relationship and spreading lies about him. Cole was surprised she hadn't contacted the family already. Which gave even more credence to her being shacked up with someone else. But he knew she wouldn't be able to stay away forever. Sooner or later, she would get in touch with the rest of the family, even if she never contacted him again.

Before going to bed that night, he decided to buy himself a little more insurance that she wouldn't expose him as the monster in her mind. He sent her an email that read, "I have talked to the family. You are dead to them now. Don't try to contact them." He knew that would devastate her and possibly silence her forever. He had to think about what he was going to tell his brother, Bruce. He would call him tomorrow.

CHAPTER 5

*W*ELL, IT WAS A DAY of reckoning for Abby. Her mom was coming to town. This would be the first visit AC (after Cole). It wasn't because Anne Albright didn't want to come, indeed had tried to come on many occasions, or because she wasn't worried about Abby. Her oldest daughter made it clear that she wanted space before the family descended upon her with what was certain to be a game of twenty questions, followed by each person's opinion of what went wrong and how things should have been handled. Then the Testosterone Factory, as Anne called the men in the family, would make all kinds of promises, saying what they would like to do to Cole. The entire family knew, though, that none of this would ever come to pass. While the boys talked big, they were all Southern gentlemen, the way Anne had taught them to be.

Abby and Anne talked on the phone almost daily, sometimes multiple times a day. Anne was a worrier. She also secretly was rejoicing that her sweet girl had finally had the strength to walk away from the monster. She never had liked Cole, and though she never said anything, to Abby at least, she always had her suspicions that Cole was her daughter's primary problem. She understood Abby

40

wanted, and probably in all honesty needed, time to heal before all the questions and opinions from the tight-knit family came raining down on her. They were quite an opinionated bunch. But she didn't have to like that she wasn't able to pull Abby back into the fold, yet.

Anne was pleased to know that her once-reclusive daughter was beginning to make a life for herself and was making friends with real people, not only those people she had friended online. At times, she felt like she had lost her daughter into cyberspace and was elated Abby was resurfacing in the real world. Mostly, Anne was excited to get to see Abby and to lay a mother's eyes upon her, to reassure herself Abby was indeed on the mend and back among the living.

She kept reminding herself to curb her enthusiasm a little bit and to avoid overwhelming her still-skittish daughter and to enjoy her visit. Anne had bought housewarming gifts and was packed and ready to head out. One call to Abby, to let her know she would be there in about four hours, a nice stack of CDs for the road trip, and she was on her way.

Abby was in a state of panic. The apartment was clean, and the food for the weekend prepared, as much as could be prepared ahead. But her mom was coming. Despite them talking on the phone every day, Abby was a bundle of nerves. She wondered why all daughters felt this way when their mother or mother-in-law was coming to visit. She realized her biggest fear was not that her mom would criticize her new haircut, judge the size of her apartment, or its neatness, or even her food selections. What worried her was how she was going to entertain her mom for a full weekend, keeping her busy enough so the subject of her soon-to-be ex-husband wouldn't come up. They already had talked the situation to death. Her mom already knew all Abby was willing to tell her, and Abby didn't want to rehash the whole thing over again on this visit. She didn't want *him* among them this weekend.

Suddenly, she had an idea. *All my new neighbor friends have said they want to meet mom, so why didn't I think to plan something?* Well, she had four hours. Surely she could put something together, and maybe the cast of characters who had become her new friends could keep her mom off the subject of Cole, at least for an afternoon. She was ready in a dressy white T-shirt, a new pair of sandals, and a pair of paisley Capri's she knew her mom more likely would approve than her normal denim or khaki shorts. Her hair and makeup were done, so she grabbed her keys, put a leash on Prissy, and headed out into the neighborhood to see if she could make something happen.

Her merry band of friends, as she called them, all lived within walking distance, and she stopped by each of their apartments to invite them for coffee and dessert the next afternoon. Since she had not planned for this, it would mean a trip to the grocery store, some baking, polishing of silver, and maybe making a flower arrangement with clippings from the community flower garden. That should do to keep both her and Mom busy for the morning, and she was certain that even after her friends left later in the afternoon, if Mom wasn't worn out, she would at least have a whole cast of people to talk about, other than *him*.

Abby was eternally thankful for all her neighbor friends every day, for so many reasons. But never more than today. Linda, Laurie, Diana, Wendy, Carolyn, Judy, and Suzanne all said they were available and would love to come. It was going to be fun, they all knew each other, and although some were closer friends than others, it was sure to be a lively event. She never dreamed they all would be available at two o'clock on a Saturday afternoon. So now her biggest problem was how she would fit them all into her tiny apartment.

Luckily, she was also friendly with the apartment manager, so she dropped by the office and asked if it would be possible to use the clubhouse the following afternoon. As luck would have it, it was available, no problem, and it would only cost her a piece of the dessert. Abby was so excited for her mom to meet all her new friends that she forgot to be nervous. She never thought to stop and think about what the conversation would be among the eight women.

Anne loved the small complex where Abby decided to hang her hat for the time being. She still hoped she would be able to convince her daughter to move back home to Roanoke, but for now, this place would do. She understood it would be easier on Abby to be here until the legalities of the divorce were completed.

It was a nice gated community with beautiful landscaping and only fifty apartments that looked like little English cottages. It suited Abby. The complex offered a swimming pool, a walking trail, a community flower garden, and a vegetable garden that all the residents helped tend. There was even a small fenced-in dog park, so the neighbor dogs could visit and play.

As soon as Anne pulled into Abby's driveway, the door opened, and Abby came bounding out. Prissy, however, flew past her and made it to Anne first. Anne smiled, reached down to pet the little furball, and cooed greetings to her before reaching for Abby. Anne grabbed her daughter in a fierce hug.

"Abby, you look great! I can't remember when you looked this good. The haircut looks great on you, and I can tell you've been out walking — you have a little color. I do hope you're remembering to wear your sunscreen, though."

Abby hugged her mother. She fought back tears at how good it felt to be hugged and to hear her mother's appreciation for her transformation.

"Oh, Mom, it is so good to see you, too. I've really missed you. Even so, I appreciate you giving me time to get my head on straight, or as straight as possible. At least it doesn't feel like it's spinning on my neck like some low-budget horror flick."

Both women chuckled. As Abby grabbed her mother's suitcase out of the back seat of the car, her mother went to the trunk and pulled out several bags. Then she reached into the front of the car to pull out her stack of CDs. Anne never went anywhere without her music.

"What is all that, Mom?"

"Oh, just a few things I thought you might need. Let's get inside and look to see what's in here."

Following a tour of the new apartment, which took all of less than ten minutes, including discussions in each room of Abby's plans for someday fixing things up, they returned to the small kitchen for a glass of iced tea.

Anne began pulling out bags. The first bag, of course, held a pair of pretty new kitchen towels. A gift of kitchen towels seemed to be Anne's signature. Each time she visited any of her children, she brought pretty kitchen towels because, she said, everyone needs them, and no one buys them for themselves. She also brought a framed painted tile to hang in the kitchen that said, "Martha Stewart doesn't live here," and a front-door sign that said, "The South... The place where... 1. Tea is sweet and accents are sweeter. 2. Summer starts in April. 3. Macaroni & Cheese is a vegetable. 4. Front porches are wide and words are long. 5. Pecan pie is a staple. 6. Y'all is the only proper noun. 7. Chicken is fried, and biscuits come with gravy. 8. Everything is Darlin' 9. Someone's heart is always being blessed."

The last bag held a new pink and purple printed argyle T-shirt for Prissy. Abby laughed, told her mom she loved it all, and they set out to hang the new additions on her walls and dress Prissy in her new shirt. Mother and daughter then took Prissy for her regular evening walk and talked about Abby's new community.

"Abby, your new little community is just darlin'!" Anne said noticing the flower beds in front of each apartment. It was obvious each resident was allowed to tend the areas themselves as each one was uniquely different.

"And it's quiet, too," she observed.

"It is. It's an all adult community. Most of the residents are single women. Every once in a while, there are visiting grandchildren in the afternoon or weekends. But it's very quiet. Most everyone gets out and walks and visits."

"It feels like a neighborhood from the '50s or '60s when we knew our neighbors," Anne added. Abby nodded her head, barely remembering those days.

"We have a monthly birthday party in the club room, there is a fitness center, a community vegetable garden we all help tend, a fenced dog area where the pups can play together, and we are discussing a monthly potluck. It's great because it's giving me some entertaining on a really thin budget."

"You all should do a game night. Or cards. Do you remember playing bridge with us when you were young? No one could believe you could play at such a young age," Anne reminisced.

"I do remember, it seems like I could barely see over the tabletop. But I haven't played in decades and don't remember anything about how to play."

"I bet it would come back to you. But you could play other games too."

As Abby began preparing dinner, they talked about her new neighbors, and she told her mom about the little get-together they were having so Anne could meet her new friends. Abby also told her it was a last-minute idea to have it the following afternoon, so they would need to do all the preparations in the morning. While they ate their light summer dinner of chicken salad, fresh sliced tomatoes, and cantaloupe, and blueberries, they debated what dessert they should fix for their company the next day. They finally decided on a flourless dark chocolate cake with fresh whipped cream and raspberry purée and, of course, coffee and iced tea with lemon slices and fresh mint leaves.

Early the following morning, they went to the farmer's market for raspberries, fresh farm eggs and butter, the fruit, and mint. After, they stopped by the grocery for the remaining party ingredients.

Once back home, they made the cake, and while it was baking, they stood at the kitchen sink and polished the silver tray, pitchers, and cutlery. While they worked, they discussed what was going on in Abby's sister Merry and brother Mick's lives, as well as all the news about the grandchildren. Abby's son Kendall and his wife Brenna lived in Boston, Merry's son Rusty and his wife Chelsea lived in Williamsburg, Virginia, and Mick's twin daughters Montana and Savannah were freshmen at the University of Alabama.

As the finished cake, complete with whipped cream, was setting up in the fridge, they went to the community garden and cut flowers for an arrangement, then shuffled the pretty china plates, cups and saucers, tea glasses, the iced tea, and dessert to the clubhouse and made the coffee. Done with only fifteen minutes to spare, they sat down for a glass of iced tea and to catch their breath before their guests arrived.

As their guests arrived, everyone introduced themselves while they talked about the weather, Abby's new haircut, Diana's blouse, and Laurie's new car. They all got comfortable with their drinks and desserts in the beautifully decorated clubhouse. Designed to feel like a home, albeit a magazine spread quality home, they were all comfortable there. Soon shoes were kicked off, and everyone was curled up on the sofas and over-wide chairs, and they chatted like old friends.

"You know, I would love to introduce Abby to my son," said Carolyn. "I think she would be the perfect daughter-in-law. The only problem is; my son is already married."

Linda laughed. "I would love to introduce Abby to my son, too, for the same reason. But I suppose it's an even bigger problem that I don't have a son." The group laughed uproariously.

Not to be outdone or left out, Suzanne added, "I don't have a son either, but I do have a gay daughter. Any chance you're a switch-hitter Abby?"

Anne had to add her two cents worth. "I'd like to meet the girl you're talking about. I DO have a single son."

"Mom!" Abby screeched. "We don't marry our brothers here, and besides, Mick is not my type." Abby chuckled her reply to the others. "I'm flattered, but no I'm not a switch-hitter, and I don't date married men or imaginary ones, either. I also am off the market, as you girls well know. Men are bad, and I've had my fair share. No more men!"

"I'm so glad we got to meet you, Anne," said Wendy. "We adore Abby, and as I guess you can tell, we all think of her as family."

Diana added, "We call her *Baby Girl* since she's younger than the rest of us. But in all honesty, she's the one who takes care of us all."

Laurie spoke up. "We do love our Abby. We aren't sure how we got along without her. She's sure livened things up around here. You raised a beautiful daughter, and we all feel blessed to know her."

"We like her cooking, too," Judy chimed in. "It sure adds something to our little events. And we love getting her recipes."

Abby gave them all a sheepish look, blushed, and replied to them all, "Ladies, thank you, but please stop. You're embarrassing me. I do love being called Baby Girl, though. Not many people are called Baby Girl at the ripe old age of fifty."

Before they knew it, the sun was beginning to set, and they realized it was six o'clock. They all pitched in to clean up the clubhouse and returned all the dishes and leftovers to Abby's apartment. Then, hugging one another, the party broke up.

When everyone had gone, Anne walked up to Abby and hugged her tightly.

"Thanks, Mom, but what was that for?"

"I am so damn proud of you Abby, and I like your friends. The party was fun, and I feel so much better about you being here now that I have met them all."

While Abby warmed a pot of homemade marinara sauce, heated a jar of Judy's home-canned green beans, boiled the pasta, and toasted the garlic bread for their dinner, they talked more about each of the ladies and how each one was special to Abby.

After dinner, Abby showed her mom the crocheted lace crosses she was making for her new friends. Anne was stunned. She had no idea Abby could crochet, especially something so fine and delicate as the lace crosses. "I learned how to do it online, Mom. You know, you can learn how to do almost anything from online videos."

Not long after, they decided they were both exhausted. So they agreed to go to bed as they wanted to get up early and have some more time to visit before Anne had to return home.

The next morning, they ventured out to the doughnut shop for a breakfast of hot doughnuts and coffee. Anne still was talking about the get-together the day before and how magnificent the clubhouse was.

"You know, Abby, we haven't had a big family Christmas in over ten years. Maybe we could have one here and use the clubhouse. Would they allow that? If you feel up to it, I'll come a day or two early and help with everything."

"Oh, that would be wonderful to have everyone together for the holiday. Let me think about what it would entail, and I'll check with the apartment office tomorrow and see if the clubhouse is available. But I think it's a grand idea. Are we all coming to your house or Merry's this year for Thanksgiving?"

"Merry wants to have it at her house. Especially since this is the first Thanksgiving since Rusty and Chelsea were married. I think she's afraid, and probably correctly, that once the grandbabies start arriving, Chelsea will want to have her own Thanksgiving celebration. You know, that's the way it works. As families grow, it gets harder and harder to get together."

"Okay, Mom. I can't wait for the holidays so we can all be together again. And thank you for coming, for the beautiful things you brought me, and for a fun, no-stress weekend." Abby hugged her mom as Prissy sat on the porch looking mournful that Nana was leaving.

"I am so proud of you Abby. It seems like you're finally leaving the past behind you. I do wish you would think about coming back home to Roanoke, though."

"Mom, you're the only thing I have left in Roanoke. I think I will move from here once the legal work is finished, but I want to try to get nearer to Kendall. I can't afford to live in Boston, but maybe I still can get closer to him. I hope you understand."

"Of course I understand. I might even consider going with you. All my kids and grandkids have gotten so scattered out. I would like to be closer to all of you, but I apparently will have to pick, unless we can all move near each other again. But seriously honey, I know Kendall and Brenna are very bright, but they live in the North now. For generations, we always have lived in the South. I don't know how well I would do as a Yankee."

Abby all but choked laughing. Then she reminded her mother, "Southern is a state of mind, Mom. We all know you'll forever be a belle, wherever you may go."

After Anne left, Abby took Prissy for a walk around the flower gardens, sat on a bench, and watched a beautiful hummingbird feeding from the nectar of the flowers. She watched and marveled at how the magnificent little bird could hover, then fly backward. Abby was so entranced, she decided to go home and research more about the little bird she always had loved to watch.

CHAPTER 6

THE OLDER GREY BROTHER, BRUCE, was sixty but he looked years younger than Cole. Cole had followed in their father's footsteps, with his love of parties and self-medicating any little bump in the road with alcohol. Bruce stayed away from the stuff. He saw what it had done to his father, what that lifestyle had done to his mother, to their family, and he wanted no part of it. But he loved his brother, despite his well-known love of the sauce.

Bruce was a widower with three sons. Life wasn't perfect — and they had experienced the usual share of ups and downs. His oldest was mature, steady, and reliable. But his two younger sons had run the gamut of drug and alcohol problems and mental illness. After his wife's death, the younger boys never seemed to grow up much. He had one son who was bipolar and one who was bulimic. He figured it must be hereditary as Cole's oldest son had some of the same problems before his death.

Bruce didn't spend much time with Cole because, even though his sons were now grown, they still seemed to suck up all his time. Bruce could never figure out what went wrong with the kids in this family. They all seemed to have issues, and he didn't think it was due to parenting styles. He parented very much like his mother, and Cole always worked at being his sons' best friend.

~

Cole knew how his family felt about Abby. They all loved her so much, which in the beginning made him proud. But he knew his mom always would be on his side; she would see Abby's leaving as a betrayal. A weak, spineless, selfish betrayal. No matter how Alice felt about Abby, his wife had changed all that by leaving.

His brother was another story entirely. He knew Bruce loved him and always had been there for him. They didn't talk regularly, but they both knew if either of them ever needed the other, all they had to do was call. But as far as Cole was concerned, Bruce had a bit of a holier-than-thou attitude. For one thing, he didn't drink. He knew in the battle against Abby that swaying Bruce to his side was going to take a lot more than the tactic he used to get his mom riled up at Abby. So he thought it out carefully and planned fully what he would tell his brother. Cole also knew that this discussion called for some high-drama poetic license. As well as being mindful of the half-truths he had shared with his mother.

The one advantage he had was that he likely could get to all the family members before Abby did. He felt sure she would try to turn them against him, because, he thought, that is exactly the kind of bitch she had become. If he could get to the family first and lay the proper groundwork, nothing Abby could say would sound credible to them, and that was what he had to do. He couldn't have her telling them he was a monster or trying to turn them against him. He had seen it happen in his family with Bruce's first wife. Because Bruce cheated, his ex-wife remained close to his family after the divorce, until her tragic death from cancer. Cole wasn't going to let that happen to him.

He called Bruce early on a Saturday morning, hoping to catch him before he got busy with his day.

"Hi Big Bro, how are things in your neck of the woods?"

"Overworked and underpaid, and a daily clock that doesn't have enough hours, just like everyone else. What's happening with you, Cole?"

"I am not doing well at all. Abby left me and the family."

"What?"

"Yeah, you know Abby was diagnosed with PTSD several years ago, and things have been going steadily downhill ever since. The medications they gave her for the depression and anxiety made her totally crazy. They keep adjusting them, but she hasn't been right in a long time."

"Yeah, Cole. I heard about her troubles and know it's been difficult."

"Well, Bro, she dropped out of therapy and started taking all these herbals and stuff. She wasn't the Abby we knew. The other day, she showed up with her family members and two moving trucks, packed up her stuff, and left. I have no idea where she is, who she's with, where she's going, or what she's doing. She won't answer my phone calls or emails. In fact, now she's even changed her phone number, so I only have an email address to contact her. If she answers that at all, it's a simple one- or two-word reply."

"Wow, I don't even know what to say about that, Cole. I'm sorry. Do you think this is permanent, or was she pissed off about something? Although, I guess that's a stupid question if she showed up with family and moving trucks."

"Bro, she's been flipping out lately. She doesn't leave the house. Ever. All she does is talk to her stupid 'friends' online, play games, and read books. A month or so ago, I told her I thought she needed to get out more, and she threatened me with a kitchen knife. I seriously thought I was going to have to call the cops to take her to a psych ward or something. Then she suddenly laid down, went to sleep, and when she woke up, everything was as normal as it ever is with her."

"Wow, that is odd and frightening."

"I'm beginning to wonder if she's developed a split personality or something. One minute she would be working on the house, the next she would be crazy, undoing everything she recently had finished. She was calling me at work several times a day, acting all crazy, accusing me of all kinds of things. Man, I go to work, call her during my lunch hour, and come home after work, unless she needs me to stop at the store for something because she doesn't leave home."

"That sounds pretty bad."

"I'm not sure what's wrong with her, but she's definitely been getting worse. Before she changed her phone number, I was calling her and trying to get her to come back home. I even told her we could start slow, I would like to take her out to dinner. But she wouldn't even consider it." Cole sounded defeated.

"Is there anything I can do to help? Is there anything you need?"

"Not at the moment. I'm stunned and in shock, I think. But I told Mom I'm going to an attorney this week to file for divorce. I may not know what is wrong with her, but I know something is up. I have to protect the house, the bank accounts, and myself. I can't trust her anymore. But there is one thing you can do for me. If she calls you, will you let me know? And try to get contact information from her."

"Of course. And if she calls, I'll try to find out where she is. Hang in there, Bro. You're going to be okay. It sounds like you've got a plan. I know this is hard, but if you need anything at all, you know we are here for you."

When Cole called to tell him Abby left, Bruce was shocked. *I know how hard living with someone like Cole can be, but Abby is Cole's rock. She's a beloved part of the family and seems to be the only one able to keep Cole grounded.*

Cole seemed to be so much better as long as Abby was in his life, and Bruce feared what would happen to Cole, now that she was gone. To Bruce, Abby always would be part of the family. He hoped she would call. He loved his brother, but he wasn't sure he believed every-thing he was telling him.

Abby threatened Cole with a knife? That sure sounds a little far-fetched. I haven't heard them so much as argue. He couldn't tell for certain over the phone if Cole was simply distraught, drunk, or hungover. But if he were that impaired at 8:00 a.m. on a Saturday, it would explain a whole lot. Bruce decided this needed some investigation. So he called his mom.

"Hi, Mom."

"Hi, Bruce. What's going on with you today?" Alice didn't sound like her usual upbeat self.

"Well, I'm planning to take the grandkids to the park later, followed by the normal grocery shopping and weekend errands. I called to see if you've heard from Cole." Bruce decided to get right to the point.

"Yes, I talked to him last night." Alice didn't say any more as Cole had said he wanted to tell Bruce, and she didn't know if he had called his brother yet.

"I just got off the phone with him, and something didn't seem right. What do you know about Abby and her leaving?"

"Well, I was surprised by the news. I always thought the girl was more substantial than that."

Bruce could tell right away that Mama Bear already had her back up. "I was surprised too, Mom. It doesn't seem like Abby. In fact, not much of what Cole told me sounded right. I know you talk to her and see her more often than I do. Have things seemed as bad as Cole made them out to be?"

"Bruce, you know she's been a blessing to me since your father died. But the things Cole told me about her, accusing them all of stealing her medications, about her being reclusive, those strange online friends of her's — just don't sound like Abby. But why would he make them up?"

Why indeed? Alarms instantly went off as he realized what Cole had told their mother, and the stories Cole had related to him, were different. He decided to dig a little more. But it was becoming apparent to him that Mom's opinion had been swayed already. He would have to tread carefully, though, and was determined not to share with Alice the things Cole had told him, but not her. He still wanted to get the full scoop on what his mother knew, so questioned her in detail. Bruce needed to know what Cole told her.

"Mom, when you talked to him last night, did he sound like he was drinking?"

"Why do you always assume he's drinking? So what if he is? Distraught and lost is how he sounded. Whether he was drinking last night or not is irrelevant to the fact that the girl picked up and left him with no warning."

Well that certainly answered my question, didn't it? "Mom, I was only asking because, when I talked to him this morning, I couldn't decide if he was super distraught, drunk, or hungover."

"Well of course he's distraught. Why are you always so critical of him? Have you already forgotten how you felt when your wife left, and you were suddenly alone? That is how I'm sure, Cole is feeling now. I would think that of anyone, you could appreciate his grief right now, and as his brother, you should be looking for ways to be supportive, not questioning his every statement."

"Honestly, Mom, I don't think we're getting the whole story. I'm going to call Jeremy and see what he knows. And I'm a little worried about Abby. It surprises me that even if things were so bad she felt she had to leave, she wouldn't call any of us. She should've known we would've done whatever we could to help. Cole said she has no money and no place to go. Don't you think under those circumstances something had to be seriously amiss for her to up and leave like that — with no warning?"

"Well, I don't think you should call Jeremy. Cole said he, Jenny, and the kids were really upset and felt Abby had abandoned them."

Alice decided she didn't want to let Bruce or anyone else know Abby called her several weeks ago and mentioned to her that the marriage was in danger. Abby didn't tell her she was leaving, but she said it was too hard watching Cole self-destruct. Alice couldn't let anyone know she didn't take the girl seriously about how upset she was. She wondered if she had been a bit more supportive, would Abby have left — would they even be having these conversations.

"Okay, Mom, I have to go pick up the kids. I'll talk to you soon." Bruce desperately wanted to get off the phone with her now. Since talking to his mom, he had even more questions. Their discussion had opened up a huge can of worms. It made the whole situation seem even more questionable.

Bruce decided he was going to call Jeremy, but he also knew it was too early to call the boy. None of them ever got out of bed before noon. He would call him later.

Meanwhile, in Greenville, Jeremy and Jenny were still adjusting to moving in with Cole. Jenny knew she would have to give it some time for things to settle down, but right now, she felt like it was fraternity old home week among the men in the house. They sat outside either with a bonfire, in Cole's truck, or their van, listening to loud rock music and drinking until late every night. She had hoped things would have settled down by now into a more normal routine; however, she was beginning to think it never would.

She decided to try to broach the subject with Jeremy. They were having a discussion in their room, on the far end of the house, where they were certain they couldn't be overheard. It was a sweet deal for them to live here. There was plenty of room for them, and they could live rent-free. It was a nice house, one they could never afford on their own, and they loved being able to have friends come over and show it off. But they were beginning to have a few personal issues.

Jeremy also had a bit of a drinking problem. And if Jeremy and Jenny were both drinking, they were like two sailors fighting over the one available girl in port. That didn't happen often, because someone had to watch over the three kids, ranging in age from three months to four years.

When Jeremy wasn't drinking, he couldn't stand to be around his dad if Cole was drinking. But if Jeremy was drinking, the two men spurred each other on, and they both ended up barely coherent. Jenny hated it when Jeremy got that drunk, though she didn't have a problem with him having a drink or two. She didn't understand why Jeremy couldn't or wouldn't understand she felt the same way about him that he felt about his dad. A little alcohol was fine, and most times even fun, but these benders were too much for anyone to deal with.

"You know, Jeremy, I understand why Abby left. Cole used to be a fun drunk, but now he's mean. You're getting mean too — I guess from his influence. If something doesn't change, it's not going to be good for us to be here, regardless of the free rent."

"I know why she left him, too. I've lived with my dad all my life, and it isn't easy. Especially when he gets like he's been since Grandpa died. But I don't know what to do about it. It isn't like he's going to listen to me."

"Look, Jeremy. All I know is something's going to have to give. And if anything should happen to me, where I can't be here with the kids, please don't leave our kids alone with Cole. I was extremely thankful Abby was around when I was in the hospital having the baby. She was great with the kids, but I wouldn't want Cole watching them alone."

"Oh, he would never hurt the girls. He loves them; they have him wrapped around their little fingers." Jeremy took another swig of his beer.

"I never said I thought he'd hurt them, but they don't need to see him like that. And when he's had that much to drink, he is forgetful of what he's doing and can't possibly keep up with all three girls. They should never have seen the fight between you two or seen their grandfather crumpled on the floor that way. Neither of you was here for the aftermath of that little episode. The girls were terrified, and it took me two days to get them right again."

"Whatever. My phone's ringing," he said, dismissing her.

"Hello?" Jeremy said as he paced the floor, clearly irritated by Jenny's comments.

"Jeremy, it's your Uncle Bruce. How're you guys doing?"

"We're okay. How about y'all?"

"We're fine. I'm calling because your dad called me this morning and told me about Abby leaving. It shocked the hell out of me, and I'm trying to make some sense out of it. I know you all were closer and saw more of them. Your dad didn't feel like talking this morning about what happened. Is there anything you can tell me about how this could have happened? Did you guys see it coming or see anything, for that matter, that would've led to this?"

"Well, it blindsided us, too. It kind of surprised us she left but surprised us, even more, the way she did it. No warning. It's dad's fault, I think. Jenny was just telling me how hard I am to live with when I start acting like him, so I guess there is something to that. I know they were arguing a lot. Not really arguing because Abby would simply go to her room. I never saw her yell or pitch a bitch about anything."

"Man, Jeremy. That sounds unpleasant."

"Yeah. Dad would say she was in one of her moods, then he'd go on and do whatever he wanted. He kept saying she was so drugged up she wouldn't know or care what he did. But it sure didn't strike me that way. Then, one day, I came by for a visit and overheard him tell her he wanted a divorce. I think he was bluffing, but apparently, she didn't think so. Two days later, she moved out."

"Cole said he wanted a divorce, then she moved out? That's what you just said, right? So there were some issues, and then she left. Am I understanding this correctly?" *Wow, this is a different spin, isn't it?*

"Yep, that's what I saw and heard. Like I said, I never saw them fight. Jenny says Dad and I both get mean when we are drinking, but it's most likely because we don't want to see those disapproving looks from our women. If a man wants to have a drink, he should be able to have a drink. It doesn't hurt anybody. Well, at least until someone gets pissed off." Jeremy laughed.

Bruce wondered about Jeremy's remark. "Did you ever see or hear of any violence?"

"Do you mean did Dad ever hit her? No. I am pretty sure he wouldn't do that."

"What about Abby? Would she have ever hit him, slapped him, anything like that?"

"Oh hell no! Abby preached to Kendall and me that a man never raises his hand toward a lady. But if a female hits first, she isn't a lady, and it's okay to defend yourself. I think she would've been too afraid to hit Dad."

"Not even in the heat of an argument?" Bruce wanted to know.

"No, I don't believe so. Not even in the heat. Abby wasn't like that. She didn't even yell. If she got mad, she pretty much kept it inside. She hardly ever raised her voice to Kendall and me growing up, and I doubt she ever would to Dad. Hey! Why all the questions? What's with the third degree?"

"As I said, I'm simply trying to make sense of the whole situation. Have you heard from her since she left?"

"Yeah, I have, but don't tell Dad. He's so mad at her, it puts him in a really bad mood to even think about her, much less hear about her. She messaged me after I got hurt at work to make sure I was okay, then she messaged me a Happy Birthday. She always asks about the girls and Jenny, too. I think she's playing it smart by not answering Dad's calls and emails because he's usually been drinking when he contacts her.

"You're probably right about that, Jeremy."

"Uh-huh. The whole drunk dialing thing and then mean, hateful messages, emails, and texts when she doesn't answer. He always tells me what he says because he thinks he's so cool, but he isn't handling things right, in my opinion. He wanted me to take him to her house, and I refused. That resulted in a knockdown, drag-out fight. I figure she's had years of practice putting up with all his shenanigans, is tired of it, and doesn't want to deal with him anymore."

"So you know where she is and have contact information for her?"

"Well, I know what complex she's living in. I saw her pulling in there one day, and I've seen her truck parked there from the main road when I drive by. But I haven't told Dad. I don't think it's a good idea for him to know where she is. I haven't heard from her since Dad said she changed her phone number, so I doubt the number I have will work anyway. I know he emails her, but I don't have her email address."

"Okay, Buddy. You guys need anything?"

"Nah. We're good. Thanks for checking on us." Jeremy always had liked his uncle, and he was glad the family all knew what was going on now. Maybe they would be able to help his dad cope with it.

Now Bruce was even more convinced there was a lot more to the story. Also, he had to figure out what, if anything, he should do about it. On the other hand, maybe it was best to let sleeping dogs lie. It sounded to him like Abby did what she needed to do, and he felt sure she had a plan. He also decided he was going to call his mom back and set her straight on the situation.

"Hi, Mom. It's me again."

"Hi, Honey. I'm sorry I got so angry earlier. I'm seriously worried about Cole. He hasn't dealt with your father's death very well, and I don't know how much more he can take. You know he's so tender-hearted and sentimental and has never been as strong as you."

"Well, that's why I'm calling. I know you said I shouldn't call Jeremy, but I did, just to check on them and see if they were okay. In the discussion, Jeremy volunteered that he overheard his dad tell Abby he wanted a divorce. He said two days later, she moved out. So Cole saying she up and left with no warning doesn't ring true, and I think there is more to the story. Anyway, I've decided I'm not going to pursue it any further. I don't much see the point. However, if Abby should call you, I wanted you to be aware there is probably more to the story than we know, and maybe we should listen to her side.

Mom, she's family too, even if not by blood, and we need to support them both. I'm sure Abby is going through a tough time, as well as Cole."

"Yes, Son. I imagine she is, and if I hear from her, I promise I'll listen to what she has to say. I love you, Son."

"I love you too, Mom, and I'll talk to you soon." Bruce hoped he had given his mom something to think about. What he most hoped was in the event Abby did reach out to them, whoever she called first would be supportive and kind.

CHAPTER 7

*A*s Abby fell asleep that night, reflecting on her mother's visit, she thought about how different she felt since leaving Cole. For so many years she struggled to get better, to be her old self, and after just a few weeks away from Cole's daily influence, she finally felt like she was getting there.

That night, she dreamed of packing, traveling a long distance, and moving. The dream was alive with sunshine and vivid blue skies. It was colorful with lots of flowers and a hovering hummingbird. When she awoke, she felt refreshed and remembered at least parts of the dream. She always had read and believed that we dream in black and white, but remembered the almost electric hues from this dream. *Hmmm. I guess scientists don't know everything yet.* What she did know was that she felt energized and renewed. It was time to start making plans for her "afterlife." The life after Cole.

After taking Prissy for her morning walk, Abby sat down with her first cup of coffee of the day, started her laptop, and went directly to Google. She was trying to locate someplace within driving distance of Kendall and Brenna in Boston, a place that could avoid Boston's high price tag. She researched the cost of living, retirement communities, and quality of life. As she found possible areas, she researched rental listings, looking for anything she thought she could afford on her meager income. Prices were so high that after rent, utilities, insurance, and gas money, there clearly wouldn't be much left. She was frugal, always had been, but now things were uncomfortably tight, and there was no room for any extras, savings, or unexpected expenses. She knew it was going to be a miracle if her fifteen-year-old SUV would make it much longer. Plus, it was a gas hog. But there was no room in the budget for a car payment, and with no savings, paying cash was out of the question.

Abby was good at research, especially with the Internet now available. But she tended to get caught up in it, and one thing always led to another. She always learned new and interesting facts, but sometimes she ended up in a direction far from where she started and lost hours.

Throughout the next week, she made phone calls to all her immediate family members to discuss holiday plans. While she was managing to keep the conversations focused on the holidays as much as possible, there was always one question that every single one of her tight-knit family wanted to ask, and they found an amazing number of different ways to ask the same question. The question — "What now Abby?"

Since no two questions sounded exactly the same, she wondered if they had sat down with a dictionary and thesaurus on some family conference call to hash out their individual scripts. She would think it was funny if it weren't so exasperating dealing with them all. She did have a standard answer for them all, and as she was trying to satisfy them with her inconclusive response, she contemplated starting a daily mass email that said something like, "No, I'm not sure yet. Yes, I will be leaving Greenville, but I don't know yet where I'm going or exactly when. I'll let you know as soon as I decide."

Her mom, of course, wanted her to come back to Roanoke. But following her visit, Abby was pretty sure her mom understood she didn't want to return there. She also didn't want to go anywhere Cole might have a common interest. Not that she was running from the past or memories of Cole, although that clearly held a lot of appeal, but because she had no way of knowing where Cole might go next. She suspected he wouldn't be able to keep his job in Greenville for long if he kept drinking like she had been told. But Abby was certain of one thing: she wanted to go where Cole wouldn't, in any way, be part of her future. She didn't even want to see his name in the paper, let alone run into him somewhere.

The week after Anne's visit, Abby's sister Merry tried to persuade her to come to Roanoke, then admitted her family might be moving away soon. *No thanks,* thought Abby.

Then, her brother Mick tried to talk her into coming to Lexington. "Nope, I'm fairly certain I'm afraid of blue grass. I like my grass green," she had laughed with her brother. Besides, Mick was a pilot, and now that his girls had gone off to the University of Alabama, he was taking long-haul flights and was hardly ever home.

Her nephew Rusty and his wife Chelsea were in Williamsburg, Virginia. It would be a nice place to live, but Rusty also was fielding interviews to move to a better coaching job. Therefore, who knew how long they would remain in Williamsburg.

The last thing she needed was to move somewhere else where she didn't know anyone, right? She knew they were all trying to help and were being typically protective, but nothing struck her as a place she wanted to live. Maybe she didn't know what she wanted, but she desperately needed to get away. And she was tired of making mistakes. Mistakes at this point would be not only expensive but counterproductive, as well.

She realized that her responsibilities and obligations now were pretty much over, at least until Kendall and Brenna started producing grandbabies. Reading all the philosophical and motivational messages that appeared hourly on her Facebook sites, Abby tried to remember what any of her dreams had been. Sadly, she came to the deeply depressing realization that she didn't have any dreams.

Abby also was tired of seeing articles about really living life, too. What exactly did that mean anyway? For her entire adult life, she had been working to get from one day, one month, one year to the next. She was in a place now, where except for the limitations of finances and her health, she could do anything she wanted. She remembered the movie, *The Bucket List,* and tried to form one. She could think of only two long-standing desires. The first came up when she was in the fourth grade when they studied the Galapagos Islands — with the giant tortoises and blue-footed boobies. The second was to visit Ireland.

These two things she knew for certain were not on any "obtainable goals" list unless she won the lottery. So to inspire her to come up with an "obtainable" bucket list, she decided to do an internet search for other things she might find of interest. But try as she might, Abby couldn't get the Galapagos Islands out of her head. She decided to search *Galapagos,* instead — she didn't even know if it was a place you could visit or if it was purely a sanctuary these days.

While perusing photos of the area and reading about the various islands, she recalled that the Galapagos Islands were part of Ecuador. She also remembered a conversation she had with an old college friend, Beth, about Ecuador. So, she searched *Ecuador* and discovered Ecuador had been the *International Living* Magazine Best Place to Retire for four years running. She read more.

In her reading, Abby learned a lot of Americans were following *International Living's* lead and retiring to Ecuador. No, not the rich and famous, not the folks who had been expatriates for most of their lives and jumped from exotic location to exotic location, but the average Joe trying to live on Social Security and maybe additional small pensions. She discovered the cost of living in Ecuador was a fraction of that in the U.S. So she researched the weather.

Abby discovered that, in Ecuador, you could choose your weather. Ecuador had it all, from coastal Pacific beaches with a tropical climate to the Andes Mountains with year-round moderate temperatures, to the Amazon jungle with cloud and rain forests.

She joined some online groups of ex-pats living in Ecuador and discovered there were some interesting and helpful people living there. So Abby reached out to her friend Beth again and asked her some pointed questions about life in Ecuador. As they talked, Abby became intrigued. She started wondering if this was something she actually could do.

She never had done anything remotely adventurous — she'd never even left the U.S., didn't even have a passport. Maybe it was time for her to do something wild and crazy. If not now, then when, right? She shook her head and couldn't believe she was even contemplating something so drastic, so different, but she felt an excitement nothing else had triggered. It could be time to do something she wanted to do, instead of something she needed to do.

For three solid days, she was Reclusive Abby again. Glued to her computer screen reading blogs from people who had moved to various parts of Ecuador, asking questions in online forums, and talking to Beth. Beth sent her folders full of pictures — everything from architecture, stores, open markets full of delectable fresh fruits and vegetables, festivals, parades — every aspect of living in this fascinating country. Abby only left the house three times a day to walk Prissy. And she didn't mention to anyone the idea floating and bobbing in her head. She had been called crazy for far too long to want to give anyone an excuse to think she was out of her mind. She had to admit, if someone told her they were thinking of such a move, she would've thought they were nuts.

After a week, Abby's family and her new friends started calling to check on her. She told them she was okay; she was suffering from her fibromyalgia pain, one of the more frustrating ailments that emerged following her PTSD diagnosis. She read that the weather in the Andes region seemed to help arthritis and fibromyalgia pain. Several people with these afflictions moved there and seemed to be leading active lives with fewer pain days and significantly less pain.

She began making a bucket list of all the things she would love to do, that she discovered she could do living in Ecuador — the travels, the adventures, the sights and culture she would be able to afford to do there, but couldn't afford while living in the States. She included skydiving and bungee jumping on her list. She investigated the requirements for a permanent resident visa and couldn't believe it was so easy. She also learned she could take her aging Prissy with her, and without any quarantine. The small dog even could fly on the plane in the cabin with her. She immediately began some online Spanish lessons.

Then she got another instant message from Lizzy.

LizzyG: Abby, are you there?

AbbyG: Sure girl, what's happening?

LizzyG: Forest just came back from Cole's. I swear that man is crazy. He's drunk as usual, but Forest says he's decided you left him for another man and told Forest you were cheating on him.

AbbyG: Oh for crying out loud. When was I supposed to have time to be cheating? The man called me at least eight times a day while he was gone to work, and if I didn't answer, he would leave work to come home and check on me. Cole knew where I was at all times. You're right. He's crazy as a loon and getting crazier by the day. I guess it's true that alcohol kills brain cells.

LizzyG: You're right, but Forest says he was cleaning guns and saying he wouldn't put up with anyone cuckolding him, and if he couldn't have you, no one would. Forest says to lay low.

AbbyG: Not a problem, I will. Our court date is in two weeks. Then we'll be divorced. The divorce he said he wanted. Maybe when it's over, he will find something else to obsess over. I can't believe he's still ranting about me. Maybe he'll find another woman, though I can't imagine any who would put up with him.

LizzyG: Oh, Abby, he blames you for everything. I really think you should move away from here. Why can't you go where Kendall is?

AbbyG: I can't afford to live in Boston. Everything there is too expensive. But I'm thinking about moving when the divorce is final. I still have to figure out where I'm going and save up the money to do it.

They talked for another half hour about what was going on in

Lizzy's life and then finished their conversation with Lizzy's promise to let Abby know if she learned anything else.

Abby realized at that point that if she moved somewhere now, she would never have the money to move to Ecuador. She wasn't willing to let the thought go. She decided if she had a year or so, she could make it happen. What many people did who moved there was to sell everything, make the trip, and start over. She could do that if she had the time. She would continue studying Spanish and plan to travel when her lease expired the following year. That gave her about sixteen months to prepare. Surely, she could survive for that long here in Greenville, especially with her new community of friends.

She managed to go this long without running into Cole, and if she kept to her practice of staying close to home on weekends and holidays, she should be okay. Abby decided she was not going to tell anyone about the big move. Although none of her current friends knew Cole, and none of them ever would want to betray her, having a friend moving to Ecuador would seem like an interesting conversational item. Somehow, someone who knew Cole could end up hearing the information. After all, this was a small town, and Cole worked for the largest employer. She didn't know why, but she thought it would be a bad thing for him to know. She also had to remember that none of her new friends knew the darkness lurking in her past. She wanted to keep it there and not allow it into her future.

Well, Abby realized, the decision was made. That night she slept more soundly than she had in years and dreamed again of piercing blue skies, pure white cotton candy clouds, rising mountains, colorful flowers, and a giant tortoise with a hummingbird hovering overhead.

CHAPTER 8

COLE WAS SITTING AT HIS desk, waiting for the day to end, and all he could think about was tonight's football game. The Raiders were playing the Cowboys. Cole's team was the Raiders, and he believed his team would take the Cowboys this year. On his way home, Cole stopped by the liquor store and bought two cases of beer. When Cole pulled into his driveway, he noticed his son still wasn't home.

Feeling a little perturbed, he walked into the house and turned on the TV. *The boy doesn't have a job, where has he gone, he knew we were supposed to watch the game together tonight, and instead he's out wasting gas he can't afford, so I have to buy it.* His mood started its daily decline. The game was going to begin in less than an hour, so he popped open a cold one and sat down on the couch. He leaned his head back to try and get rid of the headache, the one that seemed to plague him every day when it was time to come home.

Jeremy opened the door yelling, "I'm home, is anyone here?"

"The game is about to start. Get your ass in here!" Cole shouted from the living room.

Jeremy rolled his eyes and walked into the living room where he

69

sat down on the couch. His two oldest kids came running, yelling "Daddy! Daddy!" Jeremy fell on the couch with the two kids in his arms. Jenny came into the room carrying the baby and kissed Jeremy on the cheek. Cole glared at her and wondered if she was going to do something with those kids tonight so they could watch the damn game. Maybe for once, Jeremy would suggest it, so he wouldn't have to tell her.

"Can you make yourself useful and get me a beer?" Cole said to Jenny.

"Yes, Pop, I can do that for you. You want one too Jeremy?" Jeremy nodded.

Cole barked a few more orders for the lazy bitch to do while she was in the kitchen. Jenny looked at her husband to see if he was going to say anything and was disappointed when he didn't.

Once she was out of the room, Cole said, "Your wife is the dumbest broad I know. She doesn't know how to do anything. I don't know what you see in her. I told you, you needed to get laid, not get married. If you had listened to me, you would be better off."

"Like you're one to talk!" Jeremy snapped at his father. "You couldn't even keep your marriage together, and you're giving me advice! What a laugh. By the way, how is that working for you?"

Cole hated that Jeremy could use this on him. Furious at Jeremy's comment he jumped up, intending to hit his son. His mind flashed back to the last time he tried that, then sat back down with a thump.

"I'll find the little bitch and make her pay. You wait and see. Nobody disrespects me and gets away with it! You need to remember that. She may think she's in control, but you watch and see what happens."

Cole's thoughts were now all on Abby. All he wanted to do was make her disappear. That would solve his embarrassment.

"Jeremy, do you love your wife or is it primarily about convenient sex?"

"Well, I like to have sex, so I guess that would make it a convenience. That getting laid you mentioned earlier led to my first daughter, which led to marriage. Why?"

"No reason. I was curious."

If I could get rid of that sniveling, lazy whore, I would be able to get the kids out of here and plan my revenge. I wish I had never let them move in here. I could use it as a practice run for Abby. I know I can take her out, and nobody will be the wiser. Cole smiled at the thoughts spinning around in his head.

"Dad, what are you thinking? You have a shit-eating grin on your face. Kinda like you just had sex — you better not be thinking about my wife!"

"Oh, nothing. I was having what you might call a happy thought. And no, I wouldn't touch your wife with a ten-foot steel pole." Cole got up and went to his home office to enjoy his thoughts. His interest in the ballgame vanished.

When Cole left, Jenny came into the room, crying.

"What the hell is the matter with you now?"

"Why didn't you stand up for me when your dad was screaming at me? I sometimes think you don't want us around. You always take his side and treat us like shit. Then at night, you still want me to have sex with you. I don't work that way."

"What the hell are you talking about, Jenny?"

"The whole time we've been here, you've been drunk, taking after your dad. I can see why Abby left. I want to do the same thing. I can't stand this craziness anymore, and I wish we had never moved here. And another thing, if you think I'm going to have sex with you ever again, you're sorely mistaken. Not unless and until things change. Remember, you'll be paying child support if we do go down that road. If you ever do get a job, with three kids, I'll be getting a large chunk of your paychecks."

Jeremy jumped up and started yelling. "You want to leave, go ahead. You couldn't get past the fucking driveway. You're too stupid to figure out what to do, and you know you can't do anything without me. So go ahead, leave."

Jenny left the room in tears, running to her bedroom. What she didn't know, was that Cole, standing barely out of sight, was listening to their fight. He had a smile on his face so big he thought his face would crack.

Cole returned to the home office wondering what he would have to do to get rid of his slut of a daughter-in-law. *That bitch can't clean or cook.* In his eyes, she was nothing more than a tramp who had gotten pregnant and trapped his son. *I can do this. There is no way I can get caught. All I have to do is pick the right time and place and work out the logistics. Now, where do I start?*

A few minutes later, a knock on the door brought him back from the darkness of his thoughts. "Dad, you in there?"

"Yeah, what do you want?"

"I need to talk to you for a minute. Is that okay?"

"Sure, what is it?"

"I'm done. I'm gonna file for divorce and get rid of that bitch forever. I think it's for the best, don't you? But I think I need your help in proving Jenny's an unfit mother. I don't want her to take the kids. I want to keep them."

"I do think it would be best for you to be free of her, but a divorce isn't going to end it. It's really hard to prove a mom is unfit, and it's a risky proposition. If she gets the kids, then there always will be child support and visitation and the nagging that comes with it. Abby and I didn't even have kids together, and I'm forced to give her my hard-earned dollars every month. So I'm still not rid of her. You need to look at some other options — need to get *rid* of her if you can follow what I'm saying. It's what I should've done. Learn from my mistakes." Cole's tone was intense.

Jeremy gave his dad a questioning look. "What are you saying Dad? All I want is to get her out of my life in the easiest way possible."

"What I'm saying is, you help me, I'll help you."

Jeremy finally realized exactly what his Dad was saying. "Let me think about it tonight. I'll give you an answer tomorrow."

Cole smiled again. Now he would have help. He knew his son. And if he played his cards right, he knew Jeremy would help him.

The next day, Cole went back to the liquor store and picked up some more beer. When he pulled into the driveway, Jeremy was standing outside waiting.

"What you're thinking is crazy, Dad. What makes you think we could get away with it? I mean, I would like to be rid of her, and I would rather not have to turn my paychecks over to her, but that sure seems better than rotting in jail."

Cole smiled. *Jeremy is in. He's going to help.* "Well Son, it's easy. We'll get away with it because we're smarter than the dip-shit cops in this town. These country bumpkins can't find their ass with both hands already on it. All we have to do is make sure all our bases are covered."

Cole started laying out his plan to Jeremy step by step. "I think we should do it this weekend. I also think we can shoot her and tell the police it was a gun-cleaning accident."

"Whoa! Whoa! Whoa! Wait a minute, Pop!" Jeremy shouted. "What in your right mind makes you think Jenny would ever, and I mean ever, pick up a gun, let alone know how to clean it? I think you should put that out of your head right now! We should start a rumor that she's going on a trip, just her. She's always wanted to go to the Bahamas or someplace like it. We can say I can't go because I have to work. Then she could disappear and never come back. I saw a case like that on the news this last week."

Cole started laughing. "Work? You can't go because you have to work? When are you planning to get a job to make that story feasible? And there is something else, where are you going to get the money? You can't even afford to buy diapers and food for your kids. Geez, and you thought my idea wouldn't work."

Jeremy jumped up, his face red. "What the hell? You asked for my help. I don't have to sit here and listen to this. And don't forget — I can make your life just as miserable as you can make mine."

Cole stopped laughing. "I brought you into this world, and I can take you out, make another one who looks just like you. So you had better watch what you say. Do we understand each other? I will not tolerate you being disrespectful to me."

Jeremy sat down, glaring at his father. They had a few more beers and continued brainstorming and refining their plan. When they were finished, they looked at each other and smiled. They had a plan, and it was a good one. They would be rid of the lazy bitch in less than six days. Jeremy would have his kids and a whole lot of sympathy and support following his wife and the children's mother running off and leaving them. Then Cole would focus solely on Abby. That bitch wouldn't know what hit her.

As he was shoveling the last of the dirt to close the makeshift grave, Cole's mind was a tumultuous mix of thoughts. *The stupid bitch deserved it. She was unmanageable, rebellious; she lied, and was lazy. She didn't clean, was a poor cook, and refused to listen. My son didn't deserve that kind of wife; my grandchildren didn't deserve that kind of mother. Everything will be better now with her gone. And it was so easy.*

The grave finished, the freshly turned ground covered with fallen leaves and debris, he decided he deserved a cold one. He went inside, popped a top, and sat, dry firing his favorite pistol. By the time he finished the first six-pack, Jenny was but a distant memory. Except now, his constant thought was he should have done the same thing with the bitch who thought she could leave him. But it wasn't too late. Yes, that was his new plan. All he had to do was locate her, and he was sure he could. After all, she couldn't go very far. She had no money. If she did go anywhere it probably would be back to her mommy, or to where Kendall was living. Abby wasn't as smart as she thought. She was a stupid bitch, too. And that damn divorce attorney wasn't worth the air he was breathing, either.

Come to think of it, with the three of them gone, his life would be great. He had a plan. *Work the plan.*

One Sunday morning in late October, Abby's phone rang. When she looked at her phone it was Kendall. She was surprised to hear from him this early on a Sunday because he usually was involved with the church.

"Hi, Kendall, what's up? Is everything okay?"

"Well, I don't know. Before we were leaving for church, Brenna went online to check her Facebook messages. Something is up with Jenny. We don't know what's going on. I've tried calling the house and Jeremy, but no one is answering. I tried Cole's cell number and was told there was no one there by that name." Kendall's rapid-fire delivery alerted Abby that something was seriously wrong. He was normally the calm, reasonable one in the family, hardly ever getting ruffled feathers, but today he sounded like he was on the cusp of frantic and terrified.

"What makes you think something is wrong? I think you left that part out," Abby spoke slowly, hoping to calm her son down. She found it unnerving that he sounded so anxious.

"Jenny and Jeremy's timelines have posted saying, 'If you've seen Jenny, please call us immediately. She's missing.'"

"What?!" Abby felt a sudden shock, then a foreboding feeling began to creep through.

"Yeah, there are comments posted that say she went to the lake yesterday to go fishing alone and didn't come back. Supposedly, they have looked everywhere for her and have called the police. They're acting like maybe she left, even saying she had postpartum depression. Apparently, the sheriff's department has divers in the lake to see if she drowned."

"Well, I guess either scenario could be true, Kendall. I certainly couldn't live with either of those men. Although she isn't perfect, she does love those kids. I have a hard time believing she would walk away from them voluntarily."

"The thing is, Mom, Friday night and Saturday morning, Jenny was posting jokes on her page and was planning for a friend from Oklahoma to come for a visit. That doesn't sound like depression or someone planning to run."

"Wow, that is a little unnerving. I am no longer online friends with anyone in the family, so if you hear anything, let me know. I'll call Lizzy and see if they've heard anything. If I hear any more details, I'll call."

Abby immediately sent Lizzy an instant message.

AbbyG: Lizzy, are you around?

LizzyG: Yes, I was about to message you. Forest is on the phone with Cole. Have you heard what's going on?

AbbyG: Kendall called a few minutes ago and told me what's posted online. What are you guys hearing?

LizzyG: It's interesting, confusing, and frightening in my opinion. Cole called Forest a couple of hours ago. He told him Jenny was missing. They think she ran away. But the rub is, when he called earlier, he said she was home last night but was gone this morning. Now they are saying she never came back from fishing yesterday and have called the police. Divers are searching the lake.

AbbyG: Well, that certainly sounds suspicious.

LizzyG: Forest says Cole sounds drunk as usual, even though it's only ten o'clock on Sunday morning. Oh! The other odd thing is earlier this morning, Cole told Forest that Jeremy had been fishing with her yesterday. but came home before she did. Now, Cole is saying *he* was fishing with her yesterday. It sounds to me like they should have gotten their story straight before they called the cops. But I have a real bad feeling about this.

AbbyG: Me, too. Let me know if anything else develops.

By that evening, the story had changed yet again. Now, neither man had gone with her. All anyone could do was sit and wait — and pray the girl was safe.

CHAPTER 9

THE LOCAL SHERIFF'S DEPARTMENT RESPONDED to the call. The house and grounds were swarming with officers, as was the lake across the road.

Cole took the lead in explaining to the officers what happened, explaining that Jeremy was too distraught and was trying to take care of his three small children.

"Mr. Grey, when did you last see Jenny?" A detective asked Cole.

"Honestly, officer, we were drinking yesterday. It was Saturday, you know how it is. Jenny wanted to go fishing, so we told her to go ahead, we – that's Jeremy, my son, and I would watch the kids. Once the kids went to bed, we might have drunk too much. I guess we fell asleep."

"I see," the officer said, "what time was that? That she went fishing, I mean."

"I don't know. It was after lunch but before dinner. Anyway, when we got up this morning she wasn't here. We looked for her every-where. I went to the lake. We thought maybe she went back this morning. That girl does love to fish like nothin I've ever seen. I found her fishing pole and her flip flops on the bank. I don't think she would have left them there. That's when we decided to call you guys."

"Mr. Grey, can Jenny swim? You know if she fell in the lake or something?"

"Oh, yeah, sure, she's a strong swimmer. But that damned lake is full of water mocassins." Cole replied thoughtfully.

The sheriff's department called in the volunteer search and rescue folks, who started diving the lake and searching the area. They had been there for a few hours; so far, nothing had turned up.

Once Jeremy had the bigger girls in high chairs eating breakfast and the baby in a clean diaper and settled with a bottle in her swing, he returned to the front porch where his dad was talking to the officers. He was visibly shaken and appeared both frightened and distraught.

The detective turned to the younger man.

"Jeremy, have you and your wife been having any issues?"

"No sir. But I'm worried. After our second daughter was born Jenny was diagnosed with oh what do call it, baby blues."

"Postpartum depression?" the officer asked.

"Yeah, yeah, that's it. Anyway, we just had our third. Last time it got better when she found out she was preggo again. But you know, her mom just died too. She's not been herself lately. She's been lazy, sleeping all the time, no energy, and snappy. You know with me and the kids. She just wanted to be by herself all the time. We thought her going fishing would help."

Although the two men appeared to show the proper amount of concern, something didn't feel right to the officer in charge. He asked them to come down to the station to answer some more questions. The officer wanted Cole and Jeremy to talk with a detective who could initiate an investigation to locate her.

"Sure, officer, we can come down to the station. Jeremy's mother's on the way from Roanoke and can look after the kids. As soon as she gets here we'll come to the station."

The officer wondered about that. He had not seen either of them use the phone since his arrival, and he was first on the scene. So it appeared to him that they had contacted family before calling the authorities. He decided to give that information to a detective instead of asking the men about it himself.

"The volunteer fire department is in charge of the search. We'll see you at the station, shortly. Be sure and call us if you hear from her."

Once the police left, Cole called the attorney who was handling his divorce and left a message explaining the situation. He felt they needed an attorney to accompany them to the police for questioning. And then Cole waited. A half-hour later, the attorney called him back, saying he would meet them at the station in two hours.

Jeremy's mom arrived to stay with the children, so Cole and Jeremy spent the time calling all their friends and family to let them know what was going on and to ask if anyone had seen or heard from Jenny since yesterday. No one had heard from her. Of course, they knew that this would be the response, so they intentionally didn't call anyone from Jenny's family.

They posted on Facebook that she was missing and asked if anyone had or did hear from her to please let them know. They knew they had covered themselves, had done what any normal person would've done, and they prayed no one in her family saw the posts until later.

If the police started contacting her friends, they would learn Cole and Jeremy had already called asking about Jenny. Jeremy had never talked to anyone in her family except her mother, so it wouldn't seem suspicious for him to not call them. He didn't even have phone numbers for them; those were all on Jenny's phone. And, they assumed, Jenny's phone was wherever she was. The more time that went by before her family got involved, the better.

The previous year, Jenny's mother died from cancer. She and Jenny had been very close and talked daily, so if Dawn was still alive, their plan wouldn't have worked as well. Jenny's only remaining family was her common-law stepfather in Montana, a stepsister in Kentucky, and a drug addict half-brother. No one knew where he was living from one day to the next. Most of Jenny's communication with her stepsister was online; they had not seen each other in years.

When developing their plan, Cole and Jeremy knew if they acted fast enough, the family wouldn't know anything and wouldn't have much legal input into the situation. They felt sure that if the police investigated, all the family members would be interviewed. However, they were counting on the small county sheriff's department not having the resources to conduct an investigation that spanned several states. Cole and Jeremy simply had to make sure there was enough doubt and suspicion in the authorities' minds concerning Jenny's stability that they would determine she had run away. The men prayed the police would want to close the case as fast as possible.

Father and son met their attorney at the sheriff's office later that afternoon. Douglas Wayne III, attorney at law, was a small town jack-of-all-trades. He would represent anyone, take any type of case, as long as the client could pay his fee. Counselor Wayne didn't know why Mr. Grey thought he needed an attorney for this particular inter-view, but billable hours in a small town didn't come along often. Espe-cially weekend billable hours he could attend to after he finished his weekly round of golf. He knew all the officers from the city police department, the county sheriff's department, and all the local judges. This was a little town, and the circle of law enforcement and attor-neys was small.

The responding officers separated the two men into the only two interview rooms in the small county office and assigned Detectives Carter and Patterson to interview them. But because the men had arrived with one council for both, the interviews couldn't be conducted simultaneously. As far as the sheriff's department was concerned, this chain of events pleased them, as it would allow the other officers to watch both interrogations. Especially since the deputy who responded to the scene had voiced some concerns and suspicions.

"What time did Jenny go fishing?"

Jeremy answered, "She left about one o'clock after the kids had lunch and were down for their naps."

Cole Answered," Not long after lunch, I think. I know it was before dinner. The kids were napping when she left. I didn't pay attention. I didn't know it was gonna be important."

"Did anyone go with her?"

"No, I did walk over and check on her. I asked her if she wanted me to cook something on the grill for dinner. She asked if I would just feed the kids and if Dad and I could fix something for ourselves. She said she would eat when she got home. I said I would feed the kids. I do that most nights lately anyway. She's always so tired," Jeremy answered.

"While Jeremy was feeding the kids dinner, I walked over and took her a beer. She said she didn't want it. I asked her how long she was going to stay at the lake and she said, not much longer. I'll be home by dark probably. I went back home," Cole explained.

"Is there a reason she would leave?"

"Not a good reason," Jeremy said. "But like I said, she hasn't been herself. I guess not having her mom to talk to has made the new baby more difficult. She complained about being stuck in the house all day every day with three preschoolers. Don't all moms complain about that? I mean, I know she loves them. But she's been sad. So, I don't know," Jeremy answered.

"You mean other than being sick of doing laundry, fixing three meals and two snacks a day, a baby that cries all the time? Look, the girl was lazy. She loved being pregnant, all the attention. But you know how people get puppies, and then when they start growing and being a problem and have to be walked every day they get sick of them and abandon them. Well, that's starting to sound like our Jenny now," Cole said.

"If she left, where would she go?"

"I have no earthly idea," Jeremy answered. "I mean really, my family is all she's got now. Her stepfather raped her. That's when she ran away and came here. Her mom is dead. Her brother is a drug addict living on the streets somewhere, no one knows where. She has a half-sister. But I don't think she would go there. That girl's father is the guy who raped her."

"She had to have help from somewhere," Cole suggested. "She has no money, she didn't leave in a car, she didn't take anything with her. But I have no idea who that would have been. Kids these days and their online stuff…I have no clue who she's been talking to."

"If she was upset or decided to leave, who would she tell?"

"I called all her friends from back home this morning. No one heard anything from her," Jeremy told them sounding frustrated.

"I don't know. Jeremy called her friends that he knows, we called family. But she has her cell phone. We didn't find it anywhere, so we can't check that. Maybe she would have called my soon to ex-wife, but she changed her phone number and we can't call her. Besides she never like Jenny and Jenny didn't like her," Cole answered wondering why he hadn't planned all along to cast suspicion on Abby for Jenny's disappearance.

The detective asked for Jenny's phone number and who the cell service carrier was and for contact information for any friends or family they could think of and Jeremy made them a list.

"Well, the search of the lake and the surrounding area hasn't turned up anything. Since she has a history of running away and there's no evidence of foul play, we have to assume she disappeared on her own accord. We will contact everyone on the list. Maybe they will tell us something different than they told you if they know of any plans she had. You folks are free to go, we'll contact you if we need anything else."

"Will you tell us if you find her?" Jeremy asked. "The kids are going to be asking about her. I don't know what to tell them."

"Yeah, we'll let you know," the detective answered.

Cole, Jeremy, and the attorney left the station house.

The only thing the detectives found curious was the attorney who had been hired to accompany them to the questioning. But they knew this family was not originally from the small town, and some of these city folks who watched too many legal shows on television sometimes felt they had to hire an attorney whenever they were talking to police. It was the first time they could recall family members bringing council to answer questions about a missing person. But they hadn't had very many missing person cases in their county, either.

Television and movies had alerted the general public that spouses and parents were always the first questioned. It sure made their job harder, now that all the real criminals were privy to the fact. They did run background checks on both the husband and the father-in-law. They saw where there had been a call recently involving some type of altercation in the home, but that had been between the father and son. There were no domestic disturbance calls concerning the husband and wife.

Jeremy and Cole stopped to talk to the attorney in the parking lot. They thanked him for answering their call so promptly on a weekend. He told them he was sorry for the distress they were going through and to call if they needed any more assistance.

Returning to Cole's car, they made a stop at the liquor store on the way home. They were going to need some liquid courage to get through the next hours and days of phone calls and people coming to the house to offer comfort and ask questions. Thankfully, they didn't know many people in town. They continued to rehearse their story, speculating on the questions they would face from everyone. And then they laughed. They felt they had done a good job with the police, and except for keeping up the appearance of being distraught, they had done their job, they had worked their plan, and they had no reason to think it wasn't going to work.

Cole took a week off from work. There was a revolving door of people coming to offer help, bringing food, and volunteering to help watch the little ones. It seemed everyone wanted to come in and stay awhile, probably to dig for more information, Cole thought. It was a hard week to keep up with the concerned charade, and they pretended to be frustrated with the lack of diligence from the police, but they managed to pull it off. After a week, all those concerned coworkers and neighbors they had never met before returned to their normal lives, and Jeremy and Cole were allowed to return to theirs.

It did work for them, but the relationship between Cole and Jeremy was starting to deteriorate. Jeremy was feeling remorseful and was getting a little overwhelmed at what it was going to mean to his life to have to care for three young children, all the time. Plus, he discovered having his dad around wasn't going to be much help. And Cole, picking up on Jeremy's weak, spineless guilt was afraid he was going to have trouble with the boy when it came to enacting his plan for Abby.

Meanwhile, the sheriff's department fielded phone calls from Jenny's stepfather and stepsister. They both claimed there was no way Jenny would have left her children voluntarily. The officers explained to the family that all evidence pointed to her leaving of her own accord, and after hanging up, would roll their eyes and mutter, "That's what every family member says."

Jeremy determined there was no way he could work and raise three daughters on his own. His mom, who worked via the internet and could work anywhere, moved to Greenville. Jeremy left his father's house and moved in with her so she could help care for the girls. At least, that's what he told both his parents.

CHAPTER 10

OLLOWING JENNY'S DISAPPEARANCE, EVERYONE ENCOURAGED Abby to get out of town. But Abby had a secret plan. If she left town now, everything would be lost. While on one hand she was terrified and wanted to run as far and as fast as she could, on the other, she was determined to keep Cole from stealing her dream. It was the only remaining dream she had. Well, the only dream she had, except for the dream of survival.

She didn't want to be another statistic, killed by an ex-spouse with all the friends, family, and neighbors interviewed on the news saying they couldn't believe it, he was such a good man, no one would have ever suspected, and on and on, ad nauseam. But she also didn't want to be a paranoid alarmist. She kept telling herself that, realistically, he was so messed up it was unlikely he could follow through with any of his myriad of threats, especially her demise.

She determined her first step was to talk to her beloved Kendall. He was wise, and she often sought his counsel. He was the one thing she was having trouble walking away from, as well. She needed to know if he would be okay with her decision. She never, ever wanted him to feel she had abandoned him, but he was an adult now, was married, had a demanding job, a wife, two precious fur babies, and an active social life. He didn't need her often, but she wanted him to know that no matter where in the world she was, she always would be there for him. She hit his number on speed dial.

"Hi, Mom. I was thinking of calling you in a bit."

"Hi, Kiddo. Does that mean you have some free time to talk?"

"Sure, Mom, what's up?"

"Do you remember a few years ago you talked about wanting to live in a Spanish speaking country since your minor was Spanish?" He was fluent and had hoped to get to use it someday. But that was before he got married. She hoped maybe it was still a dream of his.

"Sure. Brenna and I still talk about it from time to time. It would be fun to spend a year somewhere before we start a family. I would love to get the opportunity to use my Spanish. Why?" Kendall's curiosity was piqued. But he never knew what his Mom would come up with next.

"Well, when you talk about it, do you think about where you might go?"

"We've talked about Puerto Rico or Costa Rica. Why? What's up?" He hated the game of twenty questions when he knew it actually was going somewhere. He was getting frustrated and wanted to know where the conversation was leading. But he also loved his mom with all her quirks. But she was a storyteller and could drag out the most mundane things.

"Have you ever thought about Ecuador?" She knew he was starting to lose patience, but she needed to cover the ground in just this way for both of them.

"No, but it's an interesting thought. Are you ever going to tell me what this is about?" Kendall was ready for the punch line.

"Well, to be honest Kendall, I'm thinking of moving there. I'm wondering how you would feel about that."

"Seriously! You're thinking about it, or it's a curiosity? What brought this about?" Kendall was surprised. He had never once heard his mother mention living anywhere other than the good old U.S.A., the Southern U.S.A., to be specific.

"I've been reading about it and talking to people who have done it. I need to get out of this town and as far away from Cole as I can. But I also don't have much of a life or future here. I'm barely making it since I can't work. The cost of living there is significantly less than here, and I might have some fun. I'm ready for a life that's interesting and worth living." She tried to make her case in as few words as possible as she wasn't sure how much time she would have to convince him.

They talked for about an hour, Kendall asking questions, and Abby answering them. Kendall told her his stepmother's parents had moved to Ecuador a few years ago and didn't like it, but they had lived in Quito (the capital near the Colombian border) and now were looking at other places to retire. Their reasons were the same as hers. So, no, he didn't think it was a totally crazy notion, but he would like to reserve judgment until he had some time to think about it and research it.

None of that surprised Abby, in the least. That is who her son was. He never made rash or uninformed decisions. However, the fact he didn't sound shocked or ask if she was crazy felt positive to her. She felt almost jubilant and she realized — *free*. She asked if they might consider spending their year in Ecuador if she moved there and they decided to live abroad for a while. Kendall said it was a possibility. That was all she needed. She felt uplifted and as if maybe this was going to be a good decision. Her excitement started building.

Her next call was to her mom. While she felt Kendall was the most important person to tell, she knew her mother was going to be the hardest. Abby knew Anne wanted to grow old with all her children and grandchildren close to her. She also knew Anne was convinced they should live together, but Abby absolutely wasn't ready for that. Everyone knew Anne bought lottery tickets every week, with the plan that if she won, they would build a big family compound and all live happily ever after.

Abby finally was beginning to get her life back. She certainly didn't want to start feeling like she merely existed until the end of her days. She was still young and hoped she had plenty of time left to have fun. The realization she wanted to live was not lost on her. She knew she had come a long way. Abby poured a cup of coffee, got Prissy in her lap, took a deep breath, and phoned her mother. The conversation was not at all what she expected.

"Hi, Abby. Have you heard anything more about Jenny?" Everyone still was hoping to hear the girl was somewhere safe, and no evil had befallen her. Although, it was the consensus among Abby's family at least that she wouldn't be found…not alive anyway.

"No, Mom. Everything is quiet, deathly quiet. It seems the information highway on Jenny has dried up. Honestly, I don't understand it. I can't believe her family is not trying to keep the information at the forefront. She didn't have any close family, but I can't believe there is no one raising a stink. There has been nothing on the local news, nothing in the newspaper, only the one post on Facebook, and all the conflicting stories Forest was able to get from Cole. When I ask Lizzy if they have heard anything, she says no, they aren't hearing from Cole at all."

"This is by far the strangest, most suspicious thing I have ever been around, Abby. I can't believe the sheriff's department isn't making a bigger deal out of it. I guess real life isn't anything at all like TV. The detectives on crime shows would've kept digging until they found her. They're much more curious and thorough than in real life."

Anne was frustrated and perplexed about the situation, and every day she prayed and thanked God her daughter had gotten out of that relationship when she did. She knew Abby felt weak for all she had allowed to happen to her, but she felt her daughter was strong. After all, she escaped. She was a survivor.

Abby laughed. "Well, Mom, I think on TV they only have one case at a time. I'm sure the real cops have more to do, although in this small town that doesn't seem very likely. But that's kind of what I'm calling about. You know I've wanted to leave this town, and I know everyone else wants me to get out of here, too. I've been researching and investigating options along those lines, and I've found somewhere I want to go. But I need to talk to you about it. I've already talked to Kendall, but I don't want anyone else to know yet."

"I assume all that prefacing means you won't be coming back to Roanoke. I understand that. With everything going on, I think you're right and need to go somewhere Cole doesn't have any ties. Where have you decided to go?"

"Somewhere that Cole not only has no ties but where they don't even have addresses or home mail delivery. I don't ever want him to be able to find me." Although Abby was teasing her mom, she was all serious, as well.

"Oh Lord, Abby! Tell me you aren't joining a cult! That is the only place I know of with no addresses or mail delivery. Unless you're thinking about Siberia and darling, the weather is, without question, too cold for you there."

"Mom! No! I've been investigating Ecuador, and I want to move there."

"Ecuador?! I don't think I even know anything about Ecuador. You said you couldn't afford to move to Boston — how will you ever afford to move abroad? Why in the world Ecuador?"

"There are lots of reasons, and I would love to share them with you. I've been researching it heavily for some time. Do you remember my friend Beth from college? She moved there four years ago. I reconnected with her on Facebook, and she's shared a lot of information with me. I have been reading blogs from Americans who have moved there, and several of them have written books. Unfortunately, a lot of the books are e-books and I don't have an e-book reader, but I'll need to buy one before I go."

"Isn't it super hot and humid there?"

"In some places, Mom, but not in the mountains. The weather in the Andes Mountains is what I have always said would be perfect for me. And you know I've always loved the mountains. Ecuador has coastal beaches and the rain forest and jungles, as well. But the mountains always have spoken to me. The cost of living there is considerably less, so my money will go much further, and it's a much healthier way of living. There are virtually no processed foods, and an abundance of fresh fruits and vegetables are available year-round."

"What will you do for money there?"

"I still will receive my monthly insurance check and can withdraw it from an ATM there, the same as here. The U.S. dollar is the currency there, so I don't even have to learn to convert the money."

They continued the question and answer session for about an hour and a half and then Anne ventured, "Maybe I'll go with you."

Abby's mouth fell open; she was speechless. That was the last thing she expected her mother to say. Her next comment, however, was not as surprising.

"I love Latin music, and I bet the music there is fantastic. When are you thinking about going, and what are you doing with all your stuff, and tell me all the details." Anne wanted to know more. It frightened her for Abby to go that far away. She was shocked her daughter was even considering it, but she still was quite curious.

Abby explained her plans. She told her mom that she had been thinking she would do it in a year when her new lease expired. But because of the Jenny incident, she was changing her move date to this March when her current lease expired. Abby asked her mom to please keep this completely private for security reasons. She would tell her sister and brother's families after Christmas.

She thought the fewer people who knew the better, at least until they could figure out how dangerous Cole might or might not be. The Jenny thing weighed heavily on their minds. They all felt something bad had happened, but weren't sure if Cole was behind it or Jeremy, with Cole covering. Either way, it was terrifying to think about.

Abby spent the next month sorting things out for her move. She took an inventory of all she had in her storage building from the house, as well as her apartment, joined several online groups that were in actuality internet yard sales, and began selling her items. She watched to see how things were priced and how deliveries were handled. She was pretty sure that selling her possessions through a Facebook group would be safer than a general listing service because although Cole frequented the "open" posting services, he never used Facebook. Also, if you had to meet someone to deliver an item, there was an online record.

She talked to the couple who managed her storage building. It had twenty-four-hour camera surveillance, and the managers lived onsite. They gave her their private after-hours phone number and told her if she needed anything, she should feel free to call. She would meet buyers there, pretty sure that she had done everything she could to keep herself as safe as possible. Since most of the stuff she had taken from the house was in storage, it also eliminated a lot of work moving things to her apartment before selling them. Anyway, she was uncomfortable having strangers come to her apartment, even in the small town.

She sent off for the documents she needed for her visa and applied for a passport. Abby continued to visit the ex-pat sites and the various online groups of people from the U.S. living in Ecuador. She asked questions and gathered information. She still didn't tell anyone else what she was doing. Abby was getting so excited, though, that it was hard to keep it from her friends. It was getting difficult to be interested in their conversations when all she could think about was the beautiful place she was going and the adventures she was going to have.

Abby traveled to her sister Merry's house with Rusty and Chelsea for Thanksgiving. It was so nice to see everyone. While she talked with them all, this was the first time she would see them since she left Cole.

It was a loud event, with all the great food, lively conversation, and the family Thanksgiving night traditions — competitive and often loud raucous rounds of board games, followed by watching a Christmas comedy. The whole family loved these holiday movies. Each year, they assigned their family members to the characters in the movie. There was lots of laughter — it was a great weekend. About thirty minutes before everyone was scheduled to depart, Merry announced she and her husband George were moving from Roanoke to Wichita, Kansas.

Abby enjoyed her car trip with Rusty and Chelsea. They also were getting excited about moving to a new part of the country. Rusty was interviewing all over the southern United States for a new football-coaching job, and he was hoping to land in an SEC conference town. It was really hard for Abby to keep her move a secret from them, but she needed to tell everyone at the same time. That was how it was done in this family.

Thanksgiving had been a profusion of family relocation news. Kendall was on the shortlist for a position in Seattle, Merry's husband George accepted a position in Wichita, Rusty was interviewing for a new coaching position — it would've been the perfect time to tell them she was moving, too. But she wasn't ready. Despite the positive results of talking to Kendall and her mom, Abby was still fearful of the family's reaction. She was surprised that, among all the other news, she hadn't slipped and said something. And she was, even more, surprised her mom hadn't blurted something out.

She and her mom still talked daily, and Anne joined the ex-pat Facebook groups, plus followed all the ex-pat blogs. Kendall started reading all the available books written by ex-pats, and each of their conversations was peppered with, "Mom, I read such and such, how will you handle that?" She finally determined he wasn't so much worried about her moving as he was ensuring she was aware of all the differences, plus making sure she was prepared to deal with, and be happy living, in a developing country.

He told her about the cultural differences in Latin America — stuff he had learned through his studies. She really loved that boy. He was by far the best son ever. They made plans when he came home for Christmas to go through all his childhood boxes. That way, he could take the things he wanted to keep, and she could dispose of the rest. She knew those were going to be the hardest things to part with and was not looking forward to it. It was going to be an emotional time, but she could only take two suitcases with her, and that had to include everything she would need. It's a good thing she had started to adopt a minimalist attitude, a necessity as she had thought she might need to suddenly leave her home with Cole, taking only the barest of essentials. It did make parting with all her treasures a tiny bit easier.

When she returned home from the Thanksgiving holiday, she found a little blue folder in the mail — it was her ticket to freedom. She so wanted to post a picture of it on Facebook, as it was now her most prized possession. But she knew she couldn't, and didn't. She did leave her new passport out on the desk for a couple of days to look at and cherish before locking it away in a safe place. Her passport to freedom, to a new life, to living, and her very own personal adventure.

CHAPTER 11

$\mathcal{C}$OLE WAS IN A STATE of glee when he thought he was in the clear for Jenny's disappearance. *What a deal! I told Jeremy it would work. The cops here don't know anything. They don't have any experience with serious crimes. Now I can start on my plan for Abby. I think I might need to enlist the help of my old friend, Amory. I wonder if I still have his phone number.* While he was searching for Amory Hunter's phone number, Jeremy came into the office, startling Cole, who didn't know his son was stopping by.

"Dad, I'm getting nervous. The police keep asking me when was the last time I saw Jenny." His voice cracked.

Cole turned to him, angry. "Dammit son, all you have to do is keep to the story and don't lose your nuts, and everything will be fine." *Why couldn't I have a son with some balls? Oh, wait. I did have a son with balls, but he's dead now. Damn. The wrong son had to be the one to die, and now I'm stuck with this sniveling little chickenshit who is so much like his mother. Actually, I think his mother has even more balls than this kid does."*

"Jeremy, why don't you make a beer run for us? I have to think." Jeremy left, realizing he had been dismissed.

Now, where was I? Oh yeah, I was looking for a phone number, shit,

94

who's number, ah yes, Amory Hunter, here it is. Cole shut the office door, dialed the number, and discovered it was no longer working. *Damn, what did I expect? I haven't talked to the guy in at least five years. Hey, I bet Bruce is still in touch with Amory. I'll call him for the number.*

"Hey Bruce, it's me. Do you still have Amory's number? I need to talk to him?" Typical Cole. Not even any pleasantries, and no thought of asking how his brother or his family was.

"Well, hello Brother, it's good to hear from you, too. Yeah, I have Amory's number; it's 945-555-0176."

"Thanks, talk to you later." Cole smiled and disconnected the call.

Bruce shook his head and continued with his day, secretly pleased he had not gotten dragged into a long dramatic conversation with his very troubled and morose brother.

Amory Hunter was Cole's childhood best friend. Amory had been a cop until a few years ago when he was fired for use of excessive force. Cole knew Amory was the person he needed to call. Amory was a cop, but not a cop, they had a long history, and he felt he could trust him. He knew, though, that he would have a little buttering up to do because it had been so long since he had talked to Amory. Cole stopped answering Amory's calls years ago because when Amory got in trouble and lost his job, he called constantly. Frankly, Cole had been tired of hearing his whining.

"Amory, man, long time. How are you?"

"Cole? I thought you dropped off the earth. You changed your number. It's been what, five years?" Amory was surprised to hear from his long-time friend.

Cole felt a little chagrined. "Yeah, I know. I'm sorry; you know how life gets in the way. I moved to North Carolina, had a new job, we were working on the new house, Abby was sick, blah, blah, blah — you know how it is. Did you get reinstated? Are you working?"

Amory hated that question, and it always came up. "No, still in proceedings, waiting for trial. I don't know how many more post-ponements they can get for one trial. Whatever happened to a speedy trial? I'm working private security now, which sucks."

Cole felt he was going to make his old friend's day. "What would you say about a little freelance work? Abby's gone off the rail. She went a little crazy, has left, and I don't know where she is. Do you think you could find her? I can make it worth your while."

"Cole, buddy, I sure hate to hear that, she was the best thing that ever happened to you. I certainly will see what I can do. What info can you give me?"

"Her full name is Abigail Albright Grey. She may be back in Roanoke. She also could be in Boston, Alabama, or Kentucky because she has family in those places. I need to find her and see if I can get her back, man." Cole knew he had to sound as calm and as sincere as possible. If Amory knew the truth, he never would help him, and Cole knew this was his best shot at finding Abby.

"I'll see what I can find out. You should hear from me in a few days. Promise"

Amory had no clue that this was not about love, but an obsession. A cruel, wicked, dangerous obsession. Plus, he had not heard about Jenny's disappearance and all the suspicion that surrounded it.

As Cole was hanging up the phone, Jeremy returned from the beer run. The two men had a beer together before Jeremy said he had to get back home to the kids.

With Amory now working to locate Abby on Cole's behalf, Cole was free to plan and prepare for her punishment. He opened a fresh beer, kicked back in his recliner, closed his eyes, and thought about what he would like to do to her. Jenny had been easy and quick, with no hassles. But quick was too good for Abby. No, he wanted it to be slow and torturous, the same way she had done him, Jeremy, and the babies. Slow would take some careful planning, though.

The first thing was to find her, then he would grab her. He decided he needed someplace he could keep her for a while. Someplace safe, where she wouldn't be able to escape, someplace where no one could hear her screams, and with no access to the outside world.

Right here on this property would be the best place. It would be easy for me, and there are no neighbors around, no traffic. It can't be in the house or the garage or the existing shed. It would be too easy for someone to hear or find her. I'm sure it won't be long until Mom will come for a visit, and Jeremy and the kids are always around. Near Jenny's grave would be ideal. I need to get one of those prefab storage buildings and put it out there among and under the trees. I know I've seen a place that sells them on the highway a couple of towns over.

Cole opened another beer and sat down at his computer to research the small buildings. He located a seller about thirty miles away that had payment plans — and they delivered. There was a section on the site about how to prepare the ground underneath, and he printed out all the specifics. Then he looked through the catalog to decide which building would be the perfect one for Abby's new home. Once he had decided which building, he also printed out the specifics for it.

He called Jeremy and told him he had a job for him. He would pay him, but he needed him to come by so they could talk about it. Jeremy explained the kids were in bed for the night, and his mom had gone out. He agreed to come by the next day in the afternoon after his mom did the grocery shopping and could watch the girls.

Cole felt like he had accomplished something today — Amory was looking for Abby, and Jeremy would do the building prep work. Now he could apply for financing and buy the building on Monday. By the end of next week, he could have it all outfitted and ready for his little wife to arrive whenever he was ready to grab her.

The next morning, he turned his attention to an Internet search. He first searched *kept wife captive* and was amazed at all the news stories that came up. He read several of them, marveling at how stupid these men had been to get caught. Then he searched *ways to torture*. Basically, what surfaced was a history of torture devices through the ages, but at the bottom of the page were more search suggestions. *Ways to torture people mentally* was right there; he clicked on the link. He read and clicked more links and read and clicked until he heard Jeremy calling for him.

Cole closed down his computer and called to Jeremy that he was in the office. He pulled the printout of ground prep instructions and the layout of the building he was going to buy. He explained it all to Jeremy, told him to take his credit card, and buy whatever supplies were needed to do the job, and put Jeremy in charge of getting the prep done before the end of the week. Then, they went out to decide exactly where to put the new building, making sure there was a clear path for the building delivery.

"Dad, why are you getting a new building? You have plenty of room around here with all Abby's stuff gone. Why do you want one out here so far away from the house?"

"You know, Jeremy, you ask too many questions. I want it because I want it, and I want it out here because I want a place away from where your nosy kids run around. Is that all right with you, because if it isn't, too fucking bad."

Jeremy had his marching orders; the search was on for Abby. Cole returned to his office to continue with his "research" on ways to make sure Abby's punishment fit her crime.

She's running. She hears him behind her, chasing her through the darkest night. She knows he's close because she hears the footsteps and the breathing. She runs harder. Somewhere in her peripheral vision, she sees another person running at her from the left. Now there are two chasing her. But the joining of forces behind her seems to slow them down, and she's widening the gap between them. She still can hear them running, but no longer hears the breathing. She must keep going. Then another figure appears behind her to the right.

Her legs are burning, her lungs are burning, but she pushes ahead faster. Again, the footfall behind her seems to get a little farther behind, but now there are three.

Of course, this would have to be a dark, moonless cloudy night. She can't see anything except for the large forms of the trees as she runs through the forest behind the house she had shared with Cole. The house that was supposed to be their dream home. Home, where you are supposed to feel safe.

She stumbles and falls onto the ground. It feels strange, then a bolt of lightning, lets her see momentarily what appears to be freshly turned dirt. She doesn't know for certain where she is, but she's quite sure she's nowhere near the garden. She's confused, and suddenly the sound of heavy breathing and pounding feet registers. The voices she hears send her into a momentary state of shock. *Bruce and Jeremy? This can't be real. How is it possible they are involved? Why are they helping Cole chase her?* She scrambled to get up, sinking slightly, a bit unsteady in the fresh dirt. She hears the unmistakable sound of a pump-action shotgun.

Abby bolted upright in her bed, drenched in sweat, her heart racing, her breathing labored, the all-too-familiar, and frequent knife-stabbing pain in her chest. She glanced at the clock. She sighed, realizing she'd only been asleep fifteen minutes. She wondered if she would ever be able to sleep again. Would she ever feel safe? She had to find a way to curb the intensity of the nightmares. Abby just wished she could find a way to make them stop.

CHAPTER 12

*J*EREMY HAD A REAL BAD feeling. This plan of his dad's for a new building didn't make any sense at all to Jeremy's way of thinking. But he was sure it had something to do with Abby. Because everything that occupied his father's mind these days was about Abby. Making Abby pay was all Cole talked about. Ever. It was getting old, tiring, and frustrating. He didn't understand why the man didn't get over it and move on. Jeremy knew for a fact that Cole had told Abby he wanted a divorce. He heard it with his own ears.

The irony wasn't lost on Jeremy. If his dad had spent as much time thinking about Abby when they were married as he did now, they might not be divorced. He also knew how many times Cole had left Abby at home, telling her he would be back in an hour, then not returning until late at night. He knew that because he had been with Cole on several of those occasions. He was certain those weren't the only times it happened because if he mentioned to his dad that he knew Abby was waiting, Cole always replied, "It's okay. She's used to it."

But he also realized, although his dad hadn't said anything to him in a while about his "debt" to help him end Abby, it still was lurking and looming there. He didn't want to help him and would do whatever he could to thwart his dad's efforts. He wished Abby would move away, and he prayed if she did, Cole never found her. In the meantime, he would do whatever he could to keep his dad away from her.

Truth was, he was afraid that he had to do whatever his dad told him. Although he knew and had proven he could beat the man, it was clear that if his dad really wanted to, he could surprise him with a knife or bullet, and there would be no chance at self-defense. He knew his dad was losing it, and he wished he knew how to make things better for him. He also wished his dad would stop drinking.

Jeremy could see the deterioration in the man. But right now, he was too tangled and twisted up knowing what they had done to Jenny, to his wife, to the mother of his children. His dad had said it would make everything better, but it didn't. He now had three small children to raise on his own, to have to tell them when they got older some story of what had happened to their mother. And he was really afraid of someone finding the body. That kind of shit could come back to haunt you for a lifetime. He was no genius, but even he knew there was no statute of limitations on murder.

Jeremy was not delusional. He knew sooner or later his dad would sell or lose that property. He always did, and sooner or later someone was going to start digging. His dad had dug that grave and buried the body. Jeremy had been too emotionally distraught, and it still bothered him. Cole had been able to do it as if he were planting a vegetable garden. Jeremy really wasn't sure it was anywhere near deep enough to even keep animals from unearthing his late wife, let alone a future construction crew.

Jeremy went to the hardware store and bought the list of supplies he needed, including pressure-treated wood, river rock, a long level, and for some reason his dad wanted a case of that spray foam insulation for filling holes. He returned to Cole's house and took all the materials to the new area. He began digging, removing the top earth, and trying to get a level area the size of the new building, making sure that there was an extra foot all the way around as the instructions stated. After a couple of hours of working, he was hot, tired, thirsty, and hungry. Jeremy returned to the house to see if there was anything to eat.

"Hey Dad, I've got it started back there, but I'm famished. Got anything to eat around here?"

"What? Does this look like a restaurant to you? Go out and pick us up a pizza. I have some more work to do here."

Yeah, what kind of work is that? You haven't done any work in months. But he wisely held his tongue and headed out to get some pizza. On the way back, as he was rounding the curve in front of the house, a dog ran out in front of him. He tried everything to avoid hitting the dog, but it was too close. He jumped out of the truck, checked on the dog, but it was too late. Jeremy put the dog in the back of the truck and returned to Cole's house, distraught and uncertain what to do. When he got to the house, he ran in and told his father what had happened.

"Hey, Dad. What should we do with the poor little guy?"

"Well, you should've left the damn thing in the road, but since you didn't, now we're going to have to bury it. Since you picked the thing up and brought it home, I guess you get to dig the grave. Where's the pizza?"

Jeremy, mad and in disbelief over how much his father had changed, returned to the truck, brought the pizza into the house, and stormed out. He drove to the back of the lot, where there was already one grave and the new building he was supposed to be preparing. The solution to all their problems hit him like a two-by-four between the eyes. He went straight to the first grave and started digging. He inadvertently had found the solution to all his problems.

If his dad was determined to install a building here in this area where someday someone was bound to decide to remove it, he was going to make sure no body would be found. At least not a human body. He dug until it got dark, all thoughts of being hungry forgotten. Then he pulled his truck in and turned the headlights on the area so he could continue to see. He hoped like hell his dad had, in fact, put the original body in a plastic bag like he said. He sure didn't want to see it. He didn't think he would be able to handle that.

About ten o'clock, he found the plastic bag. Even tied up in plastic, the stench of death hit him before he actually had unearthed it. After retching up what little was in his stomach, he removed the bag and dug several feet deeper for good measure. The muscles in his arms and back were screaming in pain, and the blisters on his hands had blisters, even through the heavy work gloves. He replaced the body, returned about three feet of the soil to the hole, placed the dead dog on top of it, and finished filling the grave. He hoped if for any reason anyone dug in that spot and found the dog, they wouldn't dig any deeper.

When that was done, he returned to the house, intending to tell his dad that tomorrow they would need to rent a compactor. Tomorrow, he would use the machine to pack the earth back over the grave to prevent as much settling as possible. Then he would build the platform for the building over the grave. Someday, if someone started digging, they would find the dog, assume it was a pet grave, and the original body would never be found.

He was feeling much better, but he knew he needed to have a conversation with his dad. There was no sense in putting it off. But Cole was passed out already. Jeremy returned home and figured he would finish what needed to be done the following day. The talk would have to wait.

The next morning, although Jeremy's body felt like it had been stomped and run over, his mood was much lighter, as he no longer worried about his late wife being found and him having to do time for her death. He drank a cup of coffee, went to hardware store to rent the compactor, and returned to the scene of the crime to finish his work. By the time he was done and returned to the house, Cole was home from work. So he asked his dad if he wanted to go fishing.

Cole was shocked. His son had not wanted to even hear the words *fishing* or *lake* since Jenny disappeared, and now he was asking to go fishing. Well, the tides must have changed for some reason. Cole was grateful, but curious. The two men grabbed some poles and a couple of six-packs and headed across the street to the lake.

"Dad, I should be finished with the building site tomorrow or the next day."

"Wow, good work Son. That was a lot faster than I thought you could get it done. Are you sure you're doing it like you're supposed to?"

"Yes, Dad, only I changed the location a little bit. I re-dug the hole we made a while back, you know the one, made it a little deeper, put the old bag in, refilled it about three feet, and buried the dog. Today, I rented a compactor, packed the earth real good, and placed the timbers for the building. Tomorrow, all I have left to do is add the river rock and make sure it's all level. I'm hoping if anyone ever has a reason to dig there, they will find the dog, and think that's all that's there."

"Damn, Jeremy, that was good thinking. I'm impressed. And we didn't even have to kill a dog, the dog committed suicide by truck. I wasn't going to put the building over the existing hole because we might have occasion to put something else in there. But if that eventuality comes to pass, we always can dig a new one. This time, we can plan ahead to add a *Beloved Pet* marker. Maybe we'll even make some stones to memorialize the animals." Cole roared with laughter at his own joke.

"Yeah, I've been pretty wigged out and tense ever since Jenny. I'm still pretty freaked out about what we did, but I was almost paralyzed with fear we would still be caught someday. I have three kids to think about, who no longer have a mother. If I end up in jail, they will end up in foster care, and I'll be damned if some pervert is going to raise my kids and abuse or molest them."

"I understand, Jeremy, and you did a good job." Jeremy soaked up the rare praise.

"Dad, I have to ask. I know you have plans for Abby. What exactly are they? I have to tell you, to be honest, I don't think I have the stomach to help with another snuffing of life. But I know I owe you." Jeremy treaded cautiously.

"My intention is to find her, bring her back here, and make her realize her mistake in leaving. Once she's endured as much pain and suffering as we have, if she's still alive, I expect her to resume her duties as my wife. Whether she lives or dies will be entirely up to her." Cole was matter-of-fact, exhibiting no emotion at all.

"Okay, Dad. How are you going to find her?"

"I have people working on it Son, make no mistake. There is nowhere she can hide from me permanently." Cole's voice sounded positively evil.

CHAPTER 13

*T*HE MONTH OF DECEMBER WAS a whirlwind for Abby. She organized the big family Christmas celebration, which included all the aunts, uncles, and cousins. She continued to get her documentation in order and worked tirelessly to clean out and sell all her possessions. She donated many to the abused women's shelter thrift store, and she continuously hauled boxfuls of stuff to the dumpster.

All the while, she kept up with the expat groups she followed, because one thing she was learning was that the laws changed rapidly in Ecuador — and with little or no warning. Abby tried to stay up-to-date with the necessary paperwork for her and Prissy so they could make the move successfully and with as little stress as possible. By the end of the third week of December, she had sold enough of her possessions to book and pay for her airfare.

To make her adventure real, she scheduled her move date to coincide with the end of her lease. Abby planned a week between leaving Greenville and flying out of Boston. She wanted to spend some time with Kendall and Brenna and get her final documents certified at the Ecuadorian consulate in Boston before leaving. While she didn't think

Cole really could have any authority to check if she had taken any flights — Abby figured that kind of thing only happened in movies — she decided to be on the safe side and fly out of Boston. Besides, he wouldn't think to look in Boston for departing flights, even if it were possible.

Abby had to visit a consulate somewhere in the States, and this way, she would get to spend some time with Kendall and Brenna. She had not talked with Brenna since making her decision, and she asked Kendall one day if Brenna thought she was crazy. He never really answered the question, so Abby knew it was definitely conversation fodder for them. She made up her mind she was going to tell Brenna that she was going to be the Mother-in-Law of the Year. She was running away from home to another continent, so Brenna would never have to worry about her dropping in unexpectedly. After all, how much better could it be than to have your mother-in-law live on another continent.

Once her ticket was booked, she reserved a residential hotel in Ecuador for thirty days so she could have a bit of stability until she found permanent housing. And then it became clear she actually was making this move. There was no going back now, because to have any funds when she arrived in Ecuador, she had to buy a nonrefundable ticket.

Friggin' Christmas. I hate Christmas. I have hated Christmas since I was ten years old, and Mom and Grandma were both fighting cancer that year. Abby made me finally look forward to Christmas. She was all about happy home and hearth at the holidays. It took a few years, but I finally got to where the Christmas music didn't bother me, and then I even started enjoying the holidays again. She was always so happy this time of year. Then the bitch left me. And now Christmas makes me even angrier than before.

If I hear one more Christmas carol, I may shoot whatever the sound is coming out of. I can't even listen to the radio in the car. I can't stand to go into the stores, even the grocery store is making me crazy irritable. What in hell do I have to be joyful about? I lost my son, I lost my dad, I lost my wife, and I lost my daughter-in-law. Jeremy is still not coming around much since Jenny disappeared. There is nothing in my life but emptiness and despair.

After Jenny's disappearance, Jeremy moved in with his mother so she could help with the three small children. Cole was alone. His mother and brother didn't call much anymore. They couldn't stand to listen to his anger, and it didn't help that he was always in some degree of a drunken state. He wondered if anyone would even call him on Christmas.

He tried calling Jeremy to see if maybe he and the kids would come by for Christmas.

"Hey Son, what's going on?"

"Same old stuff, Dad. Trying to take care of the kids and looking for a job. It's really hard to find work this time of year."

"If you want to bring the girls here for Christmas, I'll help you get presents for them. We can fry a turkey, have a good meal, and watch the kids play. What do you say?"

"I'm sorry, Dad. We already have plans. We're going to Grandma's. She's helping me with Christmas for the girls, and it's all already bought and wrapped. Maybe we can get together in the next week or two."

"Okay, I understand. Call me and let me know." He got off the phone before Jeremy could hear the tears in his voice.

I guess I'll be spending Christmas alone. Pretty fitting since I hate the damn holiday anyway. I better make a liquor store run before they close. I guess I can do anything I want, whenever I want, through the long weekend. I don't have to get dressed, don't have to entertain family, have rugrats running around. How in the hell has it happened? Last year, we had twenty people here for Christmas. I guess they only came because they wanted something. Fuck them all."

It never occurred to Cole that it was his own attitude and actions that caused him to be alone. In his mind, everyone else was screwed up.

This is all Abby's fault. I have hated Christmas nearly my whole life. For years, I was comfortable with that. I wouldn't have minded spending Christmas alone. She changed all that and made me like Christmas again. Now, because of her, I'm alone. I hate Christmas again, but now it makes me sad. Jeremy is exactly like his mother. Ungrateful little brat. All I have ever done is try to help that boy, and all he cares about is himself. Cole poured another drink.

I will make her pay for this. I'll find a way to make her as miserable as she has made me. There's gotta be some way I can make sure she loses everything. All of this is Abby's fault. Jenny's death is her fault. If she hadn't left, Jenny would still be alive. I would still have a good relationship with my son. Jenny's blood is on her hands. I know what I'll do. I'll call Kendall. He's a good boy, and he knows I love him.

Before Abby knew it, it was Christmas. The large family celebration included those she had seen during the last ten years only at the kids' weddings, which made the occasion especially bittersweet for Abby. She cherished seeing each and every one of them, but it was made both sweeter and sadder knowing this might be the last time she was with them all for the holidays.

Her secret burned within her, but she waited until the end of the evening to tell them her news. Abby knew they would be stunned, but she didn't want to tell them early in the celebration, as she didn't want the day to be about her. At least that's what she told herself. She didn't want to think it might be nerves causing her to delay the inevitable. The best-case scenario would be they would all have questions and be interested in the same way her mom and Kendall had been. The worst case would be they would think she was crazy and be furious with her. She didn't want to spoil the day either way, so she waited until the end of the holiday celebration to spring her news. Of course, Abby was a bundle of nerves during the entire event, wondering how her news would be received.

Once she announced she had some news to impart, they all listened intently. She told them she would be leaving Greenville in a few months, and she knew they had been waiting to see where she was moving. As she told them her plans, she watched each of their faces, looking for telltale signs of how they were receiving her news. She stared into disbelieving, stunned faces. Never had she seen her family speechless — later she would find it funny.

Except for her nephew and nieces, Rusty, Savannah, and Madison, who started laughing and were the first ones to say anything.

"Good one, Abby," the three said at the same time. They thought it was a joke. When she finally made them realize she wasn't kidding, she was met with a combination of blank stares from the older generation, who appeared to be mortified, and a passel of questions from the younger generation, who thought it sounded cool. She calmly answered all the questions.

The party broke up, and everyone returned to their respective hotel rooms. Abby, Kendall, and Brenna went back to her apartment, glad that they were not part of whatever discussions were going on at the hotel.

The next day, after the rest of the family left for home, Abby, Kendall, and Brenna dug into all the boxes of keepsakes from Kendall's childhood. Abby handled the sorting process better than she expected. In fact, the three of them had a lot of fun rehashing old memories and telling Brenna cute stories of Kendall's young antics. They sang "Little Bunny Foo Foo" and "The Never Ending Song" all through the day, until they were all sure the two songs would be stuck in their heads for eternity. What Abby had been dreading so much became a sweet moment in their lives, complete with new cherished memories.

They loaded Kendall and Brenna's car with all the treasures he was taking back, leaving Abby with two piles. One went to the dumpster, and one was to donate or sell. She would deal with those once the kids were gone, because she knew that actually disposing of the remnants that formed the quilt of Kendall's childhood would be the hardest part for her emotionally.

Cole called Kendall three times on Christmas Day, but got no answer. It never occurred to him that maybe Kendall was involved in family celebrations and didn't have his phone nearby, or wasn't going to answer because he was involved in something, or maybe it would've been rude for Kendall to answer his phone at those particular moments, or he could be traveling. Kendall never talked on the phone while driving. Cole became more agitated by the moment and sent this text message: "So, I guess you aren't going to talk to me?"

Kendall returned Cole's call the next day, explaining he had been at his in-laws' family gathering and didn't know his phone had rung. Then he tried to listen, tried to be patient, through a half-hour-long diatribe of how sad Cole's life was and how he missed all the people who had passed away. When Kendall couldn't take any more of it, and was convinced Cole was drunk again, he got off the phone and made up his mind — he didn't need this grief. Cole called him eight more times over the next two days. When Kendall didn't answer his phone, Cole started sending drunken, angry text messages.

Finally, on the third day, Cole received a message from Kendall that he would call him the following day, citing he was tied up with family gatherings. Cole decided to wait until the next day for Kendall's call. Instead of a call, he got a long email at work from Kendall. In summary, it said Kendall didn't want to have any more contact with Cole as long as Cole was drinking, and he hoped Cole would seek some assistance from a counselor, priest, rehab, or whatever he was comfortable with, to turn his life around.

Cole sent a reply: "That's fine, but your mother will pay. My life is good because I have lawyers, and I'm a Grey, Greys are winners. She's the one who is suffering. She should've never left me." Kendall read the message and chuckled to himself thinking, *if he only knew.*

CHAPTER 14

*T*HE NEXT TWO MONTHS were crazy busy for Abby. Every day she was amazed at how much stuff a person could accumulate. But she was disposing of it all systematically, one way or another. She purchased an e-reader, an undergarment security pouch for traveling, luggage locks, suitcases (the largest she could get within airline limits), a luggage scale to ensure she wouldn't incur overweight charges, and she broke down and told her closest friend, Judy, what she was doing.

She needed one friend to know what was happening, to share in her daily complications and triumphs. Abby had told her local friends only that she was cleaning out her storage building and getting rid of the stuff from her past life. Which was true, of course. However, she strategically didn't divulge her reason for the heaviest spring-cleaning she had ever done in her life. While they didn't know the sordid details, her friends did know she recently went through a divorce. Even the friends who hadn't been through one, knew how difficult a divorce could be, so no one pried too much.

But Judy was a different story. Because they were the closest, she had to tell Judy. They grew even closer and spent more time together.

Abby shared Jenny's tragic disappearance with Judy and found herself opening up a little bit about her shaded past, especially when she found out Judy had been married to an emotionally abusive alcoholic, as well. It was a shared history they both understood better than most.

Each week, they splurged and went to their favorite barbecue restaurant for the five dollar Monday night special. It was a time when they could share what was going on that week for them both. Abby would have loved it if Judy would move with her to Ecuador, but Judy had grandsons who were the apples of her eye. She couldn't imagine going that far away from them.

Judy benefited from Abby's dissolution of property, though. Lucky for her, they wore the same size shoe and collected some of the same things. Abby also benefited because she had someone to share it all with — the funny moments, the sad moments, and the apprehension of late travel and visa documents, plus all the other inevitable daily setbacks that happen when working with two governments.

Then there were the daily phone calls from Abby's mother. Her favorite was when her mom called.

"Abby, I was listening to my Tim McGraw CD today and the song *"Live Like You Were Dying"* came on. It made me think of you, what you're doing, and it made me really want to do it, too. I think I am a little too old to ride a bull or skydive, so I'm really thinking about moving around the world instead. Would you mind if I decided to join you there?"

"No, it would be great. But you know what I'm going through consolidating everything from a lifetime. Are you sure you could do that? I know how sentimental you are, and how much you love your things. It's hard to do. I think the only reason I can do it is because I want this so much."

"Well, no, Abby. I'm not sure of that at all, but I think I want to try. I could get a storage building for my treasures."

"The other thing, Mom, I'm moving to a place far far away, one that I've never been to before. It really is best if you can visit a place first to see if you'll like it there, before you get rid of everything and make that kind of commitment. Things are very different in Ecuador. You know you can't even flush your toilet paper? It might be better for you to visit there first. I can't afford to do it that way, but I'm willing to take my chances, knowing I'll have to stay probably at least three years to save enough to come back and start over."

"I wouldn't be able to afford to go twice either, Abby. I'll have to do the same thing you're doing and sell everything to raise the funds to make the move. But I was thinking. Maybe you can check things out for me, send me pictures, and tell me all about it. You'll know if I'll like it when you get there. I figure that will put me about six months behind you. Dear, are you sure you can't flush the toilet paper? I bet that is one of those silly rumors. Did you check that fact-finder site?"

"Yes, I'm sure, and no, I didn't check that site." Abby laughed. "But if you're sure you want to give it a shot, I think it would be great for you to go, too."

"I'm not 100 percent sure, but I am thinking about it. Let's not tell anyone yet."

"Sure, I understand." And so another plan began to hatch.

There were also the conversations with her nephew. He sent her an instant message that read, "OMG! Did you know there are volcanoes in Ecuador?"

"Yes, I do, but none are close to the city where I am moving, and there are no tornadoes or hurricanes. A year ago, the city where I am going got a little ash cover, but aside from some extra house cleaning, no one was harmed."

She secretly loved the fact her boys were researching quietly behind the scenes to learn more about where she was going, but she never let on to them about it. On the other hand, her nieces were so involved in their new college lives, she figured her move was the furthest thing from their minds.

When she was telling Kendall about scheduling Prissy's vet appointments for vaccines and travel documents, he ran down the checklist of all the immunizations she herself needed. She laughed and told him you only needed those if you were going to the coast or the Amazon. She explained that she had checked the Center for Disease Control website and had consulted with her doctor. He had completed a mission trip to Ecuador so knew what to do and verified she was good to go. Kendall wasn't convinced, but recognized he had hit a brick wall.

Her weekly conversations with Lizzy, were focused on the questions arising from Jenny's disappearance, Cole's running litany of complaints about everything being Abby's fault, how did she leave so quickly, and who she had run off with. She never mentioned to Lizzy she was leaving. Abby felt a little guilty about that, and she wanted to trust her with the information, as Lizzy was such a good friend. But she knew it was unfair to expect Lizzy to keep the news from Forest. And if Forest knew, it could be extremely easy for him to get exasperated with Cole one day and blurt out that Abby was gone. She knew once she reached Boston, she would have to block Lizzy from her Facebook pages. While she had not posted anything about moving or Ecuador, she knew once she arrived at her new home, she would have to post pictures and updates for her family and Judy. For obvious reasons, she couldn't take a chance on Lizzy seeing it.

She didn't hear anything from the aunts, uncles, or cousins; mostly she talked with her mom and Judy. But she did get wind her family had established a betting pool of how long she would stay in Ecuador. She thought it was hysterical that the longest time anyone chose was three months.

"For crying out loud, Judy. Do they think I would sell everything, including my vehicle, just to return in three months? They really do think I'm crazy!" They had a good laugh.

The last three weeks before her departure approached nightmare status. There was so much to do and coordinate at the last minute and, of course, everyone wanted to spend time with her before she left. Merry drove all the way from Wichita for a two-day visit, Rusty and Chelsea came for one night, and her mom planned to come for the last week to help with selling those items she needed until she left. Abby had arranged to sell her truck at an auto auction on her last day in Greenville, for Prissy's last vet checkup and paperwork, cleaning the apartment, and so on. It was a whirlwind; it was exciting; she was nervous, but determined.

Abby arranged for a mail forwarding service so she could maintain a U.S. mailing address, and set up online Skype and Internet phone accounts so she could keep in touch with everyone at home. She double-checked her reservations, and Prissy's approval as an Emotional Support Animal, which would allow her to travel in the plane cabin — all the last-minute details.

The hardest part was the packing and repacking, culling out more and more stuff so everything would fit in her suitcases without them being over the airline's allowed weight. Which, of course, resulted in more items to be donated, given away, or bequeathed to friends. Each day, the excitement and nerves grew in equal measure.

Abby was exhausted, so she indulged in a nap. Where naps had at one time been a daily occurrence, these days they were few and far between. When she awoke, she had three missed calls from one of her long-time best friends, Trent Dumas. Before she returned the call, she noticed she had an instant message from a mutual friend. "Trent is trying to call you. He's on his way to Greenville." A surge of excitement pulsed through Abby. She had not seen Trent in about a year, and she was looking forward to a visit.

They had worked together at the steel company and had become fast friends. Even though she stopped working there, they still talked on a regular basis, and she considered him one of her closest friends. They had both been married, and there was nothing romantic about their friendship, nothing but best friends who could talk about anything.

For years, while they were at the steel company, they worked closely every day. They knew about each other's families, they alternately joked and were serious and cared deeply about one another's successes and failures. They grew remarkably close as sometimes happens in certain working relationships.

When Abby first stopped working, Trent called her every few days to check on her. He was concerned because he could tell things weren't right, but he didn't know for sure what was going on. Then Abby grew more and more distant, although she always sounded glad to hear from him. Eventually, she told him about her diagnosis. After much discussion, he realized that Abby's problem stemmed from all the medications in combination with her lengthy healing process. He tried to give her the space he thought she needed, but never went too long without checking on her.

After Abby and Cole moved to Greenville, Trent let her know when he would be traveling through her area and they would meet for lunch. But Cole became more and more disapproving, jealous, and suspicious about their relationship. The last time Abby met Trent for lunch, she made sure she told Cole in advance that Trent was coming so he could join them for lunch. He declined the invitation, so Abby thought things would be okay. She met Trent for lunch as planned. As she was leaving the restaurant, she hugged Trent, told him how good it was to see him, wished him a safe trip, and returned to her truck to leave. As she was pulling out of the parking lot, she spotted Cole's truck across the street. Even from a distance she could see the angry set of his jaw and knew there was going to be trouble. She checked her mirrors and looked for Trent's truck. When she saw he already had left the parking lot, she breathed a sigh of relief knowing that at least Cole didn't have plans to confront Trent. She didn't let Cole know she had seen him and went straight home.

Abby steeled herself for the argument she knew would be coming. She just didn't know if Cole would come home now or go back to work. She prayed he would go back to work, where maybe he would have time to calm down before finishing for the day. When Cole didn't appear within about thirty minutes, she realized he must have returned to work, and the confrontation would wait.

While she waited, she realized how ridiculous this whole situation was getting. She had done nothing wrong. She had met a friend for lunch, in a public place, she had told Cole she was going ahead of time, and she had even invited him to join them. When Cole got home, he didn't quite see things the same way.

From that point on, until she left Cole, she regularly talked to Trent on the phone, but just never mentioned it to Cole. And when Trent called to say he was in the area, she always found some excuse that she couldn't meet him. It was just one more way Cole had isolated her from her friends.

Not long before Abby left Cole, Trent was promoted. As a result of his new assignment, he had not had the opportunity to travel to her area. Since she left Cole, Abby, and Trent talked more often on the phone. She told him some of her reasons for leaving, but never anywhere near the whole story. It had been over a year since she had seen him so she returned his phone call right away.

CHAPTER 15

"*H*I GUY, I HAVEN'T HEARD from you in a while. What's going on?"

"I'm headed your way, Abby. I should be there between lunch and two tomorrow and wondered if you were available. I would love to see you." Trent was hopeful, but he didn't want to take no for an answer.

"Of course I'll make time to see you. Call me as soon as you get here, and I'll buy you lunch."

She had shared with Trent a lot of what was going on, more than she had shared with anyone other than her mother, but there was still much she had not and would not ever tell anyone. They were her demons, and demons she was determined to leave behind, so there was no sense in burdening others. She was determined to be a victim no longer, and sharing her experiences only would allow Cole access to all her relationships. However, as she had told Trent of her move to Ecuador, she knew full well that was the main purpose for his visit.

She spent the rest of the afternoon and evening trying to get as much done as possible so she would feel she had free time when he arrived. She was excited to see him, so she took the time to do hair and makeup and put on her favorite teal green shirt over a white tank, jeans, and sandals. And then she waited to hear that he was in town. When she got the call, she went to pick him up.

When he walked out, he looked around as she waved to him from her truck. He came walking over and opened the passenger door.

"I didn't recognize you. You look great!"

"Wow, what a greeting! Thanks. You do too!"

He stared at her. "No, I mean you're gorgeous! What did you do?"

"Nothing. It's the same ole me." Trent was making her feel a little self-conscious.

"No, something's different." Trent insisted.

"I'm alive again. The last time I saw you, I think my soul was dead. I've also lost a little weight, that's it."

"Well, you look fantastic!" Trent was sitting in the passenger seat, with his body turned toward her, and she could feel him staring at her.

"Thanks. What do you want to eat?" She started driving.

"Anything but Chinese is good with me."

"How about a steak?" She knew steak was always a winner for a man, and for her, too.

"Hell, yeah. That sounds great."

They spent a couple of hours over lunch. They talked about his work, their mutual friends, their kids, and life in general. She asked him where he was headed, because usually when they met up, he was en route to somewhere else.

"I'm here for work, but don't have anything to do until Monday."

It was only Saturday. She tried to think of something they could do. "Do you want to go to a movie or something?"

"Or something, but not a movie because I want to be able to talk to you. I can watch a movie anytime. Since you're leaving, I want to spend time with you."

"What about the stock car races — we have a little local mud track?" Abby asked, trying to think of something they could do and still visit, without returning to her bare apartment. The only unsold furniture left were a mattress on the floor and a patio chair.

"Wow! I haven't been to the races in years. That sounds like fun!"

The races didn't start for a while, so they drove around town for a couple of hours, then stopped at her apartment to walk Prissy. She decided to grab a jacket and change into more appropriate shoes before they headed to the races. It was a beautiful night, clear skies and a little chilly, and they had fun.

All day and all night, even at the races, he noticed that if anything moved behind her, she started and looked over her shoulder. He wasn't sure why. He didn't know what was up, but something certainly was.

"Call me when you get up in the morning," he said as Abby dropped him off at his hotel.

"What time do you want me to call? I get up really early."

"I don't care if it's 5:00 a.m. or 8:00 a.m., call me when you get up. We can get breakfast or coffee, whatever you like."

Well, she hadn't planned on that, but she would deal with it tomorrow. For now, she was worried about getting home. This little drop-off had put her in Cole's part of town, on a weekend night. Her nerves were twanging. She couldn't wait to get home. She never was out on the weekends as she didn't want to take a chance on running into Cole, but she had had fun tonight and was glad she was able to see Trent before she left in another week.

He'd known her the better part of his life, but only truly saw her for the first time today. And he wanted her. Her laughter was deeper than he remembered, her eyes brighter than the stars on a clear summer night, her smile more cherished than his favorite motorcycle. But she didn't see him yet.

Back at his hotel room, he couldn't sleep for rehashing their afternoon and night. He lay, staring at the ceiling, wondering why she looked so different, and he realized there was a light in her eyes that had been missing before. Maybe she was right about her soul having been dead. Regardless, he sure was glad she was doing better. He would make her believe again, of her worth, in her beauty, in really living life, and love. It would take a long time, but she's worth it, he's sure.

She knew she still was running, still feeling hunted, after her last bad relationship. No mistake, she felt more alive than she had in years. The sun was brighter; there was joy again in her life. But she didn't trust herself to make good decisions. While she realized it was wrong to judge all men by the actions of a few, she no longer trusted her judgment in affairs of the heart and doubted she ever would.

Abby was so glad she had the opportunity to see Trent again before she left, and she had really enjoyed herself, despite her nerves jangling and twanging over being afraid of running into Cole. She knew her biggest fear was that she and Trent might run into Cole and what he might do to Trent. With all Cole's recent ranting about her having run off with someone, she knew he would have jumped to conclusions, and Trent could have been in danger. That scared her more than worrying about her own safety.

The next morning, Abby didn't call Trent as soon as she woke up at six. She walked Prissy, made her coffee, and evaluated her to do list for the day. She still had a lot to do before she left in just a week. She realized she didn't have the time to spend with Trent, and it saddened her. She called him at eight, and he asked her to pick him up for breakfast. Abby told him she couldn't do breakfast because she had a full day of errands to make up for yesterday.

"Come on, Abby. How long can breakfast take? An hour maybe.

You need to eat, then I promise I'll let you go home to take care of things."

"Okay. But if I do, the hair is in a ponytail, and it will have to be quick."

"That's fine. I promise not to keep you long."

"Okay, okay, give me thirty minutes. I'll pick you up." Abby took fifteen minutes to put on some makeup, pulled her hair up, and dressed in jeans and a T-shirt. She didn't have the time to do more.

She was running through her mind where she could take him for breakfast on a Sunday morning where she wouldn't be afraid of running into Cole. She decided on a hole-in-the-wall café downtown. It was famous for home cooking at lunch, but recently began opening for breakfast on Sundays. She hoped maybe Cole didn't know about them being open for breakfast now, and there was no place else open downtown on Sunday morning other than the churches. Abby was pretty certain Cole wouldn't be visiting any of the churches this morning, so she felt the café would be a safe place.

Breakfast ended up taking a couple of hours because the service staff were new, plus Abby and Trent talked and talked, mostly about her move to Ecuador.

"I can't believe you're moving that far away. I'll never get to see you."

"Probably not, but we can still talk on the phone. I'll have Internet calling so I can contact folks in the States at no charge. In addition, I have a U.S. phone number so you can call me. It will only work if I'm at my computer, but you can leave voice mail. I promise I'll call you back." She knew she had to reassure him as she had so many others.

"I know, but I'm here where you are now. And you're leaving. I have a meeting here tomorrow, then I go back to Roanoke for a week, and then I'll be back here for the foreseeable future. We finally would be in the same town again, and you're leaving. Do you want to tell me what's really going on with Cole? I sense you haven't told me everything, and you don't have to, but I would be interested in knowing, if you want to tell me." Trent was hoping she would take the bait and tell him what really was going on.

She did. He already knew about Cole's drinking and a few of the threats he had made, but she told him more about the threats, about Jenny's disappearance, and that everyone feared foul play.

"Oh my gosh, Abby. I knew things were bad from what you told me on our phone calls, and I sensed there was more. But I never imagined all this. I thought you guys were happy."

"Well, I wanted to believe we were. I never told anyone otherwise."

She took him back to the hotel and got out of her truck to wish him goodbye. He hugged her tightly, and it felt so good to be held in his strong arms, where she knew she was safe.

"If anything ever happens between you and that lovely wife of yours, you be sure and let me know." She was only half kidding.

"You'll be the first to hear. What time is dinner?" he said a little too seriously. Abby looked him in the eye, and he covered with a chuckle.

"Trent, really I can't. There's still so much left to be done." She really wished she had more time.

"You have to eat, and we might as well eat at the same time. You name the time; I'll be ready. We'll make it fast." Trent now was pleading.

Oh, I can't believe he's begging. That is almost impossible to resist. Of course, I don't really want to resist. His visit has been good for me, and I sense he's feeling a little panicked that I'm going so far away. Okay, scratch almost impossible, those pleading eyes are impossible to resist.

"How about six-thirty; we'll grab Mexican. We have a great restaurant here, and it's fast." Abby suggested this, yet felt a bit defeated.

"That works for me," Trent said with a triumphant grin.

She went home and repacked her suitcases again — she finally got them finished and underweight. Abby sorted all the remaining items earmarked for charity and hauled another truckload to the dumpster before leaving to pick Trent up for dinner.

They got to the restaurant and quickly ordered. She could tell something was on his mind. But she knew if he wanted to talk about it, he would. So she asked the question that had been nagging at her all day.

"How is your family handling all your new travel and being gone all the time? You said you were going to be here for the foreseeable future. How is Suzy dealing with that? Will they move here?"

"Actually, she's not. The kids miss me, and I miss them. Apparently, my being gone all the time didn't work too well for her, and she's having an affair. When I go home Tuesday, it's to sign the divorce papers."

Abby was stunned. She realized she was staring at him with her mouth wide open. He and Suzy had been such a great couple. Trent had been so in love with her, and it showed. She was surprised this had happened and surprised he had not mentioned it until now. She asked him why.

"Well, to be honest, I haven't told anyone. I haven't even told my family yet. It's been a long time coming, but the legal work has gone fast. I don't want anything but to be able to see my kids whenever I can. There isn't anything to fight over. It's not like I could get custody or even joint custody with all the traveling I do for the job. So I pay child support, I walk away with my clothes, and I can see the kids whenever I'm in town. Done. Over." Trent was pretty matter-of-fact, but his eyes conveyed the pain and sorrow beneath.

"I'm so sorry, Trent. I would never have suspected." Abby truly was shocked.

"Abby, it's been over for a while. The last two years, the only time we talked was when she needed something, mostly money. I would call her for days, she wouldn't answer, and she wouldn't return my phone calls. When I was taken unconscious to the hospital last year, the hospital called her for three days before she answered. They asked for my date of birth, and she didn't know. I knew then that she didn't care about me as much as I cared about her."

"This is so sad. So there's no chance to fix it?"

"Unfortunately, no. There were other signs too. It became clear she didn't want to see me much. I kept making excuses for her. I've been asking her for months what was wrong, what could I do different, what did she need from me? I even offered to quit my job so I could stay home with her and the boys. I knew something was wrong, but I didn't know what. And since I didn't know what the problem was, I didn't know how to fix it."

Abby's heart broke for him. He was such a great guy — family was everything to him. He didn't deserve this. By the time she dropped him at his hotel, it was eleven o'clock. Oh, she had lost a whole weekend, but she couldn't even think about that. He had promised to call her after his trip home to let her know he was okay. They promised to stay in touch.

When she got home, her phone was ringing. It was Trent.

"I really need to keep talking to you, pleeeeease. We can talk while you work, unless you're going to bed."

They ended up talking that night until 3:00 a.m. When they were trying to get off the phone, he told her, "I have never in my life talked to someone on the phone for four hours. I will call you when I get back from Roanoke."

The next day, Abby rose early to take Prissy for the final vet check and paperwork for the trip. It had to be sent express to the USDA for processing and overnighted back so she would have it before she left for Boston. When she arrived at the vet, despite having talked to them several times over the last three months, the clinic realized they were not certified to complete the needed the papers so referred her to another vet.

She went to the new office and discovered that the cost was going to be double. Then this office said they couldn't provide paperwork for a dog that wasn't their patient. Abby surprised herself and stood her ground, insisting that it all needed to be done now. Phone calls were then made between the two vets, and they told her to come back in an hour.

She returned home, to see if she could find another vet willing to supply the necessary papers based on the records from her vet. All she wanted to do was call Trent. She questioned herself, *why is that?* But she didn't know. Abby wondered why her first thought wasn't to call her mom, or Judy, or Kendall. They would've all understood her panic and helped in any way they could. But she wanted to talk to Trent. She couldn't call him. First, he would think she was crazy; and second, she knew he had a meeting today.

By the time the vets finally sorted everything out and sent the papers to the USDA, it was lunchtime. Without even thinking, she dialed Trent's number. He was as supportive as she could have asked for, talked to her in a soothing tone of voice that instantly calmed her, and told her everything was going to be okay. She didn't know why, or how he had done it, but she believed him.

That night they talked on the phone for five hours. They talked like they always had. When Abby went to bed that night, she felt apprehensive for him, for what his next few days would be like. Although she was worried about him, if she were honest, she had to admit she was sad she wouldn't be able to talk to him for the next few days. He was going to be with his kids. Despite the fact she and Trent were almost the same age, his kids were still young, while her son was grown. But she recognized his need to spend time with them, and she hoped the legalities of the week wouldn't taint the few days they had together.

She was surprised when he called her at eight o'clock on his first night home. The kids had gone to bed, so Abby and Trent talked late into the night. They marveled at how they could talk for so long and never run out of things to say. He was even more surprised than she. He had never talked to his wife for more than fifteen or twenty minutes at a time on the phone. But, with Abby, he never wanted to hang up. They both felt they were trying to grab every moment before she left.

When he called the following night, the conversation took a huge turn with one simple phrase.

"Sweetness, if I didn't know this move was the best thing for you, I would do everything in my power to convince you to stay."

Oh damn! Why did he have to say something like that? I know not to trust my instincts about men, but has a man ever put my needs before his desires? Be still my heart. Settle down, they are only words, just flirting. Her heart was racing.

"Wow, you're a charming flirt aren't you? Thank you for that. And I do think this move is the best thing for me. At least for a few years. Then maybe I can come back. Will you come see me in Ecuador?"

"Yes, I will. I would love to visit Ecuador. But we aren't done just because you are leaving. I can't stand the thought of not talking to you. You have to promise we will still talk, every day. I need to see you, too. We need Skype. I don't have a great imagination, and I need to see that gorgeous face, your smile, and hear your laugh, too. I can wait three years for you to come back, but no longer, you hear?"

It was true that she had laughed more in the past week, than in the previous ten years. Abby started to feel good about herself again, and dare she think, happy? Her heart raced, but it felt oh so different from the rapid heartbeat of a panic attack. It felt good.

CHAPTER 16

*A*BBY COULDN'T BELIEVE THE TIME had finally come. Today was her last full day in Greenville. The local charity arrived in the morning to take the few things she had needed until the last minute.

She cleaned her apartment and said tearful goodbyes to all her neighbor friends as they dropped by to say a final farewell. There were promises to keep in touch, and Abby made sure each one had her email and her new Skype phone number so they could call her. She reminded each one she wasn't sure how long it would take for her to get Internet, but until she did, whenever she had access she would post an online update. Those who didn't have computers or Facebook accounts would get their news updates from the ones who did.

Cleaning the apartment took longer than she anticipated because of all the visiting, but she knew that was an important part of the separation process as well, both for her and her friends. She knew they would be shocked when they discovered where she had moved, and she still felt bad for having to do things this way. But she also knew it was a necessary precaution.

She turned in her apartment keys to the manager and checked into the hotel where she would be spending her last night in Greenville. Judy took her to pick up the rental car for her drive to Boston and then drove her to the auto auction where she sold her truck. It was a bittersweet time for them both. But they had fun, as they always had fun when they were together. Then Judy dropped her back at the hotel, complete with fierce bear hugs and teary *I love yous*.

As soon as she returned to her room, she called Trent. He was as anxious to hear from her, as she was to talk to him. He wanted to hear all about her day, how the auction had gone, how she was feeling. Their conversations over the last week had left her feeling like something big was happening. Abby even told him she thought lightning had struck when he had been in town. But though they talked about everything under the sun, she wasn't sure Trent felt as she did. She knew she was already in love with him. She guessed it shouldn't be such a big surprise, as close as they had been for so long and now with them both being available. It probably was only natural. Logically, she knew this wasn't like a new romance, but it still seemed to be moving so fast. And she was moving fast away from it, physically at least.

That night they talked for five hours, sharing their insecurities about relationships and themselves, telling each other the histories of their past and their dreams for the future. There were no promises made about their own personal future, although there were a lot of compliments, reassurances about the other's fears, judgments about the other's partners, and how stupid they had been to let them get away. It became clear that while their situations were totally different, they were alike in that neither of them had been properly respected, cherished, or valued. She wanted to prove to him he was worthy; he was experiencing the same thoughts about her. Abby was by far the more damaged of the two, but she soon realized that behind all of Trent's talk and bravado, he was broken, too. Secretly, she was hoping that despite their upcoming distance, they might be able to heal one another.

Abby had sold, given away, donated, or trashed everything she owned that didn't fit in her two large suitcases. She had purchased an airline ticket, rented an apartment a world away, and was on the road to making some big changes. She also was covering her tracks. The rental car was loaded, and she was making a 600-mile journey to get to the Ecuadorian consulate in Boston, planning to keep to back roads, staying in cheap hotels, paying in cash. Five days to travel 600 miles. She didn't think Cole would have any way to track her, but she knew he had friends in law enforcement and a coworker who was a bounty hunter. She planned to take this trip slowly and carefully. If Cole were able to enlist help in tracking her, she was going to make sure they would have difficulty in finding a trail.

But her nights were blissful, because she talked with Trent. Every night Abby promised herself an early bedtime, but she couldn't help herself. They talked and talked and talked. And she laughed. It had been so long. The sound startled her at first, but it became a warm elixir to her soul. She found herself smiling for no particular reason, and despite almost no sleep, her eyes were alive with a discernible sparkle. She felt lighter, more agile, more energetic. Truthfully, she felt like she was sixteen again.

Trent could be totally serious one minute, talking about his hopes and dreams for the rest of his career, and then somehow the next minute, they would be arguing the virtues of Batman versus Spider-man, and in the next talking SEC football, which somehow would lead into family stories of one episode or another. The chatter went on and on, and she delighted when he turned silly. It was refreshing, yet it wasn't because he was immature, or irresponsible, it was just because he was fun.

And she was leaving. Going three thousand miles away. Wasn't this a fine kettle of fish? She was finally happy; nevertheless, she was leaving it behind. She didn't know how long the bliss would last. Abby felt sure it was arguably the newness of the situation, but she knew she would ride the happiness train for as long as it lasted. If it all came crashing down around her, it would hurt, it would hurt bad. But she was a survivor, and she had outlived and outrun much worse. She knew she would survive. But for now, she was holding on, holding on tight, and would do everything in her power to keep the relationship and the sensations alive for as long as she could. Everything, that is, except stay.

She and Prissy spent three nights on the road, meandering their way slowly from Greenville to Boston. She had to kill three days getting to Boston, because she had to be out of her apartment on the last day of her lease. It worked out as Kendall was out of town at a conference for those three days. Even with their tight schedules, she still wanted to spend a couple of days with him, Brenna, and her fur grandbabies before leaving. Abby was fully aware that it probably would be a long time before they saw each other again.

Trent started calling her in the daytime as well as continuing their nightly talks. Several times a day, in fact. But once Abby arrived at her hotel for the night, despite the cool spring evenings, she would sit outside and talk to him. Then as it got later, she would move inside, and they would talk until the early morning hours. When they finally said good night, Trent would say, "When you get in bed, close your eyes and concentrate. You'll feel me behind you, holding you, keeping you safe, and we will both sleep well." She did imagine, and they did sleep well, each dreaming of the other.

Abby and Prissy arrived in Boston just in time for Kendall and Brenna to be home from work. The dogs were all happy to see each other again, and it tugged at Abby's heartstrings to know this might be the last time the dogs would be together. Prissy was already at her breed's life expectancy, so Abby didn't figure Prissy would be coming back to the States with her, if she ever decided to move back. The humans went out to dinner and discussed the last-minute preparations and directions to the consulate, where Abby was headed the next day. After dinner, they took a tour of the kid's favorite places in Boston, as Abby had not been able to visit Boston since they moved there.

Kendall took charge, as usual. At his insistence, they obtained color laminated copies of Abby's passport and heavy-duty bug repellant for the drive from Guayaquil to Cuenca. Kendall pointed out that although Cuenca was at a high altitude with few if any mosquitoes, much of the drive was along rivers. He instructed his mom to be vigilant about the bug spray so she wouldn't get dengue fever or typhoid. Abby laughed, hugged him, reassured him that she would be fine, and promised to reapply the bug spray often.

When they all said goodnight, and the kids went to bed, Abby took her computer out on the terrace and called Trent. She told him about her day, and he told her about his before she realized she had to be up in just a few hours to make her consulate appointment.

There were only a few minor hiccups at the consulate to finalize the paperwork for her trip. The staff was nice, and it didn't take as long as she thought it might. She returned to Kendall's and called her mom to let her know she was set to leave. Abby was getting very excited, but the nerves were growing as well.

When Kendall and Brenna got home from work, they all went into the kitchen to prepare dinner. They ate while talking about what was going on in the kids' lives, their friends, and activities. After dinner, they repacked Abby's suitcases one last time and watched the three dogs play. Kendall decided there were a few more things Abby needed so they made another trip to the store and stopped for ice cream. As everything was set for her early-morning departure and her rental car return, they all retired for the night; tomorrow was going to be a big day. Once again, Abby slipped out onto the terrace to call Trent. He was off the next day, and they ended up talking until it was time for the kids to get up and Abby to leave for the airport.

At the Boston airport, Prissy collected a fan club as she pranced through the site as if she did this every day. Abby sent text messages to her mom, sister, and brother that she was at the airport and on her way. Then she called Trent, and they talked until time to board. He told her to call from her layover in Miami, and she told him she would if she could, explaining the layover was short and she knew Prissy would need a potty break.

As it turned out, the layover in Miami was extremely short, so Prissy's potty break resulted in a sprint through the airport, a quick visit outside, and a repeat pass through security. There was barely enough time to send text messages that she now was leaving Miami, but no time to call Trent.

On the flight from Miami to Ecuador, there was a beautiful small Ecuadorian child traveling in the row next to her with his mother and grandmother. He was so well behaved through the flight, and she enjoyed watching him. His mother spoke a little English, and she and Abby talked. The mother was fascinated that Abby was moving to Ecuador and welcomed her to the country. Abby had read the Ecuadorian people were warm and friendly — it already was proving to be true. Her flight arrived in Guayaquil at 10:00 p.m. As she disembarked from the plane, Abby thought she felt her universe shift.

She made it through immigration and customs and retrieved her luggage with the help of a nice young man and exited the airport. Though going through customs and immigration was uncomfortable and a little frightening, as she exited the airport doors and stepped into her new country, she felt she had passed through the portal between hell and heaven.

Her host was waiting for her right outside the airport doors. He loaded her luggage and took her to his home, a bed-and-breakfast, for her first night in Ecuador. He was warm and friendly, and they talked as if they had known each other for years, even though their only previous contact had been over the Internet when she booked his services. He was Ecuadorian, but had lived in the U.S. during his high school and college years, so he spoke excellent English. The only problem was the Internet was down, so she couldn't let her mom, Kendall, or Trent know she had arrived safely.

Abby awoke the next morning to a beautiful sunny day, in a country where she was sure Cole never would find her. Not once did she look over her shoulder. Only a small handful of people in the world knew where she was. A beautiful land with no addresses. Even her eventual immigration papers would list nothing but the closest intersection, and the U.S. State Department only had her email address. Abby actually could feel a difference in the air filling her lungs. She was free...finally.

When she went to walk Prissy, she was amazed at how much brighter the colors were — the sky, the grass, the flowers. It seemed as if she was in an optical sensory overload. The people she met along her walk all spoke to her. She believed she was in heaven. Her host, Jorge, took her to breakfast as the bed-and-breakfast kitchen was being remodeled. The food tasted so good. They chatted about the differences between the U.S. and Ecuador, after which they embarked on the journey to her new home in Cuenca.

It was about a four-hour drive, beginning in the lowlands where she saw bananas, cocoa, sugar cane, coffee, and many other crops growing along the way, as well as llamas and flamingos. They then climbed through the Cajas National Park, a mountain range park where the roads seemed to drop off on at least one side of the mountain, and where they ascended higher than the clouds. Looking out the windows, it appeared as if it had snowed, but it was clouds. And it was magnificent.

Once she got to her temporary short-term housing, she had Internet so she rapidly fired off emails to family, friends and Trent saying that she had arrived and was safe. Abby also let them know she would be out and about looking for a permanent home and would contact them as soon as possible. To her surprise, she found an apartment that day, but it was unfurnished. Because she had planned to rent a furnished apartment, she had to spend part of the next three days locating and purchasing the necessities. The rest of the time was taken up with moving into her new apartment and ordering Internet service, which she discovered wouldn't be installed until the following week. She let Trent know and then completed her move.

In the coming hours and days, Abby emerged from her self-imposed protective cocoon and blossomed. She had a perpetual smile and a kind word for everyone she met on the street. She knew coming here was the right thing to do; after all, it was responsible for the better part of her emergence. But she also couldn't deny that Trent had a lot to do with it, too. While her physical freedom and security was dependent on this place, he was the one setting her soul free, untangling the web of doubts and insecurity that had imprisoned her mind for years.

She was soaring, floating through her days, absorbing her new surroundings, and relishing the feeling that she mattered, was desirable, and had worth again. A heavy, warm blanket of peace and tranquility surrounded her. *Tranquilo,* as the locals called it.

She began exploring her new city. The Old and New cathedrals in El Centro rivaled the famous cathedrals of Italy, in her opinion. She took the yellow bus tour to Turi, and she walked and walked and walked. Every day she found more to love about her new home, from the foods, to the architecture, to the slower pace, and the people. The people were so helpful and friendly, especially since she was Spanish-language challenged. The Ecuadorians were so patient in trying to decipher what she needed. It made her ashamed of the attitudes of some people in the U.S. toward the immigrants who didn't speak or were still struggling with the English language.

She spent the next month waiting for Internet service. She was frustrated, her family was frustrated, and Trent was frustrated. She would go as often as she could to an Internet cafe, post a message on Facebook that she still was waiting on Internet hookup, and was fine. Of course, she called Trent. She felt guilty she didn't call anyone else, but he was the one her soul needed to talk to.

Abby was talking to Trent and drinking a glass of champagne. "Trent, oh my gosh, this champagne is the best stuff ever. I've never much cared for champagne, but I think I could drink the whole bottle. And it's only five dollars!"

Trent chuckled. "You better be careful with that. I'll love watching you get all goofy, though."

"Who me, goofy? Never! I think I can handle a glass or two of champagne. I admittedly haven't had much to drink in the last few years, but this stuff is so so so good!"

Trent was still chuckling, but he still was concerned. "From the Abby I used to know, you better be careful. But it would be a sight to behold, I tell you."

"Okay, seriously, how much trouble can I get into, sitting here talking to you on the Internet phone?"

"You're used to drinking at about fifty feet above sea level. Now you're at 8,000 feet altitude, and it's different. Oxygen levels are lower, so you feel the alcohol more."

"I know. That's why I waited a week to drink anything after getting here. I'm not feeling the effects of the altitude so much, now. I'll stop drinking if I start feeling it. Right now, I'm barely starting to get a buzz. It feels good and tastes good, too. Like I imagine your lips might taste." Abby was feeling a little adventurous and flirtatious.

"Whoa, Whoa, wait a minute girl, I'm glad you're enjoying yourself, but hey how is it in Ecuador?" Trent tried to change the course of the conversation before Abby said something he knew would embarrass her the next morning.

"Oh Trent, it's beautiful! The air feels so clean. But I am sore from walking everywhere. It's great though — you really see more when you're walking a city than driving. I think I am going to love it here. That is, if I can ever figure out the buses. You should have seen me carrying a table twelve blocks. I never would've thought it. Before I came here, whenever I thought about developing countries, I thought of poverty, desolation, run-down places. Cuenca is amazing, and I don't feel like I'm in a developing country at all. What's going on there? What have you been up to while I couldn't talk to you?"

"Not much. Just working, wondering if you are okay, wishing you could hurry and get your Internet up and running. I miss you, and I want to sleep next to you. When you get your Internet, we are going to leave it up all night, so if I wake up, I can look at your gorgeous face. Where are you calling me from?"

"I met a friend, and she's letting me hang out at her house and use her Internet. Naturally I called you. I wanted to share this fabulous champagne with you that she introduced me to. Crap, the bottle is almost empty, and I have to go to the bathroom. Be right back."

Abby was gone a long time. When she returned, she didn't look so good. Trent shook his head.

"I told you. You gotta be careful."

"Whoa, that hit me hard out of nowhere. I didn't think I would make it to the bathroom, or back again. I was feeling fine until I tried to walk. I don't feel too good right now. I guess you were right, as usual." She tried to be as still as possible.

"Are you okay? You look a little green around the edges, and you look like you're going to be sick."

"Yeah, I feel like I'm gonna be sick, too, but I refuse to be. I haven't been sick from drinking since college. Talk to me, and it will get better, I hope. I'm going to be seriously still." She tried to chuckle.

"I guess a $5 bottle of champagne makes you a cheap date, huh?" Trent was laughing now.

"Yeah, ha ha, that would be a cheap date. Come to Ecuador, everything is cheaper. Flowers are super cheap. Roses run about four dollars a dozen. You could buy a girl flowers, a bottle of champagne, and take her out for dinner for less than thirty dollars. I do wonder if flowers are such a big deal to women here since they are so abundant and inexpensive."

"I wish I could come to Ecuador, Gorgeous, and I will someday, but I can't do it right now." Trent said forlornly.

"I know," she said with longing in her voice. "I really could get into a little cuddling about now. Maybe if you held me in those big strong arms, the room would stop spinning."

"All right, come here, I'll give you a big, fierce virtual hug. But then I have to go to bed; I have to work early tomorrow. I don't want to hang up, but I have to. Are you going home tonight or staying there?"

"Mmm, thank you. Sweet champagne dreams, Handsome. I'll call you again as soon as I can. I am going home."

"All right girlie girl, have a good evening, I'll talk to you next time. Be safe going home,"

~

Once her Internet was installed, she had even more time for exploring her new city. It was more beautiful, more magnificent, more friendly than she ever could have imagined. And when she wasn't out exploring, she was talking to Trent. Her life seemed glorious.

Despite some serious sleep deprivation from her hours and hours talking with Trent, she awoke happy, full of purpose, and looking forward to what each day would bring. She still shook her head in disbelief when she took the time to look back and ponder.

She had Trent, who seemed to make her his whole purpose, twenty hours a day, never failing to keep up the litany of how beautiful she was, how sexy, how funny...all the things she had not heard in years. Then there was his selflessness. First, he gently nudged and encouraged her to join a musical theater group. No, she had no experience in theater or performing whatsoever, was shy, and was so trained to remain behind the scenes that the limelight's harsh glare made her cringe. But she was finding she loved it and excelled at it. Abby also loved the mental exercise this brought, as for the past few years, her brain had felt like mush. And she thrived on the camaraderie with the group.

Next, Trent pushed her to join a geocaching group. The exercise, the fresh air, the group dynamics, the exploration, and the beauty of her new home revitalized her in a way she never could have dreamed. And he seemed to know these things would be good for her. He encouraged, cheered, and even pushed when necessary, despite the fact all these things took away from her Skype time with him. He wanted to be connected to her at all times, except when she was involved in one of her activities. She felt more alive than ever before.

~

When Trent reconnected with Abby, he was awestruck by her beauty. They had always been friends, good friends, even the best of friends. But that day, he saw her in a whole new light. The ensuing days, he discovered even more about her, how suppressed, damaged, and fearful she was. And torn down, cynical, withdrawn, afraid, and almost reclusive. Except when they talked. As time went on, she opened up to him. As she became more active and involved with others and interests around her, he saw the complete metamorphosis of this beautiful woman. She was blooming from the inside, and it was even more beautiful to watch than her stunning face. He wanted her with him every moment. The physical distance between them was killing him, but it was all worth it to see his frightened little bird develop into the stunning, unstoppable hummingbird he knew she could and would be. It was the sexiest thing he had ever experienced.

CHAPTER 17

TRENT COULDN'T BELIEVE HIS EYES, and he couldn't believe Abby that she had not changed anything. She was beautiful in a way he had never noticed before. Abby said it was because the last couple of times she had seen him her soul was dead, and now she was alive.

He got to thinking and realized that maybe his soul had been ailing then, too. Back then, his marriage had been falling apart, and maybe he was in a fog of his own. He had not told anyone about his marital problems and was shocked when he poured it out to Abby. He never planned to tell her. Not now anyway, especially with her leaving. That night, he reflected on why he had told her all his innermost fears, his feelings of rejection, and all the rest of it. He thought it was because he really needed a female perspective concerning what might be going on in his wife's head. He didn't want his marriage to end, but he was tired of not having any support, any real relationship, and the arguing, whining, and complaining.

When Abby called him on that Monday to let him know about her trials with the vets, his heart skipped a beat when he saw her name on his phone. He was so glad she had called; all he had wanted to do all morning was call her. But he knew she was busy, and he was aware he had monopolized most of her weekend. He also was confused about why the urge to call her became so strong. Was he that desperate for a human connection? Was he lonely? Was it his feelings of failure and inadequacy that were a result of a failed marriage, or was it something more? All he knew for certain was that each time he heard her voice it excited him. He was feeling something he had not felt in a long time. He felt like a teenager again. Consumed by a girl. How ridiculous was this at his age?

Each night when they reluctantly hung up the phone, he marveled at how many hours they talked. Never any dead space, no lulls in the conversations. One minute they would be talking about something serious, the next giggling over something downright silly. He loved it. But dammit, she was leaving. Going three thousand miles away. Because of his job and the amount of time he spent on the road, he knew he had the patience to wait for her to return. As long as they could keep on talking, as long as he could use Skype to swim in her eyes and to know he caused her to beam that beautiful smile. As long as she really did come back. Each night he prayed she would.

His progress was frustrating, at best. He couldn't believe Cole had been able to get to her that much — to diminish her self-respect. He did not believe she couldn't see what he saw. His goal was to make her aware of her worth and to help guide her back to the strong person she had been. He knew it would take a while.

Trent understood about self-doubt and self-worth because he wrestled with it, too. But for him, the task was accepting how others saw him, regardless of what he felt about himself. He knew he was a good guy. He always tried to do the right thing, valued family most of all, and would do anything he could for anybody. But it seemed no one in his life saw him that way. Whenever anyone was in need, he was their first call. The rest of the time, he was their last thought. It was true of his siblings, his friends, and his wife. Therefore, they must see something he didn't. He accepted it, but didn't allow it to change who he was or what he believed in. Abby, on the other hand, was an exceptional lady in every way, and he would do all he could to make sure she knew it.

Over the next days and weeks, he was so thankful she allowed him to follow and be a part of her journey. He loved hearing her excitement as she explored her new home and met new and interesting people, and he wished in some way he could experience it, too. But for now, sharing the experience through her eyes would have to do.

They grew closer. He confided all his deepest secrets to her. Things no one else on the planet knew. She never acted surprised, disappointed, or judgmental in any way. He was comfortable with her. Comfortable in an exciting way. He didn't know where this was going to lead, but he sure hoped the road was a long one.

Trent wasn't ready to give his heart to her yet, but he also couldn't imagine his world without her. He wasn't sure he could ever again give his heart totally to another. It always ended badly, and he couldn't stand the thought of going through it once more. "They" say it's better to have loved and lost than to never have loved at all. "They" didn't have a clue. It actually wasn't worth it, in his experience.

What he did know was when he talked to Abby, everything seemed right in the world. And when she smiled at him, everything else disappeared, his heart fluttered, and all the crazy crap going on around him didn't seem so important.

He knew when he talked about the people in his life she held her tongue, and he knew she had to work hard at it. He respected her for it. Every once in a while though, she couldn't hold back, and her words would fly. Then she would apologize. He told her not to, because deep inside, her words made him feel like a king.

She made a difference in his nights, in his days, in his life. As the weeks went by, he became used to the fact that she worried about him. He wasn't accustomed to this, and it took him some time to consider which things would cause her to worry. Trent never wanted her to be concerned unnecessarily so he began sharing only those things he knew would keep her from worrying. It felt strange to have someone worry about him. He was the strong one. But her concern made him feel significant. He wasn't sure he had ever felt he was that important to someone, and if he had, it had been a very long time.

Abby was so beautiful and so sexy. She was caring, intelligent, efficient, and understanding. In fact, the only temper he ever saw was toward the people she felt were treating him badly. The only thing she did that irritated him was her belittling herself or believing his compliments were biased. Hell yes, they were biased, but nevertheless true. Some days he wished he could wipe the floor with Cole. He couldn't understand why the guy couldn't let it go. He had made his decisions, done exactly what he wanted, when he wanted, and everyone else be damned. Trent knew now that Abby never had been Cole's first concern, and he could not understand that. He made a supreme effort always to let Abby know how much he appreciated her. She did so much for him, and he never wanted to take that for granted or for her to ever feel that way.

For God's sake, all he ever had to do was say I'm hungry, and from three thousand miles away, she instantly would be ordering food to be delivered, before he even had processed the thought to ask. How could someone not appreciate that? How could someone not realize how rare it was in this world for a person to be more concerned about someone other than herself? He knew, without a doubt, she would take care of the people she loved until her dying breath. That's how she was, who she was, and what she did. He never ceased to be amazed at how much she found to do for him from so far away. He could only imagine how rich his life could be if she actually was with him.

Trent realized, although he wasn't ready to give himself over one-hundred percent yet, he wanted her with him. All the time. He still worried if he had habits that would irritate her — everyone else seemed to have issues with him. There were some things he was willing to change, but others were simply a part of him. He was tired of the women in his life trying to change him. So far, the only thing Abby seemed to want to change was, from time to time, she would mention gently that maybe he needed to drink more water. Well, sheesh, if that was all she wanted to change, he could tolerate drinking an extra glass of water a day to have that lovely lady beside and behind him on a daily basis. How would it feel to have someone that supportive to come home to at the end of a trying day? He had no experiences in his life that gave him anything to compare with what life with Abby would be like.

As he reflected on the whole situation, he supposed his real worry and the source of his hesitancy was the fact that two wives had cheated on him. Abby was so much woman. He couldn't see what she saw in him and felt deep down that it was only a matter of time until she, too, sought someone else. That was his real fear. It was seconded only by the fear Cole somehow would get to her and take her beautiful soul away again, and this time it might be permanent. He had to figure out how to prevent that unspeakable event from happening.

CHAPTER 18

OLE HAD NOT HEARD FROM Amory Hunter regarding Abby's whereabouts. He tried calling Amory several times, to no avail. All he could guess from that was either Amory couldn't find her and didn't want to admit his failure, or he had found her, and she had given him some song and dance that made Amory turn on him.

Well, he was tired of waiting. He had to find some other way to find her. He couldn't carry out his plan until he found her. Scratching his head, he tried to decide how to proceed. Then he realized he had never had her sign the quitclaim deed on the house. She couldn't sign one until he was ready to refinance the house and remove her name from it, which he was supposed to do "in a reasonable time period" according to the divorce papers. This certainly seemed like a reasonable time period.

Cole knew Abby had a bank account at the same bank that held their mortgage, but figured the bank wouldn't give him her new address. However, if he filed some sort of lawsuit against her, and they tried to serve papers at her old address, the process servers or court or attorneys or someone should be able to get her new address, right? He first had to find out what kind of suit he could file and where she would need to be served. He made a mental note to call the attorney in the morning, and if that didn't work, he would try the bank. He had to admit that serving her papers was much more satisfying because he knew it would cause her stress.

It actually took him a couple of days to get around to setting up a meeting with the attorney. When he finally sat down with Mr. Wayne, they first had to dispense with the attorney asking about Jenny's disappearance, if they had ever found her, and if Cole and Jeremy had encountered any more problems from law enforcement regarding her case. Cole told him, in as sad a voice as he could muster, that no, they had not found any trace of her, and no they had heard nothing from the law since a week after her disappearance when they had ruled it a case of her running away on her own. Cole told Wayne that the detective handling the case told him the case was closed for lack of evidence.

When Wayne asked Cole what he could do for him, Cole explained Abby had not signed the quitclaim deed on the house, as was stipulated in the divorce decree. Plus, she had moved, changed her phone number, and didn't answer his emails. He wondered how they could find her, and if there was any legal action he could take against her.

The attorney knew the easiest and probably best way to locate Abby, as well as the fastest, would be to hire a private investigator. But in a nanosecond, he discounted that thought because he wouldn't be able to bill for a P.I. So he quickly scanned his internal memory index of charges they could file against Abby. What immediately came to mind was a contempt of court charge, because she had failed to comply with the divorce decree. He said it would take him a couple of days to get the paperwork drawn up and filed with the court. They could use the address the court had from the divorce to file against her, and the process servers would query the apartment management or neighbors as to her present whereabouts. Wayne asked Cole if he felt Abby was still in the state, or if she might have moved.

Cole explained to him he couldn't imagine she would go far. Her mom and sister were in Roanoke, and her son lived in Boston. He thought the apartment manager could to give them a forwarding address. He sure hoped they could get this worked out and soon.

Wayne thanked Cole for coming in and told him he would have the paperwork filed within a couple of days. He also told Cole it sometimes took several days for the process servers to get complete service, but as soon as he heard anything, he would let him know.

Cole left the attorney's office feeling absolutely giddy. He had a feeling this was going to work. To prevent suspicions from arising, he might have to put his plan on hold for a little while until the court case was completed. On the other hand, he would know where she was and eventually could end this saga. He would have liked to go out to celebrate, but there wasn't anyone he wanted to be around much. So he stopped by his home-away-from-home liquor store, purchased a nice bottle of premium whiskey, and headed home. He and the dog would cook a steak and celebrate, knowing that in a matter of days, Abby would figure out he had tracked her down. He couldn't wait to see her realize that she would never escape from him. Then he spent the rest of the evening daydreaming of all the ways he was going to make the bitch pay for leaving him.

It was the following Monday before Cole heard back from the attorney. Wayne didn't have good news. He said the process server had gone to the address on file with the courts, and Abby had indeed moved a month ago. He questioned the management office, and they explained Abby had left no forwarding address.

Cole, turning beet red, steam seeming to come from every orifice, yelled obscenities, and asked the attorney what in the hell were they supposed to do now.

The attorney thought Cole was overreacting quite a bit and couldn't imagine why this bit of news was so catastrophic. They had known it could work out this way, and surely the man knew he wasn't going to give up that easily.

"Mr. Grey, please. We still have more recourse. This was just the fastest, least expensive, easiest way. All we have to do at this point is run ads in the newspapers with a legal notice. If she doesn't respond, you can win a default judgment."

I don't give a damn about the judgment, I need to know where she is, thought Cole, but he was wise enough not to express that to the attorney. Well, this attorney was proving to be about as useful as the women in his life. He guessed he was going to have to move to Plan B.

Abby had been up all night talking to Trent. Nothing unusual about that, but she needed to get up early this morning for a play rehearsal.

When she returned home, it was almost five o'clock. When she started her computer, she found an email from the manager at the Greenville apartment complex.

Dear Abby,

They came to serve you papers today. It looked like they were from your ex-husband, and they looked like divorce papers. I told them you've moved, and you left no forwarding address. He asked if he could ask the neighbors, and I told him I would have to check with my corporate office first. I don't know anything about the law on that kind of stuff, but if I can legally keep him out, I will. Let me know if there is anything else I can do to help you. If you want, connect with me on Facebook, and we can chat, or you can call me. I hope you're doing well. We all miss you,

Bianca

Abby immediately responded.

Dear Bianca,

They can't be divorce papers; I'm already divorced. I can't imagine what other kind of papers they could be. There is nothing left for us to fight about. I appreciate you covering for me and your efforts. Maybe he won't come back. I miss all of you too.

Abby

Then she connected her Internet phone and called Trent. She was shaking, but tried to keep it out of her voice. Of course, with Mr.

Observant on the other side of the connection, she should have known better.

"Hi Handsome! Sorry I'm late getting home. How was your day?" She made sure she was smiling.

"My day was fine, Abby. What's wrong?" He was seriously concerned.

"Nothing, everything is fine," she replied, making sure to keep the smile in place.

"Abby, don't bullshit me. I can tell something's wrong."

So she told him about Bianca's email.

"That doesn't make any sense. Could the papers be from someone else or for anything else you can think of? Usually a process server doesn't let anyone read the papers. How does she know all this?"

"Oh, you don't know Bianca. That girl is clever, sneaky, and can be nosey when she needs to be. I imagine she batted some eyelashes at the guy and then did that sultry, droopy eyelid thing and was reading the papers in his hands." Abby chuckled.

"Well, if they can't find you, whoever it is will get a default judgment. So you have two ways to play it. You can call the courthouse and try to see who is suing you, or you can ignore it. You have to decide what you want to do, what you are comfortable with, what will cause you the least amount of stress, but most important, how you can stay safe."

Abby took a deep breath and released a sigh, "What would you do in my place? What do you think I should do?"

"I can't tell you what you should do, Abby. I can tell you what I would do, I can tell you what I hope you will do, but I cannot and will not tell you what you should do. That has to be your decision based on all the things I have already mentioned. Nevertheless, I would like to truss Cole up like the chicken he is. I believe with all I am that the man is all talk and no action. I think he's a bully and a wuss and his only role in whatever happened to Jenny was only to help Jeremy cover it up. Personally, I am not willing to take that chance with you. In my opinion, whatever is going on with the courts here, you can straighten out if and when you ever decide to return to the States. And we both know my opinion —"

Abby cut him off and finished his sentence, "— is the only opinion that matters," and she laughed. Because, this time, his humor really struck her as funny. She was sure it was the tension, but she was thankful to have him help keep her emotions and worries from boiling over.

"I think you're right, tomorrow is another day. There will be time to clean up whatever messes are made, if and when I return. For now, I want to be irresponsible, footloose, and carefree. I want to snuggle into your arms, listen to you breathe, and not have another care in the world."

On the computer screen, she saw Trent lean in close and open his arms wide.

"Come here Abby, I'll wrap these arms around you and never let anyone take you away from me."

She loved that, like her, he could be silly and imaginative in their virtual relationship. She never would have dreamed Skype hugs and kisses would be a part of her daily life.

Having made the decision to let whatever was brewing brew without them allowed them to move on — to discuss what had transpired in each of their days, the humor and the beauty. They talked about the tragedies in the news, and they talked of their wishes to be together.

CHAPTER 19

"*WELL DAMN!*" SOMEHOW THAT STUPID bitch had bested him again. He was getting really tired of being a day late and a dollar short. He was sick of waiting on others to get the job done. As his grandmother always said, "If you want a job done right, you have to do it yourself."

He couldn't believe a former cop and an attorney had trouble finding one stupid, broke, mentally challenged female. He still deposited her whopping $200 alimony in her account every month. While it chapped the hell out of him to do it, he was also realistic enough to know she still didn't have the funds necessary to totally disappear.

Cole emailed his boss on a Sunday afternoon, saying he needed to take a week or two off to help his mother prepare her house for sale. He had planned to do that for the last year and a half since his father's death. His boss knew that, but with everything else going on in his life, Cole had not had the time. His boss never would catch on that he had no intention of seeing his mother.

There was one thing he knew for certain about Abby. She wouldn't go far from her family. She couldn't afford to live in Boston, where her son Kendall was, so she must have returned to Roanoke, or at least somewhere near there. The second thing he knew for certain was she was always in daily contact with that crazy mother of hers.

He remembered reading on one of the disaster preparedness websites, one of the ones called *SHTF* or *Shit Hits the Fan,* about places online to buy listening devices and bugs. They were illegal, but within the SHTF community, you could buy nearly anything needed to live off the grid, be self-sustaining, or prepare to fight martial law, from prescription medications, home protection, and weapons to emergency food supplies. He started searching for what he needed: a lock pick set, a telephone bug (he believed her mom was the only one who still had a traditional landline phone), and some listening devices he could plant in the others' houses. He found what he needed and arranged for his order to be delivered via next-day air. Since today was Sunday, the equipment would arrive by 11:00 a.m. on Tuesday. He would leave for Roanoke as soon as his package was delivered.

In case he was able to locate and grab Abby, Cole decided to finish outfitting her new "little cottage" as he was calling it, on the back of his property. He and Jeremy had painted it on the outside after it was delivered so it couldn't be seen from anywhere, including the sky. It was camouflaged with the trees and natural earth in the area. They even had placed pavers in a winding path out to the Spartan little cottage in the woods, but they had been spaced far apart and covered with pine needles again to prevent detection. They were there so Cole would have good footing to get back and forth without rutting out a path in bad weather.

He went to the local discount store and bought a blow-up mattress, a camping toilet, a blanket, one towel, a gallon jug of hand sanitizer, and a five-gallon jug of water. That should do it. Should be all she'd need. On second thought, he went to the cleaning supplies section and bought a large bottle of bleach, some garbage bags, a package of cleaning rags, and a scrub brush. Since she would have nothing else to do, she could keep the little cottage spic and span. He knew she not only hated the smell of bleach, it seriously affected her asthma. He would expect that cottage to smell lemony chlorine fresh every night when he returned with her one meal of the day. He added paper plates and bowls and plastic spoons and cups to his cart. She wouldn't be getting any fine china, forks, or knives she could possibly brandish as a weapon. He was not a fool. Then he went to the pet department and bought one of those shock collars and enough cable to surround the cottage. He hoped she liked the new necklace he got for her. He made a mental note to have Jeremy come over and install the cable before he left town.

On Monday, he spent the day using the spray foam insulation to cover the shed's interior walls and ceiling. Just in case. He knew it would provide some sound protection if anyone were to go walking through the woods. He never once saw anyone out there, but it was better to be safe than sorry. He laughed out loud thinking about Abby having her very own padded cottage.

Jeremy came over and they installed the cable that would shock Abby through the collar Cole intended to permanently fasten around her pretty little neck. This would come in handy should she somehow escape the cottage. There was one window in the original shed design, but he already had removed the glass, welded in metal, and covered it all inside and out with the spray insulation. He didn't need the sun reflecting off the metal, or for her to be able to get access and eventually work it loose. She was, after all, going to have a whole lot of time on her hands.

Cole figured by the time she was broken and convinced her place was with him, when he felt like he could release her back into the main house, she would be so thankful for something to do, he wouldn't have to worry about her cooking or cleaning again. He made a mental note to remind himself to purchase enough of the perimeter barrier cable to go around the property before time for her to be released.

When he and Jeremy were done, they locked the shed with the triple locks they had installed on the only door. No, she wouldn't be leaving her new little home until he decided it was time for her to go.

At 10:30 a.m. Tuesday, he headed to Roanoke. His plan was to watch Abby's mother first, then if necessary, her sister. He was sure Abby had to be staying with someone in the family. He had spent hours searching the Internet for her, to no avail. So, he figured, she probably had no utilities in her name, meaning she was living with someone else. On the off chance she was shacked up with some guy, or had indeed moved somewhere else, the listening devices should let him overhear phone conversations with her — someone was bound to say something. Even if she wasn't living with them, if she was in the area, he figured within two weeks' time at the most, she would show up for a visit at one of the houses, or one of them would go to her. He had two weeks. If he spent four days following her mom, and four days following her sister, and nothing was revealed, he would take the next four days and go to Williamsburg to follow her nephew.

By five o'clock that evening, he had found a place up the street from Abby's mother where he could sit and watch for her to leave. He knew it was going to be tempting to follow her the first time she left home, but the first time, he needed to get into her house and place the listening device in her phone. He figured that would be the only one he would need there, as she only used her cell for emergencies, which meant she never used it. He sat there until eleven, when he figured there was no chance the old lady was going to leave home, and went to find food, a restroom, and a place to lay his head until morning.

By 8:30 a.m. the following day, Cole was back at his self-assigned watch station. Waiting. Waiting for anything to happen. Waiting to see Abby, or for Anne to leave home. A little before ten, Anne did leave home. He had no way of knowing where she was going or how long she would be gone, a general listening device would've been good to get that kind of information, but he had not thought of that. He quickly went through backyards to get to Anne's rear door, let himself in, and installed the phone bug. He left, making sure everything was as he found it and returned to his car. Since he figured there was no more information to glean from Anne's until she returned, and he had no way of knowing how long that would be, he traveled the four blocks to Merry's house and found a place to watch. If Merry left home, he could bug her house, too. He thought it looked like no one was there, but he didn't want to risk it.

He sat outside Merry's house until 6:00 p.m., when a car pulled into her driveway, and a lady got out. It was someone he had never seen before. The lady went up to the side door, inserted a key, and let herself in. *Who was this? It's definitely not Merry.* He sat there the rest of the evening until all the lights were out. No one else had come, and the lady was still there. Judging from the shadows on the windows once the lights were on, the lady was the only occupant of the house. *Was this possibly a house sitter?* He would return in the morning, and when the lady left, he would put the devices inside and maybe figure out what was going on.

The next morning, he returned to Merry's house and watched the lady leave, presumably for work. He went in and installed the listening device. Once in place, he knew he could get the recordings from both the devices at Anne's and Merry's on his computer, so he decided to hit the hotel and get a little rest. He was exhausted and in severe need of a beer.

Thursday morning, Anne's telephone bug emitted a signal to Cole's computer. He began listening. It was Merry calling her mother. *Oh yeah, this is it.* With any luck, he could figure out where Abby was and when she would be returning home.

"Hi Mom, have you heard from Abby?" Cole couldn't believe his luck — that they would get right to the information he wanted.

"Yes, I talked with her last night, Merry. She's doing really well and said to tell you hello."

WHAT?! How was that possible? Cole had checked the device, and it was working now. But there was no record of any calls last night at Anne's house. Something wasn't right here.

Suddenly he couldn't believe what he was hearing when he tuned back into the conversation.

"Hey, Mom. Are you still going to come see us next week? I have

157

the guest room all made up and ready for you. I found some cute shops here I think you'll like."

Son of a bitch. Merry had moved away. Now he didn't know where she was. He continued listening to see if maybe her location would be mentioned or he would hear anything else that might help him find her. Nothing. Since she had asked Anne if she had heard from Abby, he assumed Abby wasn't with Merry.

Well, the only thing he knew to do now was return to Merry's house, or rather what used to be Merry's house, retrieve his devices, and add them to the equipment at Anne's house. He decided he would go to Williamsburg tomorrow and add devices to Rusty's house. There was no sense in letting moss grow under his feet. Abby obviously wasn't living with her mother, so he had to find where Merry was and check out Rusty. He decided it was pretty safe to return to Merry's old house now to retrieve his bugs, since it looked to him like the lady who lived in the house had a fairly routine work schedule. It also appeared she lived alone.

When he entered the house, he paid more attention to the furnishings and surroundings. Then he knew for certain Merry no longer lived there. *Damn it! I'm tired of all these problems. Why can't something work right for a change?* He retrieved his devices, got back in his car, and returned to Anne's to watch for her to leave again.

He was getting even more frustrated as he realized, one more time, he wouldn't be able to follow Anne. However, he thought it was more important to install the extra device in her house. Apparently, she was using her cell phone now, which might indicate that wherever Abby was, it was a long distance call. He needed a clue to begin looking. Cole was beginning to think he should have spent the money on video surveillance as well as audio. *Oh well, nothing I can do about it now.*

He waited outside Anne's until 10:00 p.m. He knew if she hadn't left home by then, she wasn't going to. He returned to the hotel and checked his computer for recorded calls from Anne's phone. There were several, but they were all to her little old friends and held no useful information, except for one call that let him know she would be attending a Bible study breakfast at seven the next morning at a local diner. *Perfect.* He could get in, install the listening device, then go to the diner and follow her from there.

Sitting outside the diner, Cole sure wished he could go inside and order something to eat. They had a right fine breakfast, and the tequila he drank the night before was swimming around in his stomach. But he wasn't ready to tip his hand to Anne by being seen in town, although he would have loved to see her face. Maybe when he was done here, he would "run into her" somewhere. He chuckled thinking about it.

When Anne left her Bible study breakfast, Cole followed her to the nail salon, then the grocery, and back to her house. *Nothing helpful there.* He was beginning to feel he was spinning his wheels. He stayed until 7:00 p.m., and figuring Anne was in for the night, returned to the hotel.

After ordering a pizza and opening a beer, he sat down to listen to Anne's day on his computer. The lady must be losing her hearing — she had her music turned up so loud, he thought he would lose his mind. That's when he remembered, the woman always had music going, but today, she was in a country kind of mood and it made him want to pull all the hair out of his arms. He couldn't stand country music, had never liked it. Country was all Abby ever listened to and whenever he heard it since she had left, it made him want to beat his head against the wall.

Then, he heard Anne talking. It sounded like she was on the phone, but the phone had not rung. *Oh my God, that's Abby.* He could hear her plain as day. *What the hell?* He knew she wasn't there; he had been following Anne all day. It sounded like they were talking on the phone, not in person. *Anne must be using the speakerphone on her cell. But she always had a dinosaur phone that didn't have many features.* Now he really wished he had a video device.

He stopped and paid attention to the conversation. They talked about Anne's day, and Abby told Anne about a lunch she went to with some friends he had never heard of, but there was no mention of where she was, or even the name of the restaurant where she had lunch. Cole was beginning to feel defeated again, and he began to believe that this particular plan wasn't going to work. He decided that he would drive to Williamsburg the next day, and if nothing turned up there, he would know he needed to spend his second surveillance week in Boston.

When he arrived in Williamsburg, he discovered Rusty no longer lived there. Seeing the empty apartment, he asked a neighbor if he knew where they had moved. The neighbor said they had moved out of state, but he didn't know where.

What the hell? He wondered if he could do a web search for Rusty and find him. Maybe since he was a high school football coach, there would be something online about him. He also needed to search for Merry's husband George. He guessed this little trip was over and for nothing. Cole didn't even bother to return to Roanoke to retrieve the listening devices from Anne's place. Instead, he decided to drive home and drown his sorrows. He knew the listening devices wouldn't work if he returned to Greenville, but he figured they were useless now. He would have to do some more research to locate her family members or find another way to locate her.

CHAPTER 20

𝒶BBY'S MESSAGE PROGRAM DINGED HER phone:

LizzyG: Abby, Cole is going crazy again. Forest was over there a little while ago, 10:00 a.m. on a Sunday morning, He was already drunk and going off on you. You're the cause of every problem he has. He's found out you've moved away and thinks you're either in Kansas or Alabama. He says he's got an attorney looking for you, and he will find you. He says when he does, he's going to kill you.

AbbyG: Oh great. My whole family has relocated to different states since I left him. How in the hell does he already know where they are? I am not there, I don't have to be afraid of him anymore, as long as he can't find out where I am, but I don't want him going after my family as a means to get to me.

LizzyG: In some ways I wish I knew where you were, but I'm glad I don't and understand why you haven't told me.

AbbyG: Yeah, Lizzy, it's definitely better you don't know. Even though Forest and Cole aren't aware you talk to me, you never know. Despite him knowing where my family is, I can't imagine why an attorney would be looking for me. The divorce is over, there is nothing left. So I think he's blowing smoke. I'll give the family a head's up. Let me know if anything else materializes. Especially if you hear of him taking any trips.

LizzyG: Forest said he was sitting in a chair, dry firing his gun, saying over and over, I should have killed the bitch. Forest kept trying to change the subject, but Cole kept repeating it over and over until Forest finally gave up and left. That man is crazy and scares me to death. He's getting gross as well. I can't stand to be around him. He's always falling down drunk and has wrecked two cars. The one he's driving now is held together with duct tape, and he always says he can't remember what happened.

AbbyG: I'm so thankful to have you, to let me know when he starts getting belligerent and obsessing over me. I don't understand, for the life of me. He wanted a divorce. He wanted to live his life the way he wanted. I can't imagine why, after all these months, he's still concerned with what I am doing. Don't forget to delete these messages. I'll do the same. Stay safe. Thanks again, you are the best.

LizzyG: I will, you too. Talk to you soon.

Abby took a deep breath. She really was lucky. Lizzy always let her know when something big was going on. The problem was, it was on such a constant and regular basis that Abby was becoming weary with it. She felt safe, though, now she had left the continent. Even if Cole tried to get to her, he most likely wouldn't be successful. First, the airlines probably wouldn't let him board because he always reeked of alcohol; second, she had no identifiable Ecuadorian address; and third, she knew his passport was expired. If he discovered where she was, he would be cooling his jets while he had to wait for a new passport. And, if he said anything to Forest, Lizzy would be able to let alert her in plenty of time to move, if necessary. She really hoped it wouldn't come to that. She loved Ecuador — the friends she was making, her busy, fun, active life here. But now she had to fear for her family, and she wondered how in the world he had found them.

She sent off emails to her sister Merry in Kansas and to Kendall to let them know what was happening and to be aware there was a possibility that Cole knew where they were and might try to get to them to find out where she was.

Amory Hunter was frustrated with his lot in life. He had to work in what he felt was a demeaning job because of a whiny criminal who charged him with excessive force and brutality. The opportunity to get back to what he loved exhilarated him.

He began his search for his long-time friend's errant wife with a web search. Since he was no longer a member of the force, he didn't have access to all the tools of his trade, but he still had his investigative skills. A search on Abby's name netted him nothing.

Next he tried Facebook. Bingo. There was Abby. He sent her a friend request. His Facebook account didn't have his full name; he used *AM H* as his online identity, so there was a chance she might agree to his request. Within a couple of hours, she accepted. He didn't message her right away. Instead, he stalked her page looking for information and clues about where she might be. It *looked* like she was in Ecuador, but that couldn't be right. There were pictures of her there and posts about being there, but he thought she might have been on vacation. To make sure, he began perusing her contact list. She sure had a large circle of contacts, and they were scattered worldwide. However, a large percentage was in Ecuador, particularly in a place called Cuenca.

He waited a couple of days before messaging her, watching her posts. Most of them had to do with some game she was playing, occasionally there would be a post with a picture of something she saw or a mention of what she had done that day. He noticed the people commenting on these posts mostly lived in Ecuador or were her family members.

Abby had been careful with her Facebook accounts, before leaving for and after coming to Ecuador. Before she left, there was nothing about Ecuador, her moving, or any other clues posted to her Facebook accounts. The night before her flight from the U.S., she deleted anyone with whom Cole might have access, including Lizzy Grant. All her security settings were set to the max. But her downfall was that she loved to play web-based games and always accepted requests from fellow players. She received the request from *AM H*, thinking it looked like an online gamer account. It came in amid requests from people who had mutual friends and played her favorite game. Until late one night, when she received a private message from an *AM H*:

AM H: Do you live in Ecuador?

While this question normally would not set off any alarms, as she had talked to several of her gamer friends about Ecuador and belonged to several online groups for expats in Ecuador, when she saw the message, the hair prickled on her neck, her breathing changed to short rapid gasps, her heart began racing, and a general sense of panic and dread set in. She sat looking at the message for several minutes, before responding. She didn't know why, but her initial response was wary.

AM H: Do you live in Ecuador?

AbbyG: Who is this?

AM H: Amory, I'm a friend of Cole's. I lost track of you guys a few years ago and was trying to find Cole.

AbbyG: Amory Hunter? I'm sorry. I can't talk to you. Cole and I are divorced now. And, quite honestly, he's drinking again and gone crazy. For my safety, I can't answer your questions about my where-abouts or anything else for that matter.

Crap, crap, crap, how in the heck did he find me? And why? Damn! All Abby could remember was Amory had been a cop and been fired for some abuse of authority or another. They had not been good friends. Cole had said Amory was crazy, and he had stopped talking to him years ago.

AM H: I understand. I'm sorry to bother you. I'm not surprised you're divorced. I figured it was only a matter of time before you saw the dark side of Cole. I swear I will not tell him I was in contact with you. I'm glad you got away from him. We've been friends since childhood, but that man is messed up, and I know it full well.

AbbyG: You know what happened to his daughter-in-law, right?

AM H: Jeremy's wife? No, I haven't talked to him in about five years. What happened?

Even though she was suspicious and frightened, she continued the conversation long enough to tell Amory about the girl's mysterious disappearance and the circumstances surrounding it. She bid him good night and immediately deleted him from her contacts. She never answered his question about where she was living, either. She also went back through her online account and determined most of her posts about Ecuador, thankfully, didn't point to anything more than a tourist visit.

All she could do at this point was pray Amory would keep his word. She felt she had been able to impress upon him the dire situation should Cole actually find her. As an officer of the law, at heart at least, his "protect" instinct toward her might be stronger than his "serve" instinct toward an old friend who had anger issues, at the very least. She also hoped, if somehow Cole had reached out to Avery to help locate her, the news about Jenny would give him pause.

Amory sat stunned, rereading the conversation, and trying to figure out whom to believe. He decided to sleep on it. Before getting back to Cole, he would make some contacts regarding the information he had learned tonight. He began another web search, looking for the story of the young woman's disappearance. Abby said her name was Jenny. Then he would decide whether or not to tell Cole he had found Abby.

The next day, still uncertain following his conversation with Abby, Amory sat staring at his computer screen. He had seen the dark side of Cole on numerous occasions, especially in their younger days. He knew there were issues, and he knew that as a young man, Cole had been charged with attempted murder following a brutal beating episode. Some good attorneys ensured he was acquitted, despite his cohort being sent to prison. And it was never mentioned, by anyone, ever again.

At the time, Amory thought it had been a fluke. Cole said Abby had gone off the rails, his terminology for she had gone crazy. But a pattern emerged. According to Cole, all the people in Cole's life were going crazy. Amory didn't much believe in coincidences, and when he had been around Abby in the early years, he didn't get any feelings she was anything other than a pretty, capable, strong, intelligent lady. So what had gone so wrong?

Then there was the story Abby told him about Jenny. Jenny was the wife of Cole's youngest son Jeremy. Abby told him the girl had disappeared under suspicious circumstances. In the first days following Jenny's disappearance, the story of who saw her last and what happened during the time leading up to her disappearance changed multiple times. The story went back and forth from Cole was the last one with her, to Jeremy was the last one with her. Abby also told him that although the police officially ruled her a runaway, a close friend with ties to the police department told Abby the case was still under investigation. Amory found it even more suspicious he could not find any online news reports. He checked the newspaper from the small town where they lived, as well as the paper in Roanoke, and found nothing about the disappearance of Jenny Grey.

Wow, what a tangled web this was, and he still had to make a decision about whether to tell Cole he had found Abby or not. He already had been dodging Cole's calls for two days, and he still wasn't sure. As his web search had turned up nothing, and since he was *persona non grata* in all police forces now, he didn't know what else he could do. Contacting any of the family members wasn't going to be helpful. It was a tight family, accustomed to covering for each other, and he knew that this long after the fact, there would be only one story.

Amory was still a lawman at heart, and he knew he had to do the right thing. He didn't have enough information to make an informed decision, but he had checked the court records and discovered there was a divorce, so Abby and Cole were no longer married. Weighing the choices, he realized if he erred in favor of Abby, Cole would be mad, but likely no one would be hurt. If he erred on the side of Cole, there could be the possibility of devastating consequences. While he hated making uninformed decisions, the ramifications were clear. It didn't bode well for Cole that he had omitted the fact they were divorced, and had not even mentioned his daughter-in-law's disappearance. That was unlike Cole, as typically the man would bemoan how unfair life had been to him so he could elicit as much sympathy as possible.

Amory made his decision.

～

Abby's Internet phone rang; it was her mom. She had not talked to her in a few days.

"Hi, Mom. How are you doing?"

"I am doing well, Abby, but I want to hear more about what you're doing — all about life there and what it's like. I'm really still thinking about coming down. Can you really not flush the toilet paper? Inquiring minds want to know."

Abby laughed. This week, I have a newcomer's lunch, where people who have been here for a while and new people get together. Some of the people I met online before I got here will be there, a couple I have already met in person, and lots of new folks. It's mostly all gringos, but a few Cuencanos come, too. It's usually fun. And I'm planning to attend the free symphony on Friday night. Mom, can you believe it? The symphony is free! The president here thinks everyone should have access to the arts, so in addition to free symphonies, most museums also are free."

"Oh Abby, that sounds wonderful. Do they have concerts too? You know I love my music."

"Yes, Mom, they do have concerts. There is live music in the parks on most weekends, and there are all kinds of performances — every genre of music you can imagine. A lot of restaurants have live music, too. Last year, Marc Anthony even did a show. There is no shortage of music here, that's for sure." Abby knew her mother would follow music anywhere.

"Well, how are things with that man you've been talking to back home?" Anne didn't much like this budding relationship because she was afraid it might cause Abby to return to the States. While a month ago she was devastated at her daughter's departure, now she wanted her to stay in Ecuador. The wise lady had a bad feeling about Cole. Also, if she were honest, her own excitement at moving to Ecuador was building.

"His name is Trent, Mom. Not 'that man,' and he's very good to me. I am enjoying him a lot, and he encourages me to get out and do things. He's a good man, Mom. I think you would like him, even though you've never liked the men I dated."

"Well, no offense Abby, but all the men you've dated have been losers and not good for you. And I worry about this one, too. I am afraid he'll want you to come back here, and I think you're doing much better where you are."

"Well, so far, he hasn't mentioned me coming back, though he's mentioned coming here for a visit. We'll see. It's a pretty safe relationship with three thousand miles separating us, don't you think?"

"I suppose. Well, call me Saturday and let me know how the symphony was — and of course your lunch, too."

"Will do, Mom. I love you,"

"I love you too, sweet girl."

CHAPTER 21

$\mathcal{A}$BBY AND TRENT WERE A well-matched pair. Neither one was Hollywood beautiful, but they were both attractive and well maintained. Trent was auburn haired, with a strong jawbone, long forehead, and strong brow line. He had a beautiful contagious smile, and his sparkling blue eyes danced when he was happy. Abby had dark brown hair, with golden-green eyes, high cheekbones, and plump cheeks when she smiled. If she was truly amused, her eyes glistened, but that didn't happen often. She was quick to smile at others, but most of the time, it didn't quite reach her eyes.

On their daily video chats, they each spent a lot of time staring into one another's eyes and smiling. What amazed Abby the most about Trent was how observant he was. It was sometimes a little disconcerting how he never missed anything. If she changed something, he noticed immediately, and when he noticed over their Skype that she had changed her nail polish color, she was totally freaked out. She realized she wouldn't be able to sneak anything past him. It was the first time ever that she had been around a man who always noticed everything — but in a good and positive way. He noticed she was losing weight before she did. There was never a day that went by that besides calling her *gorgeous,* he didn't *tell* her she was gorgeous as well.

One day he seemed especially stern. "Abby, listen to me, and listen good. I have something to tell you, and I'm only going to say this every day. You are gorgeous."

She couldn't help the nervous giggle that escaped, because she was absolutely sure he was going to tell her something dire from his initial tone of voice. And then she realized, to him, what he was telling her was monumentally important. She knew he was trying to convince her of her beauty and her worth. He was most serious about it, and about the only thing that ever irritated him was when she would belittle, brush off, or contradict his compliments.

In the beginning, he had done the same thing with her praise of him. Then he realized what he was doing and slowly began to accept the compliments. He, too, started believing them.

Each of them felt overwhelmed with what they felt for the other. And, slowly, they started opening up and realizing the admiration was mutual. There were times they felt totally overboard and, maybe, even obsessed. They definitely felt like teenagers. Obsession was never a good thing was it? They both wanted all of the other. The good, the bad, the past, the future. All they had for now was the present. And there was never enough.

They progressed from talking all night every night, to talking in the daytime, too. Maybe it was the distance, but Abby felt as if they were in the same room twenty-four hours a day.

Abby was limited to their time together because she could talk only via computer. But Trent wore a headset and took her everywhere with him. If he went for a walk, he would ask her if she would like to join him; if he ate, he would invite her to dinner. She always accepted his invitations with an abundance of enthusiasm, even though they both knew she couldn't see the scenery on the walk or taste the food. It mattered to them both that they did it together.

She even was connected to him during work and meetings. And she didn't feel the least bit tethered or smothered. Abby wanted to know everything that happened in his day. Trent felt if he couldn't hear her voice, he would suffocate. Her voice had become as essential to him as the air he breathed. He began to resent anything that took him away from her, in *his* life anyway. But he was always happy for her to get out and socialize with her new friends, explore new things, and be involved in her new community. Abby wasn't sure how to make him realize that he was the only thing in which she was truly, deeply, passionately interested.

She told him one day, "I love that you want me around. It still amazes me you want me around as often as I want to be with you."

"Well, Abby, to be completely accurate, I only want you around twenty-three hours and fifty-nine minutes a day."

"What the hell, Trent? What are you doing for a whole minute a day without me?"

"Well, I have to go to the bathroom sometime." They both laughed, but the laughter was full of the warmth and affection they shared.

He always asked about her daily goings on, he knew the names of all her friends, and indeed he felt he knew all their personalities, because if she didn't tell him everything on her own, he asked. He was pretty absorbed in all things Abby Grey.

Their feelings frightened them. Neither had experienced a relationship so intense. They constantly questioned themselves. How long could it last, it was burning so hot, would it eventually flame out? Or was this the kind of love that transcended time and space to last more than a lifetime.

Finally, Abby couldn't wrestle with the fears and doubt that constantly ran through her mind whenever they were apart. She decided to broach the subject with Trent. She wasn't ready to have someone else tell her she was crazy, and she didn't know anyone she thought could possibly understand.

"Trent, some days I feel crazy again."

"Abby, you're not crazy, you've never been crazy. You were made to *feel* crazy, but you're one of the sanest people I know." When Abby went down this particular road, it agitated him.

"Oh, I am beginning to believe that now. What I mean is, I'm crazy about you, and I feel like I'm obsessed. Obsessed with you. Isn't that supposed to be a bad thing? I am loving this feeling, but does it scare you?" Abby held her breath waiting for his reply.

"Gorgeous, no way, no how, am I scared. I suppose someone on the outside would call me obsessed with you, too. I guess a mutual obsession is a good thing, right?" While it did frighten him a little, not that she was obsessed, but to admit his true feelings, he could not let her feel she was hanging out there alone. He wasn't quite ready to put all of his feelings into words for her, but he needed her to know how important she was to him.

"I sure hope so. I'm sure my family would call this an unhealthy relationship. Hell, probably everyone would, but it sure doesn't feel unhealthy to me." She hoped it wasn't her bad judgment creeping in again.

"Me either, sweetness. Let's go with it and see where it leads. Besides, my opinion is the only one that matters."

She chuckled. "Really? Your opinion is the only one that matters?"

"Sure, in my opinion."

"Okay, your opinion is the *only* one that matters then because only your opinion matters, in your opinion?" She laughed, expanding on one of his favorite comments.

Abby decided even though that was one of his little jokes, she could live with it. She could definitely live with it. They decided they could be happily weird together.

Despite the fact she was a world away in Ecuador, she took care of as many of his needs as possible. She paid his bills, the ones that could be paid online. She ordered whatever he needed online and had it sent to him, wherever he was traveling. She made his hotel reservations and always, always knew exactly where he was at all times. She acted as his navigation system when he was driving, would check online for map views to find whatever he needed, wherever he was. She was his alarm clock in the morning, and she found ways to make his work easier. Because that is what Abby did. She was a fixer.

All she needed from him was him. His voice affected her in ways nothing ever had. His smile erased all fear, all nerves, all depression, and he always could make her laugh no matter how mad she might be at someone or some situation. She desperately wanted to be near him. She wanted to feel his strong arms around her; she wanted to nestle into the dragon tattoo on his shoulder. She wanted to feel his hands running through her hair. She needed him in a way she had never needed anyone. He helped her get through the sleepless nights. He talked to her, in his soothing, deep bass voice, and usually within a matter of minutes, she was calm and sleeping like a baby. He was priceless.

He appreciated all she did for him, and he came to depend on it. But it was not what he wanted from her. He wanted her beside him when he went to sleep and when he woke up. He wholeheartedly needed to hear her talk and to share everything about his day and hers. He longed for her physically.

They were as close as a couple who had been together for decades. They could finish each other's thoughts and often did. Yet they never had touched. They wanted to, oh how they longed for it. It was the only thing missing — the one thing that would make everything complete. They often talked about how they were going to arrange for that to happen. She was perfectly willing to take a trip back to the States, as soon as she could save up the money. But he didn't want her coming there as he fully realized it was dangerous for her. But he had not figured out how to get the time off work to see her. So they continued as they were and cherished every moment they could share together.

Trent decided maybe he could reason with the man who was keeping Abby from him. If not reason with him, maybe he could get a read on Cole — if he was just talking or was a danger to her.

Trent knew a little bit about what Abby had gone through. She had told him some of her trials, and he felt he knew her situation, to a certain degree. He had grown up with an alcoholic father and understood how tumultuous a life like that could be. He remembered clearly what a hell his mother's life had been during those years. Trent had been a victim of his father's drunken verbal abuse until he was old enough to fight back. He also felt he had some knowledge about how to approach and deal with that an alcoholic. He debated for days and weeks about trying to neutralize the situation. Finally, he decided that things with Abby had reached the point that he was justified in approaching Cole. However, he had no experience in dealing with the mentally disturbed, and although possibly justified, his decision may prove risky.

Trent knew from Abby that Cole went to the same watering hole for lunch every day. He was such a good customer, they served him his lunchtime drink in a Styrofoam cup as if it were a soft drink. If someone from work happened to be there, no one would be the wiser as to his lunchtime libations. So Trent made a point to be there. Since Cole ate at the bar, Trent knew he would be able to casually approach him and start a conversation.

"Hey man, how are you doing?" Trent approached the dark-eyed, man sitting at the bar alone.

The man barely glanced in his direction. "On the downhill slide for this miserable day, so things are starting to look up."

"I hear you. It's five o'clock somewhere, right?" Trent offered his hand to the man. "I'm Trent."

"Name is Cole, and you're damn straight." When the man looked up, Trent couldn't believe the physical difference in the man. He had last seen him only a few years ago. Now, his eyes were swollen, his face red, and he looked to have aged at least fifteen years.

"Oh. Hi Cole. I thought you looked familiar. I think we met before; you were married to Abby, right?"

"You know Abby? How do you know Abby?" Cole began looking a little agitated and suspicious.

"We worked for the same company, many years ago. We ran into each other a while back and reconnected. I believe you and I met at her son Kendall's graduation a few years ago. She told me you guys divorced, but I sense maybe it's not so final for you?"

Cole sat up straighter on his barstool, his eyes narrowed, and his face turned even redder, if that were possible. "What business is it of yours?"

Whoa! This guy is a bit confused. "Well, we're friends, and I'm not sure why you think you still have any claim over her now. Why is it your business what she's doing, if you're divorced?"

Cole suddenly stood. The barstool rocked and nearly turning over. He was clearly trying to intimidate Trent. "Abby will always be my business, and you need to get your nose out of our affairs."

Trent began to realize it was going to be harder than he thought to reason with the man. "Look man, I don't want to start anything, I really think maybe you should let her go, let her be, step back out of her life."

Cole leaned over until he was almost in Trent's face and got loud. "Fuck you and the horse you rode in on, and if you know what's good for you, leave my wife alone!"

Trent realized at this point that he might have made a bad judgment call. He may have made the situation dramatically worse for Abby, but he also realized now that he had not fully understood how bad things had been for her. This was much more serious than he had suspected. "Man, I didn't mean to ruffle any feathers. All I was trying to do is give you some friendly advice. Good seeing you again." He threw a twenty on the bar to pay for his lunch and quickly retreated from the restaurant. He was going to have to find another way to make a difference in Abby's life. Abby had alluded to the fact that Cole had a jealous streak. Unfortunately, it had not occurred to Trent that his plan might trigger a jealous response.

Cole couldn't believe the audacity of some people. Abby was his wife. Divorce courts be damned, she was his, had been his, and always would be his. Despite the fact the bitch left him and the family, it didn't mean anything. He knew she eventually would see things his way and come crawling back. No one left him. And now, this know-it-all S.O.B. who thought he was going to take her from him, needed to learn a lesson. That guy never should have gotten in the middle. Now he was part of the equation, too, and would have to be dealt with. But not before he used Trent to find out exactly where the little whore was hiding.

Abby's Internet phone rang; she hoped it was Trent. He had been kind of mysterious and vague about some lunch plans he had today, and she was waiting to hear from him. But it was Kendall, which caused her heart to soar.

"Hi, Kiddo, how are you?"

"I'm good, Mom. I got some great news this week. I have two papers being published." Abby could hear the excitement in his voice — she was so proud of him. She really loved that after all this time, no matter how much he had published, each one was like the first for him.

"Kendall, congratulations! That's fabulous. Two of them? Which conference, and where will you get to go for this one?" Abby knew the drill by now. Each time a paper was published, he went to a conference to present it. He had been able to travel to some fun places, and more often than not, his papers took Best Paper awards for the conference.

"This is a big one, in Washington, this summer. I'm super excited. But I want to know what's going on with you. Do you still like it there? What are you up to?" Even though he knew she was doing well, he still worried about her. He didn't want her to slip back into the reclusive ways that had isolated her when she was with Cole.

"Yes, I do still love it here. I love it more and more every day. I went out to dinner a couple of nights ago to celebrate a new friend's birthday. I've been to a Newcomer's Lunch and met some really neat people, and I think I'm going on a trip to Riobamba and Alausi with one of my new friends. We are going to take the bus. It will be a fast trip, about thirty-six hours. It's about a four-hour trip from Cuenca, but the bus will only cost six dollars, and the hotel is only thirty-five a night, and we probably will share a room. Then we are taking the Devil's Nose train ride. I can't wait. You'll have to check my pictures when I get back."

"That sounds great, Mom."

"The other night, I went to the symphony at the Old Cathedral. The place is fabulous, and the concert was great. So yes, I'm doing much better here. When are you and Brenna going to come visit?" Abby couldn't wait to share the country with them, as she hoped they might decide to spend a year in Ecuador with her.

"We're working on that. Maybe in the fall. We can't wait to see it. Brenna loved the alpaca sweater you sent her. I think I want one, too." This was a surprise. Kendall was not one to ask for much.

"You got it, what color?" She was delighted to know of something he wanted, that she could send to him.

"It doesn't matter. You can pick. That sweater is the softest, warmest thing we have around here. Brenna would appreciate not finding her sweater on me. So, she asked if you could please send me my own." They both chuckled.

"You bet. How is Brenna doing? And my furry grandpuppies?"

"They're all good. We will post some new pictures online this weekend. I called you on my way home to check on you, but I have to go walk the dogs now. Love you, Mom."

"I love you all, too. Congratulations on your papers, and you two give each other hugs from me. Talk to you soon."

∽

Abby was hanging up with Kendall when, finally, Trent called her.

"Hi Handsome, how was your lunch?"

"Well, it didn't go quite like I hoped. I need to tell you about it, but I don't want you to worry or freak out, okay?" She could tell from his tone, something was wrong.

"Oh boy, I hate conversations that start that way. Why in the world would I worry or freak out over a lunch?"

"I went where you told me Cole goes every day for lunch. I acted like it was a coincidental chance meeting."

"Oh Trent, that doesn't sound like a good idea. I gather since you said don't worry or freak, something happened." She felt the dread and alarm rising.

"Well, it didn't go as well as I planned. He got really agitated with me. He was drinking, and things got heated. I told him I was sorry to bother him and left. I don't want you to worry, because I know you're safe now, and he has no clue where you are." Trent tried to reassure her.

"What in the world did you say to him? What did he get upset about?" Abby was really alarmed now.

"Well, long story short, I told him it was time to get over you." Trent tried to add a little levity into the situation to keep her from panicking.

"Oh no, Trent! Now you've put yourself on his radar and in the crosshairs for his anger and retaliation. And you tell me not to worry!" She was freaking out, she knew it, he told her not to, but he didn't know Cole the way she did. She was trying to remain calm, but it wasn't working too well. She was working hard at not letting her voice come out in the screeches that were echoing in her head.

"It will be fine. I told him I had run into you, and you told me you were divorced. He took the conversation from there. I didn't tell him there was anything between us, of course. He characteristically showed his ass is all." He tried to minimize what had happened. There was no need for Abby to know every word, it would accomplish nothing but upset her.

"I hope you're right, and this doesn't come back to haunt us." She sighed, trying to trust him. In that moment, Trent knew this woman meant the world to him. *Unbelievable, she's worried about me; I sure didn't see that coming, though I guess I should have.*

CHAPTER 22

OLE WAS ALMOST AT HIS wits end. He always paid his alimony, simply because he knew that bitch would love to drag him back into court, and he absolutely couldn't afford more court costs and, more important, didn't want to give her the satisfaction.

But he was almost at the point of realizing that if she were gone, it would be hard for her to file a court case against him. But he might be able to use the alimony to flush her out of wherever she was. He had the thought if he stopped paying it, she would be forced to contact him to ask him about it. That might be the best idea he had come up with yet.

He searched online for George Taylor, Merry's husband, and only turned up George's contact information at the company he had worked for in Roanoke. Cole called the company, asked to speak to George Taylor, and was told he no longer worked there. He explained he was an old college friend, and did they know how to contact him? The switchboard operator told him she didn't know the company he went to work for, but she believed he had moved to Kansas City or Wichita, somewhere in Kansas. *Well, at least that was something.*

When he web searched for Rusty Taylor, Abby's nephew and

Merry's son, he found references to his high school football coaching job in Williamsburg, but nothing yet on any new job.

He decided to send Kendall a text message. Maybe with one message he could manage to get both Kendall and Abby's addresses, if he phrased it perfectly. He sent the following text message:

"Hello Kendall. I'm sorry to bother you. I know you said you didn't want to hear from me, but I'm getting ready to sell the house. I found some things of yours and of your mom's, and I would like to return them to you both. I don't have your address or your mom's anymore. Is there any way you could send me your addresses. Thanks, Cole."

Now he had to wait and see what would happen. He called Jeremy to invite him over to watch a ballgame.

"Hi, Dad."

"Hi, Son. You want to come over to watch the game tonight? Will your mom watch the girls? You can have a kid-free, female-free night. We can get some wings and beer and have a guy night."

"Sure, Dad, that sounds like a plan. Let me check with Mom to be sure she can watch the girls. I would love to get out of the pigtail, ponytail, *My Little Pony* house for a while. I sure wish I could find a job. This being in the house with four women is killing me."

"Can you stop and pick up the wings and beer? I can give you the money when you get here."

"Yeah, Mom should be able to spot me some cash until I get home. I'll call you back in about fifteen minutes and let you know for sure."

"Great, I'm looking forward to it." Cole breathed a sigh of relief when he hung up the phone. He needed some company.

Ten minutes later, Jeremy called back and said he would be leaving in about twenty minutes. Cole was excited to have someone to spend the evening with. The empty house was getting to him this week, for some reason. He wondered how long it would take to hear back from Kendall. He was getting too old and tired for this stuff. Maybe he should forget about Abby. She was getting to be too much trouble.

Jeremy arrived, and the two men dug into the wings. Jeremy told Cole what antics the girls were up to this week. They couldn't wait for it to get warm enough to swim. And he was going through the potty-training blues.

"You know, Dad, you said things were going to be better without Jenny. I'm still living in a house with four women, and I have to do the potty training. You didn't tell me about that part. Right this minute, paying child support seems like a dream in comparison." Jeremy laughed.

"Yeah, well, sorry about that. I thought you would be happier. You were the one who said you didn't love her."

"I am in some ways. I get a lot of help from friends, and of course, Mom is helping a lot. That's help I don't think we would've had if Jenny were still here. I feel bad that I don't really miss her, not like I miss Dustin."

"Well, Dustin was your brother. Jenny was solely a good lay. I didn't think you ever really loved her."

"I thought I did, but I guess maybe I didn't. I don't know. But life is what it is. I am glad to be able to spend time with my kids. What's going on with you, Dad? I came by a couple of times and you weren't here."

"Well, I went to Roanoke to look for Abby." Cole was proud and wanted to see how his son would respond to the news.

"Did you find her?" Jeremy asked, trying to hide his fears.

"No, I didn't. What's more, her sister and nephew have moved out of state. I think Merry is in Kansas City or Wichita, but I haven't been able to confirm that yet. I have no clue where Rusty is. I messaged Kendall earlier to get his address and to see if he would give me Abby's. I haven't heard back from him yet."

"Dad, do you really think trying to get her back, or to make her pay, either one, is a good idea? Maybe you should let it go and try to get on with your life." Jeremy hoped his suggestion wouldn't light any fuses.

"Abby is my life. I don't know what got into her, but it's definitely not right. She should have never left us, and right now I'm tired, but yes, it's still a good idea, and I will succeed sooner or later. Doesn't it bother you that she up and left like she did, as quickly as she did, and she never looked back. According to the family, she hasn't contacted anyone. She said she loved you. Doesn't it bother you she so easily walked out of your life?" Cole twisted the facts a bit.

Jeremy knew Abby did not suddenly walk out of his life. Until a few months ago, she would check on him from time to time, but he couldn't tell his dad that. It wouldn't be good for any of them.

"Yes, it does bother me, but I have to figure she had her reasons, and I figure there isn't anything I can do about it anymore than I can bring Jenny back. The past is the past."

"Well, Abby is my future. She promised to love and honor me until death do us part, and I intend for her to honor that vow, even if she hasn't honored all the others." Cole was starting to show signs of agitation.

Cole's phone chimed, notifying him he had a text message. He looked, and it was from Kendall. Kendall had sent him his address at work in Boston, but said he would have to check with his mom first before sending hers.

That was all the spark Cole needed to reignite the fire, and he was irate now. Jeremy realized the text message would be the end of their fun evening, and *My Little Pony,* wasn't looking too bad right about now.

The next day, Cole received an email from Abby. He was so shocked; he did a double take at who the email was from. When he opened it, he almost exploded. It read:

"Kendall told me you needed my address. I'm sorry, at this time, I don't have an address to give you."

He paced, he drank a beer, he hit the wall, and he taught himself a few new cuss words. The following day, when he was calm, well, at least calmer, he replied to her message:

"That's fine. I need your address to pay your alimony. I can't

183

deposit cash into your bank account anymore. I have to mail you a check so I have a record for tax purposes."

"Cole, you can deposit a check into the account, as was agreed upon. You'll still have a receipt for tax purposes."

Well, that smart-ass bitch wasn't going to see another dime from him. If she wanted the money, she was going to have to come get it. Then it sunk in with Cole — he was fast running out of ideas to try and find the bitch. He was not a happy camper. Unless Trent Dumas could lead him to her, he was at a loss.

CHAPTER 23

"TRENT, I KNOW I SAID I was only coming here for a few years. But I love this place. I think about coming back to the States, and I honestly don't know if I can do it."

"I know, Abby. I sense it. I'm figuring that out. I just don't know at this point what the hell I'm supposed to do about that."

"What do you mean? What you're supposed to do about what? Are you saying you want to be with me?"

"I'm saying I want to be happy. The pursuit of happiness is what we all are after, right? I feel differently about you. I'm tired of relationships, as I've known them. I'm tired of arguing. I'm tired of all anyone ever needs me for is money. I'm tired of being the one to keep in contact, and the only time I ever hear from anyone is when they need something. I'm tired of my fucked-up life. Yeah, right now, I think things are different with you. But I can't be sure yet. Pursuing this is what I want to do. But I don't know how with you there and me here. If I come there, I give up and lose everything. I know you want to stay there; hell I think you need to stay there. At least as long as Cole is still alive. So yeah, I don't know what the hell to do, what I'm supposed to do, what I need to do, what I want to do. If I come there, I

185

lose my kids. Their mother will never let them go to Ecuador. That's the most important thing. Also, I have to earn a living. I don't speak Spanish. So what the hell am I supposed to do, how the hell am I supposed to do it?" Trent was visibly worked up, his head bent down, running his hands through his hair while simultaneously shaking his head.

"Let me tell you, Trent, as someone who has done it, given up everything, walked away from everyone and everything. It can be done, if it's what you want bad enough, but it isn't easy. But I didn't know you were at this point. I didn't know you were feeling or thinking about this. Damn men, never say how they feel, it's like a guy code thing, express your feelings, and you are at risk of losing your man card if anyone finds out. So, for sure, don't tell a woman your feelings because we all know they tell everything." Abby had a wide-eyed look of shock and surprise.

"What do you mean? I know how I feel about you. That's not the problem; the problem is, what do I do about it."

"Exactly, you know how you feel about me, but I'm not sure how you feel, because you haven't said. Yes, you've shown me in a million different ways every single day, and yes, most women say show me, don't tell me, but dammit, Trent, that doesn't mean *don't* tell me; it means tell me *and* show me. I don't know why, but we need to hear it, too. If I knew you were thinking this way, it would be something we could work out together. There are ways to handle situations. No, your kids probably can't come here, but you can go there. You could work here. With all the gringos here, I'm sure we could find some-thing you could do. Or I could come there. I can travel there three months a year; you can travel here three months a year, legally. We *can* work this out some way, if it's what you want." Her voice was settling and calming, but her heart raced at the possibilities.

"What do you want, Abby?"

"I want to be happy. I've been chasing it all my life, and I finally am happy, feel safe, and at peace. My definition of happiness is different at this point in my life, and maybe yours is too. What makes me happy is this place, the friends I am making here, the activities I'm involved in, but mostly *you*! You, Trent, make me happy, everything I do, I want to be able to share with you. I don't want to take you away from your kids. So, if we can talk about it, maybe we can find a solution that fits not only both of us, but with all our circumstances. We want to be happy, but happiness can't come with a price. Happiness is black and white; there is no gray. But that doesn't mean there is only one way to accomplish it. For starters, go buy a lottery ticket!" Abby chuckled.

"Abby, have we finally had our first argument?" There had been no angry words, only frustrated voices.

"No, we've simply had our first impassioned, heated conversation," They both laughed.

Abby was deep in thought. I am finally on the road to recovery. I feel better physically and mentally than I have in years. I know Trent is a huge part of that. Damn damn damn! I want Trent here with me so much. But can I let him do that? I'm scared he will come and begin to resent me, or it won't be the same, I'm terrified that he won't come.

These months have been the best in my life, and I think the only way for it to be better is for him to be here, where I can share everything with him. But what if it all falls apart, like all my other relationships? I would rather have him at a distance than to not have him at all. It feels like the perfect romances — the kind you only read about... usually in a novel. A mutual love, all consuming, yet supportive. I want to completely accept and cherish it, but is that wise? I'm tired of making mistakes. Dear God, please don't let this be a mistake."

Likewise, three thousand miles away, Trent also ruminated on the situation.

I didn't mean to blurt out my feelings to Abby. Do you really think you could move to Ecuador? I've been burned so many times, is this time really different? But I can't lose my kids. I have to figure that out first. Maybe I'll go for a visit to check things out. Our relationship so far is based on talking. What if she has some weird habits that drive me crazy, or the reverse?

My need to be with her is so overwhelming, but is that because I can't have her in that way? Women always say that men love the chase. I can't believe I'm even thinking about this. I definitely know I want to be near Abby, and she's in Ecuador. I absolutely cannot imagine my life without her in it, but can I do what I need to do to be with her?

Abby would have liked to sit around and do nothing but try to figure out her situation with Trent. But she had other things to do. There was a festival going on, with a parade and a big celebration, and she didn't want to miss it.

She got dressed in jeans, a short-sleeve shirt, and a long-sleeve shirt. She packed a warm jacket and a raincoat in her backpack, along with two super-huge cans of spray foam — necessary and expected at the Carnival celebration. Carnival was the same holiday as Mardi Gras back home, but it was celebrated in a much different manner.

There was a parade, there were costumes, and there were fireworks, but the highlight of the event was the spray foam. Everyone was packed into the park in the center of town, and everyone from small children to little old ladies was armed with the spray cans. Some of the cans were huge, the size of a fire hydrant. Some people also were armed with boxes of cornstarch, and they would walk by and throw the powder, which of course, stuck to the foam.

Everyone sprayed everyone else. Hair, faces, everything in the area was covered in foam. It quickly disappeared as it really was some type of soap, but everything remained wet and slick. Older ladies came by and gently patted the cornstarch powder on Abby's face. By the end of the night, it was like ice-skating on the sidewalk tile. Abby had gone with a couple of gringo friends, and they had never had more fun or laughed so much. Abby hurt all over from all the laughing, running, and dodging. It was the greatest release of tension she could imagine.

The Cuencanos loved that the gringos participated in their traditions. There were not many gringos, most had decided to stay in, bar the doors, and avoid the madness. Abby couldn't believe how much fun those people were missing. She had her picture taken more times that night than in the last fifteen years combined. It was a toss-up who enjoyed it more, the locals or the expats. When all the fun was over, Abby could not wait to get home and tell Trent all about it. She hoped that maybe next year he could be here for the celebration.

When she arrived home, she stripped and hit the shower. She was cold, wet, and sticky and was afraid of what the mixture of cornstarch and foam soap would congeal into by morning. Then she called Trent and told him all about. She had him in stitches, laughing so hard at all the crazy antics from the evening. He agreed he would love to be able to be there next year.

She posted her few pictures. She didn't have many, as she was afraid to pull her smartphone out too often. Besides, her friend had taken pictures of her with thick white streaks of foam all over her face, covering her eyes and hair and posted them online. It didn't take any time at all for her friends back home to wonder and ask what in the world was going on. Her Internet phone started ringing almost immediately, and she had to keep putting Trent on hold to explain to friends and family what she had been up to and how much fun it had been. In her opinion, it was much better than Mardi Gras in New Orleans.

She went to sleep that night with a smile on her face. *Oh, how I love this place!*

Abby began to pick up more Spanish. She was able to converse a little with the taxi drivers, and they taught her more Spanish along the way.

At one point, she joked all she knew about Spanish she learned from taxi drivers, but it wasn't far from the truth. When they asked her in Spanish, "Where is your husband," she answered them back in Spanish, "No husband." Every driver invariably would ask "Why?" sounding surprised and unbelieving. She answered, "Husbands are very bad." They would all laugh, every single time.

She received more than a few invitations to have coffee from those same taxi drivers and quickly would tell them she had a boyfriend, even though she didn't have a husband. She wasn't entirely sure if that was true or not, but it did get her off the hook from unwanted coffee dates. It seemed Trent was right, someone always seemed to be asking her out. But she simply had no interest. She thought she had found the one. The only one she had eyes for, at least until he ran away from her.

CHAPTER 24

"MY WATCH IS MISSING!" TRENT exclaimed when he called Abby on Tuesday morning.

"The one you said is your prized possession?"

"Yes. I had it last night, and this morning I can't find it." Trent was frantic.

"You had it last night at home, or while you were out?"

"I had it at the business dinner; it was in my pocket. This morning I can't find it. I don't remember having it after I got home, but I think if I hadn't I would've noticed when I emptied my pockets."

"May I ask, why is it your most important possession? You've never told me much about the watch."

"My grandfather gave it to me. His grandfather gave it to him. My grandfather was the most important person in my life. He practically raised us after Mom and Dad got divorced, and I told him I would always treasure it. I have, I do, and now it's gone. That watch is almost 150 years old!" Trent's voice was full of anguish.

"I assume you've looked everywhere at home. Have you tried calling the restaurant to see if maybe it was turned in to the lost and found?"

"Yes I did, and it hasn't been turned in. I am sure I would've noticed it missing when I got home and emptied my pockets onto the dresser, because I always put it there every single night," Trent tried to remember the night before.

"Trent, I am so sorry. Maybe it will still turn up. Could it have slipped out of your pocket in your truck?"

"I looked there, too, but I'm going to be late for work. I will have to continue to look for it later. I can't lose that watch. It's irreplaceable and has too much sentimental value. I can't believe it's gone." Trent obviously was devastated.

Cole sat in the dark room, the curtains closed. He was feeling rather pleased with himself. He didn't have any way of knowing how valuable the treasure in his hand was to its owner, but he felt sure its disappearance would have some kind of impact. What he treasured most was hoping fear would strike when it was discovered the two items were missing. He didn't know which of the two the rightful owner treasured most, but he knew he treasured the picture of Abby. The pocket watch was merely the icing on the cake.

It had taken supreme willpower for him to slip into Trent's house last night while the man was sleeping and not kill him. But before he did away with him, he wanted to play with his mind a little. He wanted Trent to know the fear that someone had the ability to end his life — and Abby's, too.

When Trent left work, he found his tires slit and a note on his windshield. "Where's my wife you bastard? I'm going to find her; she will come back to me. I'll make you sorry you ever fucked with MY wife. I know where you live."

He knew then who had done it, but couldn't prove it. However, he filed a police report and asked if they could check out Cole.

"No sir. I'm sorry, but there is no proof he had anything to do with this, and until there is, there isn't much we can do."

"Don't you see my life could be in danger, here?" He then remembered his missing watch and wondered if the two incidents could possibly be related, but couldn't imagine how.

"Well, if you have a physical confrontation with him, call us. Then we can do something. In the meantime, maybe you shouldn't screw around with someone else's wife," the officer replied, referencing the note left behind.

"Thank you, officer, for that sage advice. I'm not screwing around with anyone's wife. They have been divorced for almost a year. He's been looking for her and voicing threats against her, and apparently he's stalking us both now."

"Be sure and call us if anything else happens," said the officer as he got in his cruiser to leave the scene.

Trent decided then that it looked like it was up to him to do whatever necessary to keep the two of them safe. The realization hit him that he needed to be careful now. Cole knew where he was and, evidently, believed that he and Abby were involved in some way. So now Trent had to make sure that he in no way led Cole to Abby.

When Trent arrived home, he grabbed a soda, plopped down in his recliner, and contemplated what, if anything, to tell Abby about this. He didn't want to frighten her, but he felt she needed to know. He finally broke down and succumbed to the notion that he needed to tell her. He was NOT looking forward to this conversation. He dialed her Internet phone number from his phone, afraid if she saw him on video, she would pick up on his tension.

"Hi Sweetness, how is your day going?" He tried to mimic his usual happy tone of voice.

"I'm having a good day, that now is a great day, because you called. How was your day? Did your meeting go well?"

"The meeting was successful, and my day was fine. But I have some unsettling news I need to tell you. When I came out of work today, my tires were slit, and there was a note on my truck. I know it was from

Cole. I filed a police report, but they say there is no evidence it was Cole, and there isn't much they can do."

"Oh crap, this is bad. Trent, we have to decide what we can do. I know the cops will be of no help. They weren't for me, and they weren't for Jenny either. I have to figure out how to throw Cole off your scent. I cannot have you getting hurt or worse. Crap crap crap. I have to figure out what I can do." Abby was terrified now, not for herself, but for Trent. *He doesn't deserve this. Well, actually, I don't deserve it either. But that is beside the point.*

Trent panicked at her words. "Whoa, whoa, whoa. You cannot get involved in this. You have to trust me. I'm thinking on it, and I'll call my brother Tommy to see what he thinks we can do. Maybe his experience with the FBI will give him some insight. But Abby, Please! Let me deal with this."

"Trent, you wouldn't be in danger if it weren't for me. I need to see what I can say to Cole to make him think he's barking up the wrong tree. If I can work it out, I can send him an email. Maybe I'll tell him I am coming back to town, and we need to talk. That should get him off your tail, at least for a while. Then we can decide what to do. What did the note say?"

He read her the note, then told her, "Abby, no. That would be playing right into his hands. Plus, if he has any friends in IT, they could trace your IP address, and he would know where you are. In his distorted, drunken mind, he still thinks you're his wife. He's seriously delusional. Please, please don't do anything. Let me talk to Tommy. I'm okay, and I'll be okay. I promise. But you can't do anything that might lead him to you. I'm too far away to help protect you if he finds out where you are. You are mighty important to me, so please don't add more stress by making me worry what you're going to do."

"Please call me and let me know what Tommy says."

"You know I will. I'll call Tommy right now. I'll call you back as soon as I'm done. Can I call you when I finish?"

"Of course."

Trent called his brother Tommy, an FBI agent in Kentucky. He explained the situation as much as possible and asked his brother what could be done. He explained that Cole was deranged, and the lady he was seeing was Cole's ex-wife. An abused ex-wife who had fled the country for her safety.

Tommy told Trent to let him do a background check and see if he could turn up anything that could help. He said he also would talk to some of his agent friends who worked with victims to see if there were options in a case like this, something that would not escalate the issue. He told Trent that the official procedure was to get a restraining order, but in his personal opinion and experience, those only seemed to make matters worse. Tommy promised to call him back by the next morning.

Trent then called Abby. He told her Tommy was looking into it and would get back to him no later than the next morning, and for now, she shouldn't worry.

"I figure he's done all he's going to do for a day or two at least, possibly forever. So don't worry, okay Baby Doll?" Trent calmed down, and his tone was back to the sweet voice Abby loved so much.

Abby reluctantly agreed, saying she would wait to hear from Tommy before she panicked.

After talking to Abby for about an hour, Trent headed to the bedroom to change out of his work clothes. As he was pulling a T-shirt out of the drawer, he noticed something. The picture of Abby he usually kept on the mirror above his dresser was gone. He looked all around to see if it had fallen, even moved the dresser out from the wall to look under and behind it. It was gone. His heart rate acceler-ated as understanding dawned on him. He had not noticed the picture being gone this morning, because he had been frantically searching for his pocket watch. Could this mean what he was thinking? Was it possible that Cole had come into his house and stolen the watch and the picture? Why would he do that? Why the pocket watch? It had nothing to do with Abby. Okay, he was ready to admit to himself, he was freaked out. And he was pissed.

Trent had to think fast. He had to decide whether to let her know about this new development or not. His first instinct was Not! He knew she would totally freak out and worry herself sick. But, he didn't want to keep secrets from her. And he knew it would eventually come out, and she would be mad he had kept it from her. He was definitely between the proverbial rock and a hard place. So he decided to take a different approach. He called her back.

"Abby, can I ask you some things about Cole and how he operated his mind games with you? I hate to bring up the past, and I hate asking you things that I know could make you anxious. But if you could give me some insight, it might help us understand how to handle the current situation with Cole."

"Sure, I will do anything to help. What do you want to know?" She was willing to do whatever was necessary to keep Trent safe from Cole.

"Let's start with this. Did things come up missing, or maybe moved, and you were certain you had known where they normally were located?"

"Constantly. You think he was doing that all along to confuse me?" She had not previously made that connection.

"Maybe. Did those things ever turn up again? If so, did you find them in weird places, places you think you wouldn't have put them?"

"Most of the time. But every once in a while, I would find them where they were supposed be. And I knew I had looked for them there, of course. I would ask Cole if he had found them and returned them. Sometimes, he would say he had and tell me some outlandish unbelievable place he had found them. Other times, he would say, 'No, I didn't know you were looking for that.' How does any of this relate to slashing tires? Could Cole have thought you wouldn't notice, or he could come back and fix them in the night to confuse you?" Abby chuckled. And then she amazed herself that she had found any humor when talking about Cole. She supposed it was the Trent Dumas magic.

"Well, to be honest, I think this is more than some slashed tires. I think Cole might have tipped his hand a little too far this time, and it might give us some ammunition." Trent tried to ease into the conversation, while trying to keep them both calm and rational.

"Why do you think it's more than slashed tires? Is there something you're not telling me?"

"Yes there is. Remember my watch was missing this morning?"

"You think that was Cole too? Honey, maybe you're a little spooked and seeing ghosts where there are shadows. I know it's easy to do." Abby couldn't wrap her mind around why Cole would steal Trent's watch, or how he could have done it, especially not while Trent was there and sleeping.

"I just spotted something else is missing, too. I didn't notice it this morning in my confusion and searching for the pocket watch. I was in such a hurry running late for work that I didn't notice it until now while I was changing clothes."

"Well, what's missing? Maybe it will be a clue as to where the watch is. Maybe they are in the same place, and one or the other will jog your memory."

"Oh, it definitely is a clue as to where the pocket watch is. Abby, your picture is missing off my dresser mirror."

"Dammit, oh my gosh! Apparently, he thinks you're tied to me in some way. I don't know how he could possibly have made that connection. I know if he had seen us together before I left, there would've been immediate repercussions. Why now?" She was bewildered by the turn of events and now was convinced Cole was behind the actions.

Trent took that time to remind Abby about the story of going to see Cole at lunch. He knew she was going to blow a gasket because she had said it had been a bad idea and was going to cause them problems. Once again, she surprised the hell out of him.

"Oh Trent, I still can't believe you tried to do that to help me. But now you're in his crosshairs, too. He probably figures you'll lead him to me. I'm so sorry you have to deal with this. As long as he thinks you can help him find me, he will just play the mind games. And now I have no doubt he's behind it all, the tires, the pocket watch, the photo.

But you're in real danger now. How could he have gotten into your house? Once he realizes you can't lead him to me, I don't know what he will do. A logical man would figure he was wrong in his assumptions. Cole is anything but logical. Crap, now I'm really scared. Not for me, but for you." Abby waited for the inevitable panic attack to begin.

"Abby, calm down. Actually I think this is a good thing. I can protect myself, and I can use his games to my advantage. Maybe we can turn the tables on him and make him feel like he's the one who is crazy. It shouldn't take much to outsmart the man. His faculties are impaired, remember? Together we are smarter than he is, only not as devious by nature. We can handle this." Trent consoled her, hoping to keep her from doing anything rash that would put her in danger.

"Trent, you can't protect yourself against Cole. He only fights with one weapon. Hot steel. Hot steel is deadly, you know." She tried to impress upon Trent the seriousness of the situation.

"I know, Abby. But I think I might have a new weapon. I should call Tommy back. He has some friends in the Behavioral Analysis Unit. They may be able to give me the necessary information. Let me call him so he knows what I need, and I'll call you right back."

Tommy had contacted the BAU already. He also had phoned a friend who was a field agent in Virginia. The BAU ran a background check and uncovered Cole's attempted murder charges. It happened when he was nineteen, and he was acquitted. However, the BAU told him if Cole were, in fact, a psychopath, his biggest fears would be exposure and loss of control. If he felt he was losing control or was at risk of being exposed, he would become more desperate. To Trent's way of thinking, if this happened, it might force Cole to become careless. Maybe he could be caught before the situation escalated and he harmed someone. Unfortunately, Trent now realized that Abby was the key to discovering Cole's weaknesses.

CHAPTER 25

*T*RENT NEVER MISSED WORK, EVER. But he called in sick the next day. He needed to work with Abby on a plan for dealing with Cole, and he knew it was going to be hard on Abby. He didn't want to do it, but he thought it might be the best way to end this crazy saga and get Cole out of Abby's life for good. It was going to take some time, and he knew this would be agony for her, so he wanted to avoid his own work distractions. He would give anything if he could be with her, to hold her, to make her feel safe as they went through this process. Trent also knew she was safest in Ecuador and hoped he could deal with Cole in the U.S. to prevent any possible harm coming to Abby.

Control and exposure. Trent did not sleep at all that night. Abby fell asleep while they were on Skype. So he watched her sleep and tried to determine if he could possibly find a solution without involving her. There were lots of possibilities, but not knowing Cole's particular deep-rooted fears, each action he considered could backfire. He didn't know why, but he thought there wasn't enough time for trial and error. They needed to hit a bull's-eye right out of the gate. He certainly didn't want to take a chance on tipping his hand or irritating

Cole enough to endanger Abby or her family. He also knew if anything were to happen to him, it would cause Abby an insurmountable amount of anguish. He didn't want that, either.

When Abby awoke, she was surprised to see Trent watching her on Skype. He should have been at work by now. She looked at him with alarm and asked what was wrong.

"Nothing is wrong, Gorgeous. How can you look so pretty first thing in the morning? I'm still home because I'm going to spend the day with you, and we are going to work on a little project. But first, I know you need your coffee."

"A project? You stayed home from work to do a project? Who are you and what have you done with Trent?" She chuckled. "Okay, I'm just going to be grateful I get to spend a day with you, whatever this project is, but you're right, I do need coffee first, and I need to walk Prissy. I'll be right back." Abby went to the bathroom, brushed her teeth, made the coffee, walked Prissy, came back from the walk, and poured a cup of coffee, wishing she had a double-size travel mug like she had in the States. She returned to her computer, wide awake now and ready to do whatever Trent had in mind.

"Okay, I'm back and ready to go. Are we selecting paint colors, picking out your next new car, or taking over the world today, Mr. Dumas?"

"Well, with your help, what I hope to do today is formulate a plan to out psych the psychopath," he replied in his best game show host voice.

"Oh dear God, I think I'm going to need more than coffee. Wonder if I still have any Xanax." She laughed, not quite grasping the gravity of Trent's statement. When she looked in his eyes, she knew she had not taken him seriously enough, and her heart started a skippy beat. "Oh Trent, I'm almost afraid to ask, but what are we doing?"

"I talked to Tommy last night. He has collected a lot of information for me, or I should say with us. By the time I got off the phone, you were sleeping, so I sat here all night trying to decide if I could do this alone. I realized it would be much better if you can help. But Abby, if this is too hard on you, I want you to say so right now. Or at any point things get to you, do you understand?"

"Yes, Trent. I can handle anything with you. But are you sure this is a good idea? I couldn't stand it if anything happened to you. He definitely isn't worth it."

"Abby, I'm thinking if we can cause him to lose it, he will do something stupid, and maybe we can shut him down or have him shut down before he can get to anyone you care about. I'm worried about Kendall, your mom, and the rest of your family, as well."

"Okay, let's do this. If it is what you and Tommy think is the way to go, I'm game. What do you need from me? How can I help?"

"That's my girl. You are such a strong woman, and I admire you! Tommy's friends at the BAU told him that for a psychopath, the fear of exposure would cause them to do drastic things, some of the same things he's been doing to you. Psychopaths will tell people you're crazy and will tell them lies about you to discredit you. Also, the BAU guys said threats, stalking, and harassment are typical. We may want to stay away from that one for the moment; it might push him too far. But they said if he senses his control is slipping, it could cause him to lose it. I'm hoping that in his altered state, it means he will do something stupid. Where I need your help is to determine what might make him feel like he's losing control, without pushing him too far."

"Hmm. I'm not sure how much I can help. I don't have much of a devious or manipulative mind, and you don't either from what I can tell, but maybe if we put both of our heads together, we can come up with something."

"If it's not too stressful, try to think about what made him the angriest, or what was most important to him. Maybe we can go from there."

"Well, he doesn't like being told he can't do something or that he needs to do something. But I'm not sure how that can work out for us. He isn't big on authority figures at all. I wonder how his paranoia would fit into the equation? If we had him followed, like by a private investigator, how would he feel about that? I'm certain if he weren't too impaired, he would pick up on it. He's one of those survivalist guys who think the government is going to institute martial law at any minute. As a result, he belongs to several SHTF groups. Maybe if we could hire a cheap PI, he wouldn't be too good, and Cole would pick up on it. That might freak him out a little bit, BUT it could cause him to go postal on the poor guy, and then we would have that on our consciences."

"Okay, that's a good thought. What do you know about the DUI laws in North Carolina? I've had no need to know how tough they are."

"Well, sadly, they are pretty lenient, unless you get two DUIs in less than ten years. Cole had a DUI, but it was about fifteen years ago, so the maximum jail time is about ten days, I think. I suppose it is possible he's gotten one since I left. But he probably would've told Forest about it and, if so, I know Lizzy would've told me."

"I wonder if a PI is tailing someone who they suspect is DUI, can they call the cops and report it?"

"I don't know for sure, Trent, but they probably could. I can't imagine why he hasn't lost his job. When I was still with him, he reeked of alcohol even after his morning shower. I wonder if he got a DUI if it would affect his work? If he lost his job, it might make him feel like he's losing control, but he's had that happen several times, so I don't think that in itself would do it. It would just give him more time to drink and obsess.

"Can you think of anything else?"

Kendall messaged me the other day and said Cole had sent him a text saying that he needed my mailing address. I emailed Cole and told him I didn't have an address to give him. Which is the truth, since there are no real addresses here, but I have no idea what he thought it meant. Cole said he couldn't pay alimony anymore without an address. Kendall sent him his work address because Cole told him he was selling the house and found some things he needed to mail him. Maybe the whole conglomeration of things will start to unsettle him, but I'm not sure what he would do, if anything." She realized she had forgotten to tell Trent about the exchange.

"Okay, I need to make a couple of phone calls. Are you okay?" He was concerned about her, although she seemed to be doing fine.

"Yes, Handsome, I am fine. Make your phone calls and call me back." She realized she was honestly okay.

"No, you stay online with me while I make the calls on my phone. I don't want to disconnect from you." He realized this was the truth.

After a quick search, Trent found a PI with military background. He asked the PI if he could come to the house to meet with Abby over Skype. The man agreed and said he could be there by ten that morning.

The PI, Pierce Wellington, arrived promptly at 10:00 a.m. Trent had his laptop set up with Abby on the other end. Trent began outlining what exactly they needed from him. To start, they wanted him to follow and take pictures of Cole Grey, along with a report of the places he frequented. They also explained Cole had a drinking problem. Trent asked Pierce if he had the occasion to see Cole driving under the influence, what would be his procedure?

Abby jumped in. "Mr. Wellington, I might be overreacting due to years of psychological abuse at the hands of this man. But I don't think so, I believe he's capable of really dark, bad things. Personally, I fear he may try to retaliate against you, and I don't want to be responsible for any more lives being damaged by him."

"First, please call me Pierce. Yes, I can follow him and take pictures until we get whatever you need. If I have an occasion to believe he's driving under the influence, I'll continue to follow him to get an exact location. I have several friends in the police department and will call it in. That would be my procedure. Ms. Grey, please don't worry about me. I have tactical training, and with your warning, will know to be alert to the possibilities. If I may ask, what are you hoping to achieve with the surveillance?"

"Abby and I are sure he's performed vandalism on my truck and are certain he's somehow gained access to my home and stolen my property. If you see him break in and were able to get pictures, we would have the proof we need for the police department. No disrespect for your friends, but the PD has been less than helpful up to this point. Also, we know he's a diagnosed paranoid psychopath."

Trent further explained that Abby and her family were afraid that if Cole were unable to locate Abby, he might take his frustration out on her family and friends.

"It would be my honor to help in your situation. My sister was a victim of an SOB like this one, when I was deployed. There was nothing I could do to help her, so now I'll help Abby. I cannot stand a man who bullies a woman. And who knows how much other dirt I'll be able to dig up on Cole, as well. Consider me your teammate. We will take him down, one way or another."

Trent remembered something else his brother had told him.

"Another thing, Pierce. My brother works for the FBI. He ran a background check on Cole and discovered that when he was nineteen, Cole and a friend beat a man almost to death. The friend went to prison, but a good defense team managed to get Cole acquitted. He's had the potential for violence for a long time. This is not new. Please watch your back."

Abby gasped at this news. When Trent looked back at the computer screen, she appeared to be in a state of shock.

"Oh crap, Abby. I guess you didn't know about that. I'm sorry I blurted it out. Are you okay?" It drove him totally mad in times like this that he couldn't hold her. This long distance thing was starting to get to him.

"No, no of course I didn't know about that. And yes, I'm okay. But knowing about it makes me even more certain he had something to do with Jenny's disappearance."

"Trent, who's Jenny?"

They filled him in on the mysterious disappearance of Cole's daughter-in-law. Although Pierce was a disciplined man, and in control of his emotions and actions, there was no mistaking the flash of anger and then the determination in his eyes. Abby and Trent both knew they had found their man, an answer to their prayers.

That afternoon, Trent spent the rest of the day online with Abby. He was determined to take her mind off all the nastiness. They played at filling out those silly Internet quizzes, trying to determine each other's answers. They found satisfaction in the fact that most of the time they could predict them, and they laughed heartily at the quiz results. Trent sang silly songs to her, because he knew she loved his bass voice. He culminated the serenade with, *"I'm Too Sexy for My Shirt,"* that had her giggling. He was so proud of her and so relieved that despite everything that was happening, she actually was able to laugh. That night, he talked her to sleep, before he collapsed himself.

CHAPTER 26

TRENT MADE UP HIS MIND. There was no way he could make a wise decision about Abby and his future until and unless they had some time together. He knew the only way he was going to get any peace of mind was to travel to Ecuador. Although he and Abby had talked about him visiting, he hoped she would be excited that he was coming.

"Good morning, Gorgeous. You know you are the only person I have ever known in my life who wakes up this lovely."

"Really? How is a girl supposed to resist that kind of statement? Even if she knows the handsome man making it is lying. Good Morning, Trent. It's good to see you."

"Well it has been four whole hours since you saw me last. I, for one, think that is entirely too long. But I know you need your sleep. I am still trying to figure out how you look so good on so little sleep."

"Oh my goodness, you sure are full of it this morning. What has you in such a good mood?"

"I was up all night thinking. And I made a decision. How would you feel about me coming to Ecuador for a visit?" He held his breath.

"Well, you've been saying you were going to come since before I left the States. Why would you wonder how I would feel about it? Honestly, I think it's empty promises and chatter. I don't think you'll ever take off from work long enough to come."

"Abby, I booked a ticket this morning."

"Oh my gosh! Really? You're really coming? When? I can't believe it, oh my gosh. When, when, when? How soon?"

"Umm. Well, I guess by that response, you're okay with it" He was relieved at her response. "In six weeks. I have to tie up loose ends here and get someone to cover me at work. I can do that and come for a month. If that isn't too long for me to stay."

Without thinking, Abby blurted, "The only thing better than a month would be forever. I can't wait. There is so much I want to show you! What are you telling your family and work about being gone that long?"

"I'm going to tell them I'm going to Ecuador. They might as well get used to it."

Abby was so excited she could hardly concentrate. She immediately started a list of all the places they would go and the things they would do. Trent chuckled. He should have known she would be making a list. She made lists for everything and always had him laughing when she was trying to find the right list among them all. She didn't need to make a list to know the first thing she would do when he arrived. She absolutely couldn't wait to feel his arms around her. Her only concern was she often wondered if they ever had the time to spend together in the same place, could they be satisfied living apart.

When Trent left for work that morning, all his thoughts were on Abby, his upcoming vacation, and how happy he felt. His step was light, there was a smile on his face, and he worked hard to concentrate on his driving. He never glanced in the rearview mirror long enough or with enough awareness to notice there was someone following him.

Cole was so focused on following Trent, he didn't observe the man following him, either. But Pierce Wellington was indeed focused on Cole. He was determined to catch anything the man was doing. He noted in his logbook that Cole was indeed following Trent. Possible charge: Stalking

Pierce also had done a little investigating of his own. He found the DUI charge, but it had been in another state. If Cole were stopped and arrested, the record might or might not show the charge from Missouri. If it didn't show up, the damned DUI laws in North Carolina for a first offense were little more than a slap on the wrist except for license suspension. But Pierce already decided if that were the case, he would turn over the information to Cole's employer. He also did some reading about psychopaths, especially how a loss of control could push them to drastic measures. If Cole were charged with a DUI, that wasn't too much. He probably would continue to drive on the suspended license until caught again. But if he also lost his job — well maybe that would push him. If kept up for a long time, it might be possible to rack up a few more charges, like stalking and breaking-and-entering.

There was a veritable train of folks following one another. Jeremy also was following his father. After Jenny's disappearance, all his dad could talk about was getting rid of Abby. Jeremy was having a hard time processing and dealing with his own part in his wife's disappearance, and he didn't want Abby to fall victim as well. She was a second mom to him, better than his first in many respects, and had always been good to him. He respected her, and Kendall, too and didn't want his dad to get away with harming her.

Jeremy understood why Abby left and didn't blame her. But he couldn't say that to his father. Jenny had, and it was the last disparaging thing she ever said to Cole. He knew his dad thought he owed him something for helping with Jenny, but damn, that had been a bad idea in the heat of a drunken moment. So he had been following his father to make sure he went to work every day and returned home. Today, he noticed it looked like another car also was following his dad. But he would keep an eye out on the return trip. It was probably a coincidence, since he couldn't imagine why or who would be following Cole.

Of course, highly trained as he was, Pierce spotted Jeremy tailing Cole, as well. But he didn't know who he was or why he was following him. On the off chance it might be a detective, he parked and looked at Jeremy closely as he went by. No, he didn't think that was a detective. That kid was too young and unkempt to be a detective, but he knew a few undercover guys who looked like that. He decided to give his pal at the PD a call and see if the case was still open on Jenny Grey.

The case was still open. But something was off at the sheriff's department about the story. For example, no undercover agents were assigned to the case. He was still puzzled, though, as to who was following Cole – who else might have it out for the man? Maybe he had a lover who was having him followed, or Pierce supposed it could be a repo team. Most heavy drinkers had financial problems. Even if they had plenty of money, drinkers often forget about mundane things like paying bills. If he saw the kid again, he would get a tag and run it. *What in the world kind of drama had he gotten himself into?*

When Cole left work that evening, there was another convoy behind him. Pierce was in a different car from the one he drove in the morning. Tonight, he was driving an inconspicuous gray sedan. There were only a few thousands of those on the road. He had parked in the lot at Cole's work and filed out with all the other employees. Pierce wasn't too concerned with being right behind Cole because he had a pretty good idea where he was going. Two blocks away, Pierce spotted the young guy again. He got the tag number and called his buddy with the police department to run a check. It came back as *Jeremy Grey.* He called Trent to find out his relationship to Cole and why he might be following him.

Following Pierce's call, Trent called Abby.

"Jeremy probably isn't following Cole. Jeremy sometimes meets

Cole after work, and they go someplace together to drink, talk, or whatever. Neither one does much without the other."

Trent called Pierce back and related this information.

"That's sure not what this looks like, Trent. I have followed Cole all the way home. Jeremy followed too, until a couple of blocks from the house, then he diverted to another route. I'm down the street from the house now, and I think I see Jeremy coming in from the other direction. This looks like a tail to me."

"Well, isn't that interesting. Keep up the good work, and let us know if anything happens."

"You know I will, and a report will be included in the weekly billing statement."

Trent decided it wasn't time yet to tell Abby of the new development. He thought it was best if they gave Pierce a little time to work out what was going on.

Pierce continued to watch the house. He saw Jeremy get out of his vehicle carrying a case of beer. But there had been no time for him to pick that up. He must have had it before he started tailing Cole.

Watching this target was easy work for Pierce. They had every light in the house on, and all the blinds were open, so he could watch these people freely. Jeremy stayed for a couple of hours, then left, presumably to return to his family. While Pierce consumed a thermos of coffee, a tuna salad sandwich, and an entire bag of tortilla chips, he watched Cole. The man sat at his computer drinking beer faster than most people could guzzle water. But as the hours ticked by, Pierce noticed Cole's body language becoming increasingly agitated. He began rubbing the back of his neck, then his hands began dragging through his hair, as he made phone call after phone call, each only lasting a few seconds. Apparently no one was answering his calls.

Pierce had no way of knowing whether Cole was calling the same number over and over, or if he was calling every number on his contact list, but it wasn't long until Cole was up and pacing the floor. He never ate anything, just kept guzzling one beer after another. When Pierce used his binoculars to look around the house through the unobstructed windows, he was amazed at the quantity of beer cans piled everywhere. There was even a pyramid of them along a wall in the large dining room. Pierce made a mental note to ask Trent if they wanted him to install listening devices in the house and/or try to get the man's phone records. Neither would be legal, and no information gleaned from them would be admissible in court if anything came of them, but if Trent and Abby wanted to incur the cost, they might be able to get more information.

He sat watching the house until it went dark at 3:00 a.m. He then went home to catch a couple hours of sleep before he had to be back at six thirty. *How did a man keep going on so few hours of sleep, especially after consuming that much alcohol?*

The following weekend, Pierce still had Cole under surveillance when an interesting development took place. Cole moved out of the house and into an apartment. Pierce watched and followed as load after load was moved. Cole was drinking heavily, but Jeremy was doing the driving. Jeremy was drinking too, but not to the same level as Cole. So far, Pierce had not had any occasion to alert the authorities to Cole's drunk driving. So far, his driving had been to and from work, stop by the liquor store on the way home, and sometimes he picked up a takeout dinner.

CHAPTER 27

*A*BBY WOKE UP DAZED AND confused. *Where in the hell am I?* In the dark, she felt around for something she recognized, but nothing felt familiar. She started to panic. *Where am I?* She could smell something like bleach, she was finding it hard to breathe, there was a strong odor that made her vomit, and her heart was beating ninety miles a second. She heard a key chain rattle and a lock open. When the door opened, she let out a blood-curdling scream. It was Cole. *How did he find me? when did he find me?*

Cole smiled. "Hello my wife. This is your reckoning. I told you, you'll always be mine, and now I'll prove it to you. I am going to show you how much you want to stay. For starters, you'll clean this shed to my satisfaction. If you don't, you do not eat, so we'll start with that." Cole left, locked the door, and turned on the power for the only light in the shed. Abby cringed when she saw the mess.

There was fecal matter in the corners of the shed, and the ceiling looked like someone tossed the stuff up there, too. The walls were smeared with the disgusting matter. She couldn't hold back any more and vomited again. *I can't handle this and Cole knows it.* But if she wanted to breathe again, she needed to sanitize the place. Abby tore her shirt, wrapped the cloth around her face, and cleaned up the shed. She had found a pile of rags, some garbage bags, and a bottle of bleach. There was a bottle of water and a large jug of hand sanitizer, but there was no food. She also discovered a camping toilet and was thankful for at least that one semi convenience. When Cole returned and saw the shed cleaned, he thought, *now it starts.*

"I see you were a good wife, and now you can eat."

Then Abby let loose. "What in the hell do you think you're doing? You cannot treat me like this. I will never take you back. I'll get out of here and report you to the police. You'll pay for this you sorry son of a bitch." Immediately, Abby found herself on the floor holding her mouth, blood pooling in her hand.

"Abby, if you're going to talk like that, then you deserve to be beaten. Now, you won't eat. Take off your clothes!" Abby started to freak out, and he repeated, "Take off your clothes. Don't make me say it twice, or I'll bitch slap you again."

In fear for her life, Abby conceded.

"Now we'll see how you like being cold." Cole took her blanket and clothes and left. All Abby could do was shiver. *How did I end up here?*

Cole woke up with a smile. Yeah. That was the best dream I have had in a long time. Things will be better soon. I will have her with me, and she will never want to do anything but what I tell her. She's all mine. An eerie laugh echoed through the house.

Abby got a message from Lizzy.

LizzyG: Cole got fired today.

AbbyG: I can't believe it has taken this long.

LizzyG: He told Forest he had stopped drinking last night at eleven. But he got to work, and they popped a drug and alcohol screen on him. The alcohol screen was immediate, and they fired him on the spot. The drug test won't be in for two days, but Forest says he's pretty sure he failed that, too.

AbbyG: Well, I'm not surprised at all. I hate it, because I'm sure this will be my fault, too. Now he will have even more time to dwell on how much he hates me. I kept trying to tell everyone that with as much as he was drinking, and the metabolism rate for alcohol, he was never not drunk. No one would listen to me. And he was buying pain pills from one of Jeremy's friends, even when I was there.

LizzyG: Forest says he's pretty sure he's been smoking pot, too.

AbbyG: Well, I wonder what he will do now.

LizzyG: At the moment, he's saying he will file for unemployment, and that he's pretty sure he knows the two people who turned him in, resulting in the first drug test he's had in nine years. He says he's going to kill them.

AbbyG: Yeah, yeah, yeah. He's a regular Arnold Schwarzenegger. He's going to take his AK-47 and be rid of everyone who offends his sensibilities. I wonder if he will be the last man standing. And doesn't he know you can't collect unemployment if you're fired for failing a drug screen.

Abby knew her remarks sounded cynical. Not only sounded cynical, they were. She was so tired of his threats. She almost wished he would try and end up committing suicide by cop, but there was too much opportunity to hurt an innocent. She didn't want anyone to be hurt; she simply wanted Cole to go away.

LizzyG: He says he's going to move in with his brother.

AbbyG: Well, that's a new one. Not. Every time he gets unhappy, loses a job, gets laid off, or we got in a fight, he would say he was going to move in with his brother. The funny thing is, I never once heard Bruce even encourage Cole to move there, let alone invite him to move in with him. Bruce is not a drinker and has no patience with it. I doubt that is going to work for him.

LizzyG: Well, I don't know what he's going to do, and I don't care. He totally disgusts me. Every time we see him, he's literally falling down drunk. All I know is that he moved into one of our apartments, and if he doesn't pay the rent come the first of the month, Forest will serve an eviction notice.

AbbyG: He moved into one of your apartments? I know he didn't sell the house, because I never signed a quitclaim deed, and he hasn't asked me to sign one. I tried to give one to the bank before I left, and they said they couldn't accept it. His mom probably will give him rent money. She would rather do that than have him move in with her.

LizzyG: Yeah, he's letting the house go back to the bank.

AbbyG: Great, and my name is still on it? Now I'm mad. I made every single payment on that house until the divorce. Now it's going to wreck my credit. I don't understand. He made good money.

LizzyG: Apparently he's drinking it all. He has a roommate now to help with expenses.

AbbyG: Well, keep me posted. I'll need to know if he moves or is homeless to let family know where he may be. And thanks, Lizzy, for keeping me informed.

Cole couldn't believe he had lost his job. He knew who the bastards were that turned him in, and he would make them pay. First, he was going to finish this bottle of tequila. Tomorrow, he would go file for unemployment.

This is all that bitch's fault. If she had not left, he wouldn't be drinking, and he wouldn't have lost his damn job. Ungrateful bastards. He had given them nine years, worked through the loss of his father, his daughter-in-law, and his wife.

The next day, he did go file for unemployment. He knew he would have to wait six weeks, but he wanted to get his claim in early. With any luck, the bastards would know what was good for them and wouldn't report his failed alcohol test. Then he called his mom.

"Hi, Mom."

"What's wrong Cole?"

"I got fired yesterday. I can't believe the assholes fired me."

"Why did you get fired?"

"A couple of asshats went to the boss and told him they thought I was drunk. They popped me for an alcohol and drug screen. I had quit drinking the night before at eleven, but they said I still had a high blood alcohol level and fired me on the spot. There was no way I was still drunk, Mom."

"Cole, Abby tried to tell you, I have tried to tell you, Jeremy has tried to tell you, that your drinking is out of control. It's time you go to rehab or back to AA, whatever will work for you."

"I know. I'm going back to AA as soon as I finish the bottle I have now. I applied for unemployment this morning, but it will be six weeks before I get any funds. Is there any way you can help me out?"

"No Cole, not this time."

"And what do you mean 'Abby told me?' What do you know about what Abby told me?"

"She told me before she left, Cole, that she was worried about you. She said you were in danger. She said you were in danger from how much you were drinking, in danger of losing your job, and in danger of your marriage falling apart. I'm ashamed to say, I didn't listen. I thought she was just whining. I should have known better because Abby is not a whiner. I didn't say anything to you because I knew you were grieving for your Daddy, and I thought it would get better, that you would get a handle on it. But I thought wrong. You were so upset when you called to tell me Abby had left, I thought it best not to tell you she had tried to talk to me. I have felt bad about the fact that she came to me for help, and I brushed her aside. I should have helped her."

"Well, fuck you, Mom. You are supposed to be on my side. That little bitch will pay some day for all the grief she caused me. It's all her fault I'm drinking now. I wouldn't be drinking if she hadn't left."

"Oh, Cole, that is merely your latest excuse and you know it. She left because you were drinking. You've never stopped. That is not Abby's fault, and until you own your decision, nothing will ever change for you. If you don't get your act together, you'll lose everything."

"Thanks for nothing, Mom. Bye!"

Cole hoped he could get to Bruce before his mother did. So he called him immediately.

"Hey Bro, what's up?"

"I'm working Cole. What are you doing off from work?"

"Those rat bastards fired me. If I can't find another job in time, can I come stay with you and maybe look for a job, there?"

"Man, I'm sorry. I wish I could help you, but the inn is full here. I'm stretched to the maximum."

"Thanks for nothing Bro. I gotta go call someone who cares!"

Out of options, Cole began to get frantic. Then he received a phone call from the company that financed Abby's little cottage, notifying him they would be picking up the shed today for nonpayment. *Fuck, Fuck, Fuck.*

That day's mail brought a certified letter from the bank that held the home mortgage. The foreclosure date was five days away. Well, that didn't upset him. He didn't give a damn about the house, and the foreclosure was going to screw up Abby's credit, too. But, he supposed he better go out to the house to make sure there wasn't anything he needed to get out of there. And he thought he better get all the stuff out of the shed. The contents of the little building might make someone suspicious.

Pierce followed Cole that day — from the apartment where he had been staying, back out to the house. Thankfully, he had his high-powered binoculars and could watch. It looked like Cole was packing up more stuff to take away from the house. The curious thing was that Cole drove his truck back up into the woods behind the house. He stayed about an hour, then returned to the house and garage. He spent about an hour going through things and putting more stuff into his truck.

Pierce then followed Cole back to the apartment. He sat and watched. Cole didn't unload the truck; he just went inside. After watching for another hour, and using his telephoto lens to snap photos of the truck contents, he figured Cole was in for a while, so he went toward the house.

Pierce drove back into the woods where he had seen Cole emerge, until he came upon a shed painted to look like camouflage. It had three locks on the door, and there was some kind of crazy foam filling the window. Since the locks were open, he peered inside. There was nothing there, but the walls were covered in foam, the kind of spray can insulation foam used for filling holes. What was strange was that the walls and ceiling were covered with the foam, as was the one window. About that time, he heard a large vehicle moving in his direction. He quickly got in his truck and drove deeper into the woods where he could watch what was going on.

It was a Gator-type vehicle that came and pulled the shed out and took it away. When the Gator was gone, Pierce returned to the site. A frame of landscaping timbers filled with river rock was all that remained. It looked as if the timbers were new. The shed probably hadn't been there long. He asked himself why Cole would want a shed this far away from the house. And then he wondered, was it placed there to hide something else? Which led him to remember about Cole's daughter-in-law who had disappeared without a trace. Was it possible? He didn't know, but decided it was time for him to get out of there and return to Cole's to see if he was still sitting at home. He had an ominous feeling that he had just discovered something important.

CHAPTER 28

*T*RENT AND ABBY SPENT THE ensuing weeks talking about all the things they wanted to do when he arrived in Ecuador. Abby wanted Trent to see everything she had done since arriving — every place she walked, every neighborhood, everything.

Trent also had a list of must-dos, including places Abby had not seen yet. Trent wanted to see the Inca ruins, for sure. Abby told him there were some ruins in Cuenca, but the biggest surviving ruins were a short day trip away. They both wanted to go to the Galapagos Islands, but that would have to wait for another time.

The site they were the most interested in was each other. They would laugh, wondering if they would manage to see anything of the city or country at all. They knew the first few days, they would need to take it easy until Trent adjusted to the altitude, and that was okay with them. A couple of days to just absorb each other sounded like what they needed most. Neither of them had experienced an eight-month relationship that had no kissing, no touching, no handholding since they were probably ten years old, and the frustration level was high. They were both excited about finally being in the same city for the first time since the friendship had bloomed into a romantic relationship. They were also nervous, which they didn't talk about.

Abby couldn't wait to take Trent to her favorite restaurants, introduce him to her new friends, walk the city, take some day trips to the artisan villages, experience the nightlife, and explore the countryside. Trent couldn't wait to see Abby. But while the anticipation built, Abby's emotions intensified. Trent had a much more casual wait-and-see approach. He wasn't worried or concerned. It just was.

Trent had a business dinner one night, and Abby decided to catch up on one of her TV shows. She had heard about the last episodes of the season and decided she would watch them while Trent was otherwise occupied. She knew the main character was going to die in the episode, she was prepared for that, but what happened was so much more, so earthmoving it changed Abby's life forever. Watching the show as the character died, she realized for the first time in her life there was someone she couldn't live without — Trent. The fears, the feelings of inadequacy vanished and were replaced with new emotions. She didn't want to be without him. Ever.

Abby always had felt emotionally bankrupt concerning the men in her life. All the tearjerker movies about lost loves always made her cry. But every time she saw one, it made her feel there was something wrong with her. She never had been able to access a feeling of devastation when something happened to a man in her life. Her mom has said it was because she had never been in love, and the men were wrong for her.

Yes, she cared. Yes, she worried. And yes, she believed she loved. But nothing like this. Nothing even close to this. This loss would be earth shattering. *I can't walk away from this one. I won't walk away.*

She needed Trent more than air. She couldn't imagine never seeing him again. The tears wouldn't stop. Every man in her life always thought she needed them, but she never did until right now, in this moment.

What the hell am I supposed to do now? Why did it have to happen this way, at this time, in this place, under these circumstances?

For the next week, their schedules seemed to clash. Abby had lunch a few times with friends, and Trent was super busy at work getting ready for the trip. Abby also went on some day trips to surrounding cities. In Ecuador, the people who live in a certain city all seem to specialize in one type of trade. Abby visited Ona, a community that works together to manufacture tequila, and Chordeleg where the specialty is silver jewelry, specifically filigree jewelry, one of Abby's favorites. She also went to Gualaceo, famous for its textile weavers and orchid farms, Sig Sig, known for fine Panama hats, San Bartolomé, home to the makers of artisan guitars, and to the Giron waterfalls. Everywhere she traveled, she marveled at the beauty of the country. She wanted to share it all with Trent.

When she was away from her computer, Abby had a lot of time to focus on her life and wonder. She realized how far she had come, how much she had healed, how happy she was, but more important, how content and peaceful she felt. She understood it really it was nothing short of a miracle. She finally felt whole. She didn't know if it was the distance she had put between herself and Cole — the physical distance for certain, but the time away from his controlling influence, as well. She remembered wondering about the saying "time heals all wounds" and how much time and distance should be part of the equation, at least for some types of wounds.

Then there were the conversations with Trent that made her feel like a twenty-something, beautiful, desirable woman. There was absolutely nothing in the world she would trade for the way he made her feel. For God's sake, she was fifty years old. Was it crazy to feel this way? And then, he would manage to do it again.

Trent woke up, glanced at the computer and realized that Abby was up and putting on makeup. "Damn girl. Where are you going? Why are you getting so fixed up?"

Abby smiled. "Good morning, Handsome. Nowhere special. Just meeting some friends for lunch later."

"Really, what are you getting so gussied up for then?"

Abby blushed. "I'm not gussied up."

"Not yet maybe, but by the look of that makeup, you're going to be." Trent obviously admired the effect.

"Well, I'm having lunch with some friends and meeting some new people who recently moved here from the States. It is going to be a pretty big crowd of about twelve people, and I want to look nice."

"Baby Doll, you always look nice, I've never seen you not looking like a million dollars. So, what are you wearing?"

"A red lace teddy. Oh, you mean to lunch? Well, wait a couple more minutes, and I'll show you."

Abby put on a new dress and leggings that showed off her fifty-pound weight loss. She knew it looked good, but wanted to get Trent's reaction.

"Well, move the camera back so I can see the whole picture."

Abby complied and stood back.

"Damn girl! That dress looks *good* on you. I'll be surprised if you're not picked up at least two or three times before you get home."

Abby delighted in his response, but to his comment about getting picked up she said, "Oh please, not really!"

"Mark my words, it will happen. You might even find a new Latin lover."

"Well, I am pretty partial to my Irish lover. Even if we aren't really lovers. Yet."

"You mark my words, at least three times, someone will say something to you."

She laughed. "I'll call you as soon as I get home."

"How long you think you'll be gone?"

"With travel time and lunch and visiting, probably no more than two or three hours."

"Okay, I'll be waiting with bated breath. I want to hear about all the guys who try to pick you up. Don't hold out on telling me I was right, okay?"

"Okay, I promise. Talk to you soon." She shut down her computer.

Surfing online one day, she ran across a saying, "Absence is to love what wind is to fire; it extinguishes the small, it enkindles the great."

She wanted to frame that saying and hang it where she would see it every day to remind her of how far she had come. A new burst of excitement and energy enveloped her. She was free. Finally, free to be exactly who she was and who she wanted to be. She was going to be *Abby Albright — The Chica in Cuenca,* and she was going to start a blog to share with all her family and friends back home — her adventures, discoveries, and trials.

Trent encouraged her writing, and she learned how cathartic writing could be. She learned when she wrote about her insecurities, the process relieved her confusion. Writing down her worries and concerns made her realize how silly they seemed and how far they were from her new reality. She finally found the remedy, the outlet for all the chaos in her mind, and she was free.

Abby asked Trent one morning, "Do you think we will ever be able to talk to each other without a headset?"

"Nope, I don't think we will."

"I envision us walking around with cords dangling and microphones in front of our mouths everywhere we go."

"And when we touch, we won't quite be able to reach. There always will be a tiny fraction of distance between us, the thickness of a computer screen."

"Yep, it's going to be like having a chaperone." They both laughed.

CHAPTER 29

OR THREE DAYS, COLE SPENT all of his waking hours glued to his computer, searching for Abby or any of her family members. Nothing was happening for him, and he was becoming more agitated, really to the point of furious. He had lost his job, so his funds were more limited. He no longer had the cottage, and he didn't even want it any more. He wanted to strangle the bitch with his bare hands so badly. He wanted to feel the life drain from her, wanted to watch her gasp and struggle for her last breath.

He realized that Trent Dumas was his only lead. It was a crappy lead, a really crappy lead, but it was all he had. At least now he could devote all his time to following Trent. Sooner or later, something would happen. He cleaned out his truck and began stocking it with the supplies he would need to spend hours upon hours in it. He placed a handgun in the glove box and another under the seat. He put a flask in the console, another under the seat next to the pistol, and returned to the apartment. He got a six-pack of soda and a twelve-pack of water and was placing them in the passenger side floorboard when a sheriff's department car pulled up next to his truck.

The sheriff got out and asked if he was Cole Grey.

"I am. What can I do for you officer?"

"I am trying to tie up some loose ends on the Jenny Grey case and wondered if you had some time to answer a few questions."

"Well, as you can see, I was about to leave home. I thought the case was closed. Have you found her?"

"No sir, we haven't. I only need to ask a few questions. If now isn't a good time for you, you can come down to the station later at your convenience."

"Well, I'm leaving town for a couple of days. I have to go check on my mother. I should be back by Wednesday. Will that be soon enough?"

"Yes sir. I will look for you on Wednesday. My name is Officer Dupree. Give the station a call and ask for me. You can let me know what time to expect you."

"Okay, thank you Officer. You have a good day."

Well shit. What in the hell could they want to ask now, this long after the fact? This can't be good. I was told the case is closed. Oh well, I am not going to worry about it. Thankfully, Jeremy had some foresight when he buried the dog. They will never find her now, and there is nothing to point toward Jeremy or me.

He returned to the apartment and loaded up a sack with beef jerky, chips, and his favorite store-bought cupcakes. *That should do me for a while. Time to hit the road."*

He made sure there was plenty of food and water in the dog's bowls. He hated being in this small cramped apartment where he couldn't leave the dog outside. He had to remind himself that if he was gone too long, he needed to call Jeremy to come walk the dog. But if he did have to call Jeremy, he knew he would have to explain where he was and why he couldn't walk the dog. *Screw that. I don't have to explain shit to anyone. The boy just better do what I ask!* He got in his car and headed out to Trent Dumas' office to wait for him to leave.

～

Pierce Wellington was on Cole's tail. He was never so thankful to be on the move in all his life. Three solid days of sitting outside this man's apartment had left him almost comatose and in desperate need of a decent, balanced meal. What he wouldn't give for a big juicy steak.

Ten minutes into the trip, Pierce realized there was someone else tailing Cole again. But it wasn't Jeremy this time. At least, he hoped it was someone else tailing Cole, and there wasn't someone dumb enough to think they could tail him. About three blocks from Trent's office, Pierce was pretty sure he knew where Cole was headed. So he pulled over, parked, and let the other car take the lead. He waited five minutes, then headed for Trent's office. He drove around the parking lot for a bit and located the other tailing car. He then found a place to park where he could watch. The car had Virginia plates. He pulled them and called his buddy at the police department to run the tags.

Amory Hunter decided he needed to see what Cole was up to. The things Cole had told him just didn't add up. He needed to know what kind of crap Cole had going on. Amory and Cole had been best friends growing up; the entire Grey family was a second family to Amory. If Cole was up to something that would cause the family grief, he wanted to try and prevent it.

Alice Grey had been through enough. Her husband recently died, and she didn't need the heartache of something happening to Cole. Amory knew, as well as anyone else, that Cole was the apple of Alice's eye. And, since Amory suspected Cole and/or Jeremy had something to do with Jenny's disappearance, it appeared whatever issues Cole had, the family wouldn't be spared from the drama of his conse-quences. Either Jeremy had inherited his father's anger issues, and Cole had covered it up, or Cole was responsible, and Jeremy was afraid to speak up. Neither scenario looked good for the family. He felt pretty sure that Abby was safe, most likely she was out of the country. But he knew she had family here, and if Cole would harm his own son's wife, Abby's family could be in danger as well.

He was in the parking lot of a steel company, watching Cole sit in his car, watching another car. But he also was watching the man in the blue SUV who appeared to be following Cole, and who had pulled in where he could watch Amory. Looked like someone else was following Cole. But Amory couldn't imagine who.

Cole had been sitting and watching for two hours when his phone rang. He looked at the caller ID — it was Jeremy.

"Hi Jeremy, what's up?"

"Dad, I need you! I'm at the hospital with the girls. Mom is in Roanoke for the day, and I need help. Please get here quick!"

"I'm on my way." Cole started the car and left the steel company parking lot.

Two cars followed him out. Amory decided he needed to find out who the other guy was. As soon as the opportunity presented itself, he would confront the man and ask him.

Cole flew into the Emergency Room parking area and took off at a run for the emergency department. Pierce knew if Cole had a real reason to go to the ER, he would be there for a while. He decided to take the opportunity to go across the street from the hospital and get something to eat.

As Pierce was browsing the menu, a large burly man sat down on the other side of his booth. He extended a hand to introduce himself.

"Amory Hunter."

"Well, Mr. Hunter, what can I do for you?"

"I think we are chasing the same prey, and I wondered what your interest is?"

"I could ask you the same thing. Who hired you to follow Mr. Grey?"

"No one. I'm doing it on my own, as a friend of the family. Who hired you?"

"I'm sorry, that is information I can't disclose at this time. So the family is paying a private dick to follow the man? Care to share why?" Pierce was really curious now.

"Well, maybe if you would be so polite as to share at least your name with me, we might begin a mutually beneficial relationship. But I hate having a partner who's name I can't remember in the morning, simply because I never knew it in the first place."

Pierce laughed at the man's humor. He knew who he was, because his buddy at the PD already had given him background. What he didn't know was why Amory was interested in Cole. Maybe they could work together and coordinate information about their common prey.

"I am Pierce Wellington, and I was hired by a friend of a family member who was concerned about his friend's well-being at Cole's hands."

"Would that possibly be a friend of Abby?"

"I'm not willing to share any more information about who hired me than that, at the moment. But maybe you could tell me what Abby has to do with any of this?" Pierce hoped for some insight into what this Amory guy knew.

Amory realized this pissing contest wasn't going to get either of them anywhere. This wasn't a paying gig, so if Pierce could cover some of the surveillance and/or share what he already knew, maybe he could go back home. He only had three more days off work, and he had spent the first two days sitting outside Cole's apartment learning nothing.

Amory began explaining. "Cole and I were best friends growing up. I haven't seen him for about five years, but he called me with a sob story of Abby running off, and he wanted me to find her. I did. But what I also discovered was she's no longer his wife, and they are divorced, which Cole didn't tell me. When I talked to Abby, she told me why she was running from Cole and about the disappearance of

Jeremy's wife. I happen to have some information about Cole's past that made me suspicious of what he might be up to. His family is like my second family, and I don't want to see his mother go through any more tragedy, so I decided to come out here and see for myself what was going on. I didn't tell Cole I had found Abby, because I happen to have a gut feeling that Abby was more on the level with me than Cole. Now, how about your story?" Amory hoped his being forthright would induce Pierce to open up.

"Well, I still won't tell you who hired me. But there are some people who are anxious about what might be Cole's involvement in Jenny's disappearance, and they have a vested interest in keeping Cole away from Abby. I'm watching Cole to make sure he doesn't get to Abby, and to see if I can uncover any possible misdeeds."

"Mr. Wellington, it sounds to me like we are on the same page. What do you think the chances are we could work together on this little project?"

"Amory, I think we could make that work, after I finish eating this big juicy steak. Care to join me before I go over to that hospital and investigate the situation there?"

"Sure, and maybe you could fill in the gap as to who Cole is following and why?"

The two men determined that since Cole knew Amory, it would be best if Pierce went inside the hospital to see if he could figure out what was going on and how long Cole might be there. Amory would wait outside and keep an eye on Cole's car. They exchanged phone numbers, so if Cole started moving, Amory could let Pierce know.

As soon as Pierce got to the emergency waiting room, he spotted Cole sitting with a baby and a toddler, trying his best to keep them both entertained, somewhat quiet, and the toddler within arm's reach. Pierce took a seat across from him and watched the little girl dance in and out of Cole's reach. He smiled. When Cole looked up at him, he asked, "What are you in for?" making a subtle joke equating the ER to jail.

"My granddaughter had an accident. My son was trying to deal with all three girls and called for reinforcements while they put a cast on the oldest one. You?"

"Buddy fell off a roof trying to patch the darn thing. I dropped him off. His wife is on the way, but I thought I would stick around until she gets here, to make sure he isn't released before she arrives, or she doesn't need anything." Pierce remained eagle-eyed for anyone entering the ER he could pretend was his buddy's wife. Sure enough, in about ten minutes, a lady came rushing in and stopped at the desk to inquire about her husband.

Pierce looked at Cole and said, "Well there is the little lady now, and she looks pissed, so I think I'll quietly scoot out the door. I hope your granddaughter is okay."

"I hear you man. Avoid the little ladies at all cost, especially the mad ones." Cole laughed, thinking he was funny.

Pierce returned to the parking lot and slid into the passenger side of Amory's car. He told him what he was able to find out. They determined Pierce would stay at the hospital to follow Cole when he left, again because with both Jeremy and Cole there, the likelihood of Amory being recognized was high.

Amory offered to buy Pierce breakfast and spell him in the morning, and they went their separate ways.

By the time Cole was able to leave the hospital, he looked rough. He helped his son get all three girls buckled into their car seats and returned to his truck. Pierce saw him take a long draw on the flask from under his seat. Cole then opened a soda and drove to Trent Dumas' house. Trent's car was there, so Cole kept driving, went home, walked the dog, and was in for the night.

At 5:00 a.m., Amory showed up with sausage biscuits, donuts, and coffee, saying he didn't know if Pierce preferred sweet or savory for breakfast. Pierce opted for a sausage biscuit and took a long refreshing draw on the coffee. Amory helped himself to both a sausage biscuit and three of the donuts.

Pierce left and told Amory he would call him about four to

compare notes and confirm the time Pierce would spell Amory for the night watch. It was going to be much easier with two men splitting the shifts. Pierce just hoped he could trust Amory to share details.

CHAPTER 30

*T*RENT'S PHONE RANG AT **5:45** A.M.

"Who died? Because I know someone must have died if my phone is ringing this early."

His voice woke Abby, who still was connected over the Internet. She sat up, aware something must be wrong.

"Trent, this is Pierce Wellington. I wanted to call and give you an update. There have been some developments with Cole Grey."

"I'm listening." Trent glanced at Abby to let her know everything was okay. He hated to see the frightened, concerned look in her eyes.

"First, Cole appears to have lost his job, or be taking more vacation time. I want a job where I get as many vacations as that dude does. Anyway, he's moved out of the house into an apartment. Also, there was a shed set up out in the woods behind the house, but it was picked up, I guess repossessed. The pad that served as a foundation for the shed looks new. Cole appears to have refocused on you and began tailing you again yesterday. In the process, I discovered there is someone else following Cole. His name is Amory Hunter. Does that name mean anything to you?"

"I don't know, I'm connected to Abby. Let me see if she recognizes the name."

"Oh my gosh, Trent, that is the guy I told you about who found me on my online page. He's Cole's old friend. What's up with Amory?" New concerns plagued her thoughts.

"He's following Cole. Do you know why he would be doing that?"

"No, that doesn't make much sense to me. But hopefully, he kept his word and didn't tell Cole where I was."

Trent relayed the information to Pierce. "Well, that lines up with what the guy told me."

"Did he say why he is following Cole?" Trent was still a little confused.

"Something about being suspicious and not wanting Cole's family to suffer from his deeds. He seems like a stand-up guy, but I wanted to check with you. I think we are going to work together to split some shifts watching Cole. If you guys don't have a problem with that." Pierce knew that if Trent and Abby wanted him to, he would return to watching Cole by himself.

Trent relayed to Abby what Pierce had said.

"Well, the rule is to keep your friends close and your enemies closer. Maybe we can figure out what they are both up to. I suppose Amory can be trusted if he's following Cole. I guess he didn't tell Cole where I am, so I feel like he decided that Cole is troubled. It rings true. Amory is still good friends with Cole's mom and brother."

Trent concluded the call with Pierce, giving him their blessings to work with Amory. When he hung up, he looked at Abby on his computer monitor, and noting the wary, nervous look on her face, said, "Now, good morning, Gorgeous. At least if I had to get waked up, I get to look at you."

Abby smiled." Thank you, Handsome. I feel the same way." Then turning more somber, she said, "This is all getting to be too much. I think I have a plan to put an end to all this and remove everyone I care about from danger."

"How's that going to work? Drain the fishing lake, fill it with vodka, throw Cole in, and hope he drowns? I'll call the liquor distributor right now."

"I don't think we could afford that much vodka. He probably would just drink the lake dry and stagger home. No, I'm serious. I've been thinking about this. I think we should fake my death."

"Oh, thank goodness. I thought you were going to say something like come back and confront him. But Abby, faking your death is an equally bad idea."

"Hear me out, Trent. I know it's illegal to fake your death. And if I truly faked my death, my income would dry up, and I have no other way of making any money right now. But, what I'm thinking is, if we only tell a few strategically selected people I had an accident, maybe take out an obituary in Greenville, the word would get back to him, and he would stop looking."

"Abby, how well have you thought this out?"

"Admittedly, not much. Why?"

"First, I don't know if just anyone can post an obituary in a newspaper. I think usually the funeral home does that. Second, now everyone looks online for funeral information, and all the funeral homes have an online guest book. People love writing in the damn things, and most important, your family would be expected to act accordingly. Do you want to involve all of them and put them through that? I think we can find another way to stop Cole."

"Wow, you are right. I guess I didn't give it much thought before I blurted it out there. I didn't think of all of that. And no, I don't want to involve my family. They have gone through enough crap because of my involvement with that man, but I desperately need to find a way to end this. I've given up on the idea of him drinking himself to death. I'm beginning to think he's the devil's spawn, immortal, and everything is permanently preserved. It's sad how many kids die from alcohol poisoning, yet that man could keep a distributorship in business and he's still walking. I never saw the movie, but I understand the definition of a *dead man walking*. Maybe there is some truth to zombies, and he's one. I don't know. I'm just so frustrated and tired."

"I know Baby Doll, we will get this worked out. I promise. But you coming here or faking your death are not viable solutions. Let's give Pierce a little more time — it looks like he has some help now. He will be working fewer hours, costing us less, and have better coverage. Tell me about Amory, though. Do you really trust this guy?"

"Yeah. I didn't trust him at first, but if he's following Cole, he's chosen a side. I don't know if he would be able to turn Cole in for something like Pierce would, but he would at least try. In addition, he might be able to stop Cole from doing something drastic."

Amory watched Cole that day. Cole left home, went to Trent Dumas' house, and followed Trent to work. Once Trent was at work, Cole then went by Jeremy's house and visited for about an hour, then went through a fast food drive-in and then to the liquor store. After, he went to the sheriff's office. Amory assumed that had something to do with the officer stopping by Cole's apartment the day before. He was at the office for several hours. When he returned to his truck, he didn't look any the worse for wear. He stopped by a pawnshop and went inside for about forty minutes, but Amory couldn't see whether he was carrying anything when he went in or came out. Then Cole returned to the steel company where Trent worked.

Amory wondered if Trent might be the person who hired Pierce, and what his connection might be to Abby. But it didn't really matter. Trent was here in North Carolina, and he was pretty certain Abby was in Ecuador. When they got to the company parking lot, Trent's truck was gone. It was only three in the afternoon, and Cole sped out of the parking lot and headed back to Trent's house. The truck was not there, either. Cole waited for Trent's return. When Pierce called Amory at four, Amory told him where he was. Pierce said he was on the way.

Pierce watched Cole watching Trent's house until 9:30 p.m., when Trent returned home. Trent parked in the driveway, went into the house, talking into his phone's headset, and didn't notice anything around his place. Cole stayed there until all lights were off, except one light upstairs. Apparently, Trent was in for the night so Cole decided to leave. Pierce followed as Cole headed home, stopping first at a liquor store and then at a drive-through for some take-out burgers. Cole returned to his apartment.

Amory took over the surveillance the next morning. When he followed Cole to Trent's house, they got there just in time to see Trent get into an airport shuttle with what looked like an overnight duffel and a computer bag. His truck was still in the driveway. Cole just continued to sit there. Amory was surprised Cole didn't follow Trent to the airport, but once all the morning school and work traffic in the neighborhood died down, he understood why.

Cole backed his truck into Trent's driveway, next to Trent's truck, got out, reached into the back of his own vehicle and removed a tool-box. He then climbed under Trent's truck with the toolbox and did something that took about twenty minutes. From where Amory was parked, there was no way he could see what Cole had done, but he made a note to have Pierce alert Trent that Cole may have tampered with his truck.

When Cole left, he drove around the block, went into a backyard adjacent to Trent's yard. He was gone about an hour. Amory wished he could have followed Cole, but was still being super-careful to keep out of Cole's sight. He was a pretty recognizable fellow, and if Cole made him, his watching days would be over. Cole returned to his truck, drove away, made a beer stop, and then returned home.

Cole was both angry for being thwarted by Trent, and not knowing where he went, and delighted he had been given the opportunity to tamper with the man's truck again, as well as search his house. He was hoping to find anything that would lead him to Abby, or at least tell him about Trent's travel plans. Cole found nothing helpful. The only clue was how light the man had packed, as if he were going on a one-day business trip. What Cole couldn't figure out was, if the pair were having any kind of an affair, when did they see each other? Yet he was certain they were. He could feel it in his gut. *Why else would the man have taken a chance talking to me and had a picture of Abby on his dresser?*

What he most needed to know now was when Trent planned to return. He called the steel company and asked to speak to Trent Dumas. He was transferred to a secretary who told him Trent was away on business, and would he like to leave a message. He said no, the call was personal, and did she know when Trent would be back in town. The secretary said Trent would be back in the office on Monday.

Monday? Monday? Wait, today is Thursday. So he either left to spend a long weekend with Abby, or was away on business returning tomorrow, but not in the office until Monday. Okay, that's not so long. I should have followed him to the airport. But the number I did on his brakes should be worth it.

Cole called his son, and hoping to get some time with him, asked if he would like to bring the girls over to swim in the pool. Jeremy reminded him one of his daughters was in a cast and couldn't swim. Then he told Cole, that his mom was taking him and the girls to Roanoke to see family and some old friends for the weekend. *Dammit, another long weekend home alone. I guess I can clean my guns and watch some TV this weekend.*

Cole spent Friday doing just that. But when he went to bed Friday night, there were two 7.62 shells on his coffee table. One had the initials *AAG* scratched into it; the other had the letters *TD*. He would stake out Trent's house tomorrow morning and wait for Trent's return.

On Saturday morning, Cole started loading his car with replacement supplies for the long wait, but when Cole returned to Trent's house, there was no truck in the driveway.

What the hell? Where has he gone at six o'clock on a Saturday morning? Did he return yesterday and leave again? Dammit! I bet he's gone to see Abby. Well, maybe he will make it there in one piece, and maybe he won't. If she's more than a few blocks away, he might have some brake problems. "Oh darn, I sure hope he isn't involved in a fatal crash." Cole chuckled aloud.

At six o'clock on Saturday morning, Trent was sleeping, but he was tossing and turning. He didn't mind the tossing and turning so much, when he could watch his beautiful angel sleeping right next to him. Three thousand miles away, he couldn't touch her face, couldn't brush the hair from her forehead, couldn't smell her scent, but he could watch her sleep and hear her breathe, and for now, that would have to do.

He would be spending the day with her, since his truck was with his mechanic being thoroughly inspected. Pierce had called and alerted him that Cole had done something to his truck, so when the airport shuttle brought him home yesterday, he had the truck towed to his mechanic with instructions to find the tampered parts.

It looked like he was going to spend the day at home. But he couldn't find any reason to be sad or upset about that. He was thankful Amory had been watching and had told Pierce what he saw. He guessed they could trust Amory after all. When he heard from the mechanic, he was steaming mad. He called Abby.

"Do you know what that son of a bitch did? He cut my brake lines. I could have been killed! Thank God, we have a private investigator following him, or I could have been seriously hurt! Pierce called while I was on my business trip. Amory saw Cole take a toolbox under my truck, so I had it towed to the shop and told them to check everything. He cut my freaking brake lines! Can you believe that?" Trent was practically yelling and wasn't thinking about how his words would affect Abby. Abby had never heard him so mad about anything.

"Oh Trent. I was so afraid something like this was going to happen. I wish you had not confronted him. I had a really bad feeling about you approaching him that day. I know why you did it, and I really appreciate it, but the fallout is simply not worth it. Now, what can we do to keep you safe? I'm so sorry about your truck. This is getting to be way too much." Abby felt panicked. She was frightened and didn't know what to do, how to help, how to stop the crazy runaway train that was the man she had been married to for years. For Abby, it was one thing and bad enough Cole messed with her mind. It was another to tamper with the life of someone who had nothing to do with their marriage or its demise.

"Don't worry about me. I'll be fine, but if I see the son of a bitch around my house again, I'll kill him myself." Trent was still angry, but was calming down a little.

"Trent, the man likes nothing more than a knock-down, drag-out bar fight, the problem is, he sometimes chooses to fight with bullets. There isn't much you can do to defend against that. We have to find a way to stop him." Abby could feel the hysteria starting to well up in her, but she tried to stay calm. She didn't want to make the situation all the more troubling for Trent.

"I understand, Abby. When he was after you, I worried about you, not me. Now you're safe, our relationship has grown, and I care more about staying safe for you now. Maybe Pierce can take care of him somehow. If Pierce had been here the day Cole tampered with my truck, he would've gotten pictures. But I don't think Amory did, so we have no proof it was Cole." Trent made a mental note to get Amory access to a camera if he didn't have one.

"Trent, please be careful, watch your surroundings. We can keep the guys on him to keep him from doing something like this again. I don't understand why Amory didn't call the cops when he saw Cole with a toolbox at your truck. We need to tell Pierce to relay to Amory that anytime he sees something suspicious to call the police. I suppose Amory probably doesn't know this is the second time Cole has vandalized your truck, or about breaking-and-entering into your house. I guess Pierce needs to let Amory know those things, as well. But if Cole gets desperate, he may try to take a shot at you from a distance. I hate I got you involved in this. If something happens to you, it will kill me."

"Abby don't worry about it. I mean it. I care for you; I will protect you. I simply have to watch what I do now. I realize now that protecting you means keeping myself safe, too. And you didn't 'get me involved' in this. I came of my own free will." Trent kept to a soothing tone, realizing how panicked Abby was feeling. He knew he would feel the same if the roles were reversed.

"Lean over here, Trent, and blow me a kiss. I wish our only problem was distance. That's enough to have to deal with. But this is totally nuts. And to think he spent years trying to make me feel like I was the crazy one. At least you are coming down here soon. Maybe out of sight will be out of mind for him. I can't wait until you get here." Abby tried to move the conversation into more positive territory.

"I can't either, Baby Doll, but for now we have to sign off. I have to take care of some stuff. I'll call you back as soon as I get done."

"Okay, I'll be here. Please, please be careful." Abby was concerned about what "stuff" he had to take care of. He usually told her what he was doing. She knew that whatever it was, it had to do with Cole. She hoped he was smart about it and didn't act out of anger, desperation, or frustration.

"I will. Talk to you later, Abby." Trent disconnected the video call.

CHAPTER 31

OR SIX SOLID WEEKS, COLE followed Trent Dumas, and he was getting seriously worried. This man had even less of a life than he did. Although he apparently had a job which was something Cole didn't have. The man went to work, went home, went to work. That was it. He saw not a single solitary sign of Abby.

Maybe his intuition was wrong. Maybe there wasn't anything going on between them. He had no doubt Abby wasn't in town any more. But he had assumed she was close by, and Trent traveled to see her. Cole's plan had been to follow Trent to locate Abby. He had been certain that was a good plan.

After the first two weeks of following Trent, and little to no sleep, Cole realized once Trent was home in the evening, he never left home again. Why was that? He finally started going home after all the lights went out in Trent's house and returned two hours before he knew Trent left for work in the mornings. Trent's routine never varied. Why was that?

On the weekends, Trent usually did some grocery shopping, and once he took his truck in for an oil change, but other than that, he stayed home all weekend, too. He never went out, never had company.

241

Cole had not seen him in the presence of a female, not once. So by Cole's calculations, either the man was gay, or he had a squeeze hidden somewhere. He couldn't imagine a man not having contact with his woman for six weeks, though.

Admittedly, when he was married to Abby, they went months and sometimes even a year with no sex. The bitch wouldn't let him near her if he was drinking — some past trauma, she said. And he loved throwing that in her face, because it kept her from knowing that when he was drinking his junk didn't work so well. So he made the fact they slept in separate rooms all Abby's fault, and he didn't have to own it. And he never would have admitted it to anyone. But he couldn't imagine a man doing without by choice. No piece of ass was worth that.

Wait a minute, wait a minute! There is only one explanation! How could I not have realized? She must be in the house. That would explain it all. It's not inconceivable she hasn't left home in six weeks. She never left home when she lived with me. It is possible she only leaves when Trent is at work. I have been so busy following him that I haven't been watching the house. I was planning on replacing the watch tonight while he slept, but maybe I'll go there now. I'll have my way with the bitch while he's off working and thinking he will come home to his little woman. MY woman."

Cole went to the house, coming in from the street behind and through the backyards, the same way he did the night he took the pocket watch. He used his lock pick set to get in the back door and looked around. No signs of Abby, no sounds. *She must still be sleeping.* He went straight to the master bedroom, barely glancing around on his way. Having been there before, when he took the watch and photo, he knew right where he was going. No one was there. *Dammit! Where was she?* He began looking around. The closets, the bathrooms, the kitchen. Not a single sign of a female anywhere. *What the hell was going on here?* What if there was nothing going on between the two? His hopes of Trent leading him to Abby would be all but dashed. He had one more play left, and tonight was the night.

Cole arrived at 3:00 a.m. He let himself into Trent's house the same as before. He returned the pocket watch, making sure to place it where he had taken it from, but not the photo. That would give Trent some pause for thought. Maybe he would think he was losing his mind. He sure looked like he was sleeping soundly. Cole decided it was time to go, the mind play from the watch would be enough for now, because maybe he had been wrong about Trent having something going on with Abby.

As he was making his way out of the house, he noticed the two large suitcases by the garage door.

Well, well, well, what is this? Going somewhere, Trent? Today is Friday, and that is a lot more luggage than you took on your business trip. Maybe my luck is about to change. Cole unzipped the smaller carry-on bag and looked inside. There was a laptop, some CDs and in the inner pocket were a passport and a plane ticket. Cole reached for the plane ticket and heard the alarm clock go off. Two hours early. He zipped the bag closed and made a hasty retreat. Cole returned to his car, drove around the block and back to the front of Trent's house to watch. In all of his excitement in his new good fortune, he didn't see the man following him and taking pictures.

Trent left home, two hours early. He was so excited to finally make this trip, that he didn't notice the truck following him. He also knew either Pierce or Amory were still following Cole, so he didn't worry about it much. The truck followed him all the way to the airport and parked in long-term parking, one row over from him. Trent didn't notice the man followed him to check-in, then stepped out of line once Trent got his boarding pass.

"Ecuador? What the hell is in Ecuador? I don't know, but I'm damn well going to find out." Cole thought.

Cole pulled his last hundred-dollar bill out of his pocket and returned hastily to the ticket counter. He explained hurriedly to the ticket clerk that the man who had been in front of him in line had dropped the bill. Would be so kind as to tell him which gate the man was going to so he could return the money. The agent looked at her computer screen, clicked a few buttons, and told Cole the man's flight was departing from gate 4C. He then went to the arrival/departure board and located gate 4C. Departing for Guayaquil, Ecuador. He then pulled out his cell phone, called Virginia Steel, and asked to speak to Trent Dumas. The receptionist told him that Mr. Dumas was on vacation. *So it wasn't a business trip.* Throwing caution to the wind, he returned to the ticket counter and bought a ticket, not for the same flight, but the next one. Praying the credit card wouldn't be declined, he vowed that he, too, was going to Ecuador.

Trent disembarked, navigated through immigration and customs, retrieved his bags, and headed for the airport exit. That is when he saw her. Running hell bent for leather right for him. He dropped his bags barely in time to catch her.

Abby clung to his neck, sprinkling kisses everywhere she could find to kiss. She wore a grin the size of Colorado, and there were tears rolling down her cheeks.

Trent laughed. "Well, I believe that might be the finest greeting I have ever received. Hello, Gorgeous!"

"Bienvenido a Ecuador, Trent!" He wrapped his arm around her shoulder and hailed a porter to move his bags. They exited the airport to a waiting car. Neither of them knew that danger could be on the very next plane.

Pierce followed Cole to the airport. Of course, he knew Trent was flying to Ecuador today. He and Abby had made sure he had email and voice chat contact information for Abby during Trent's visit, as Trent's cell phone wouldn't work while he was Ecuador.

Pierce called his buddy at the police department to tell him of Cole's breaking-and-entering at Trent's house. He had long-range photos documenting Cole's break-in, and he emailed them to his detective friend. Pierce sent Trent an email explaining that he needed to notify the police, email a statement to press charges, and apprise the authorities of his expected return date to the States. Trent sent the email from the airport while waiting for his plane to embark.

Now Pierce was following Cole to keep tabs on him until a warrant for his arrest could be obtained. He followed Cole into the airport and saw the whole series of events unfold. Cole had followed Trent, then gone back and purchased a ticket for himself. He made it all the way to the gate before both the airline and Cole realized he didn't have a passport.

Cole got angry, loud, belligerent, and obnoxious with the counter attendant, who then called security. Security deemed Cole was trying to board an international flight with no passport. Cole tried to explain to them he had forgotten it at home, and his son was bringing it to him at the airport. Security arrested him for drunk and disorderly conduct because of his attitude and the fact he reeked of alcohol.

Once security placed Cole in a hold, Pierce, who had watched it all unfold from a distance, pulled an officer aside and asked him to continue to hold Cole. He explained that the police department was issuing a warrant for Cole's arrest on unrelated charges, and everyone would be appreciative if security could hold the man at the airport until the local authorities could get there. Pierce then called his detective friend and told him of Cole's activities and that security was holding Cole at the airport. The detective told Pierce he was en route and would be there in twenty minutes.

During the detective's drive, Pierce stayed on the phone and explained about the missing girl and the newly placed and removed shed at Cole's former residence. Pierce related to the detective he didn't know anything concrete and had no proof, he just had a gut feeling about the situation. The detective got off the phone with Pierce and called the county sheriff's department and talked to the detective handling the Jenny Grey case. He asked if there had been a shed in the woods on Cole's property; the detective checked the reports and said there was no mention of one. The detective then called for another warrant and to dispatch a team to dig up the grounds at Cole's house.

By the time Abby and Trent arrived in Cuenca, she had a message from Pierce. Cole had been arrested and charged with drunk and disorderly at the airport, breaking-and-entering at Trent's house, and stalking Trent. Pierce's photos were all the officers needed to press the charges. They needed Trent to testify at the trial, but that would be months away, after Trent's return to the States. Also, a judge issued a warrant to dig up the ground under the recently removed shed at Cole's house. If a body were found, there could be murder charges. Pierce said he would keep them updated as the situation progressed and wished them a great vacation. Abby replied to his email, thanked him for the best news they could have hoped to receive, and told him they were going to drink a champagne toast to him and enjoy their vacation.

And they did. The first two weeks of Trent's visit were heaven. They explored each other and a beautiful country. They didn't worry that Cole might now know where Abby was because he was in jail.

Cole was so mad he was seeing red, and nothing was in focus. They told him he was being charged with drunk and disorderly. Then another detective, from the city police department, showed up with a warrant for his arrest for stalking and breaking-and-entering.

What the hell? Where did this come from? What were they talking about, stalking? Breaking-and-entering?

Cole later learned that someone had hired a private investigator to follow him. They had photos of him following Trent, sitting outside the man's office and house, and pictures of him cutting through the backyard and entering the house through the back door, and then coming back out.

Pierce returned to the site of Abby and Cole's former home, and the area where the shed had been. He watched as the sheriff's department began digging. Slowly and carefully, one shovel full of dirt at a time. As the hole opened up bigger and deeper, a deputy who was digging yelled, "I hit something!" The smell of death rose from the ground as everyone stood around the hole. A plastic bag was carefully unearthed. There was an audible collective sigh of relief when the deputy opened the bag and revealed the remains of a dog.

Cole was arraigned on Monday morning, and bail was set at $500,000. His mother hired a good defense attorney for him from Raleigh, or the judge might have denied bail. She posted his bail, but told Cole it was on the condition he seek help for his drinking problem. He agreed, thinking to himself, *Yeah, yeah, yeah. Whatever. She will return home and won't know what I'm doing.*

CHAPTER 32

ABBY AND TRENT WERE HAVING the time of their lives. Abby was having as much fun showing Trent around her new home as he was exploring his first foreign country. He couldn't have imagined anything sweeter than finally getting to share in this adventure with her. Even though she had told him so much about her new city, he still was surprised at how beautiful it was, and how modern. It didn't feel anything at all like he envisioned a developing country, and he kept wondering why it was even designated as such.

All the things he had thought would be true about Abby were true. They had fun, the relationship was more solidified, the private moments were sweet, and she had made good on her promise to cook for him. She remembered all the things he did and didn't like, and it warmed his heart, every meal she cooked for him. He knew she poured all her love into making everything special and catered to his likes.

While exploring an artisan market one day, they came upon a booth filled with hummingbirds. Abby loved hummingbirds so they had to stop and look at all the wonderful crafts. The lady in the booth spoke English, and they struck up a conversation. She learned her

English in the U.S., where she lived for five years. Abby told her how much she loved her hummingbird crafts, and that she always had loved the sweet little birds. She told the vendor that since arriving in Ecuador, the birds had taken on a new meaning for her. They even appeared in her dreams.

The lady took a special interest, invited Abby and Trent into the booth, and offered them a seat. She said, "I would love to tell you about the hummingbirds, the little colibri, and why they are appearing in your dreams."

Abby understood the importance of dreams and spirit animals as she had a Native American friend when Kendall was small, who identified the wolf as Kendall's spirit brother. Kendall still loved wolves to this day, and through the years, she and her son read all about wolves and spirit animals. Abby never considered she might have a spirit animal or token, too.

The lady, Rocia, explained the hummingbird represented joy and peace. But the hummingbird's life wasn't easy, yet it was a strong and resilient bird, created to overcome many obstacles in life with grace and beauty. Therefore, the bird represented energy, vitality, renewal, sincerity, healing, persistence, peace, infinity, agility, playfulness, loyalty, and affection.

Abby and Trent both looked at Rocia, astounded. Abby was speechless. Trent said to both women, "Yep, that sounds like our Abby here. She's traveled a great distance, conquering physical and emotional challenges."

Abby had tears in her eyes and still couldn't speak. So much made sense to her now.

Rocia went behind the counter and returned with a beautiful hummingbird. She told Abby it was made from reclaimed copper, and she herself had hand-painted it. It was the most beautiful thing Abby had ever seen. Rocia handed the life-sized replica of the dainty little bird to Abby and told her, "Abby, always look to the hummingbird. He's your spirit totem and will always show you the way. I believe, like your man here says, you are indeed a hummingbird. I see the light in your eye, and I sense you've indeed traveled a long distance and experienced a world of healing. Always follow what the bird tells you. He will never lead you astray. And Abby, you are every bit as beautiful as the hummingbird. Let your step be light, for you float on his wings. You will triumph. It is said, on cold nights, the hummingbird dies, but when the morning sun comes, and the bird warms up, he comes back to life. I expect you've been resurrected as the hummingbird is after a cold night; you're coming back to life. Welcome to Ecuador. Go in peace."

Abby was so emotional; she was quiet for hours. Trent gave her the time. They walked, hand-in-hand, which comforted her, and she worked through all she had been told. Trent knew something momentous was happening to his lady, the one he had always called his *little bird*. He felt her healing as they walked, and was so thankful to Rocia and to the hummingbird for helping him see this transformation. Abby would be whole again. Trent knew that, now, no one would ever again be able to crush and diminish her. They walked for hours through the town and along the lush bank of the Yanuncay River. It was a beautiful, peaceful place. Suddenly, Abby looked at him, her eyes wide, and she said, "I am a hummingbird."

Trent replied tenderly, "Yes, Sweetness, you are. You're my little hummingbird, and I hope you always will be."

Abby smiled, the most peaceful, joyful smile he thought he had ever seen, and replied, "I will always be your hummingbird. You helped me release my inner hummingbird, and I'll always be grateful for you. We will soar together, and heaven help anyone who tries to knock us down."

They hugged and kissed, right there by the river, and they each knew their lives and their relationship had somehow changed. And they were happy.

~

When they returned home that evening, there was an email from Pierce. It was bad news. Pierce messaged them after Cole had been arraigned and told them all the details and about the judge granting his bail. He also told them that when the police dug up the site at Cole's house, they found the remains of a dog, so there would be no murder charges. Abby and Trent knew when Trent returned, he would have to deal with Cole, who was free on bond. But today's message sent a chill through them both. It simply read, "I hate to be the bearer of bad news, but Cole has disappeared. He's jumped bond, and the bounty hunters are looking for him. Amory and I are, too, and we will not rest until we find him. Be safe."

Trent's first fear was for Abby. Cole had followed him to the airport and tried to follow him to Ecuador. Of course, Abby's first panic was for Trent.

Trent looked at Abby, who looked stronger than ever, and asked her, "Baby Doll, I know you love it here, and I love it here, too. But do you think you need to move again? Could you move again?"

"Yes, I could. I know now that I can do anything. But I'm not worried. The man has no job and is now a wanted man. The chance of him being able to board a plane is slim to none. I happen to know his passport expired years ago, and under the current situation, I don't think he would be able to get out of the country. The only place he could get the money to come here is from his mom. Since he's jumped bail on her $500,000 investment, she won't be lending him the money to flee the country. My concern is for you. He knows where you live, where you work, and now he suspects you're someone important to me, with access to me. He will come for you."

Trent looked deep into her eyes and tried to relay all the love he was feeling. "Remember when I told you I would take care of me because you are so important to me? I sent an email last week resigning from my job. My mom is in Greenville now overseeing and packing up my house. I was renting anyway and have given my notice. I am moving to Miami, so traveling to see each other will be easier, until we decide if you're coming back to the States or I am moving here. Abby, what this trip has told me is I never want to live a day without you in my life. The Internet and the phone were fine while we got to this point, and it will tide us over again until we can be together, but it isn't nearly enough."

Abby looked at him in disbelief. "Trent, what will you do? And Miami is so far from your kids."

"There is another steel company that has been trying to get me to go to work for them for a couple of years. They have an office in Miami. I didn't take the job before because it was so far from my family, and Suzy didn't want any part of Florida. Now it is a bridge to where I want to be. The good news is that it pays a lot more, and maybe I eventually can move here with the investment capital I need and with enough put away to start a business. If you'll have me, and you want to stay here, we will make it happen. Can you give me some time to get it done?"

"Of course I will, but I also want you to realize that I know how important your kids are, and I am willing and would be happy to come back to the States with you. I know now as much as I love this place and my life here, home is wherever you are."

"Okay, that's settled, for now. Let's get on the phone and tell your family that Cole is out there somewhere, and they all need to be careful. Abby, don't worry; we'll see that man caught. This time, when he is, they'll lock him up and throw away the key. Then, we are going to buy some of that high-dollar champagne you're so fond of, and celebrate our new life."

And they did.

Click here to continue reading the next book in the *Shattered Survival Thriller Series: **Shattered Chance***

A NOTE FROM SCARLETT

First, I'd like to thank you for reading the Shattered Survival series. It's always an honor when someone spends their limited time reading an author's words.

This series is the one that will always be the dearest to me no matter how many I write. Not only was it my first as an author, but the characters are very real to me. Each character in the series, I've known personally. And what they all have in common is that they are strong. Vulnerable because they are good and caring people who have been thrust into horrible situations and through their strength and willingness to accept help, they triumph. Despite all of the emotionally and physically challenging situations they encounter, they are survivors. They are richer for their tragedies and they are prepared through their experiences to help the next person in need. And in the end, they find a place to feel safe, loved, and accepted for who they are. They find happiness again. In this series, it just happens to be my beloved Ecuador. In reality, in can be any place.

It has been my personal experience, that those of us who have endured the worst are the most willing to help the next person faced with unimaginable challenges and obstacles. I hope if you ever find yourself in need that there is someone there who can help you through, and that then you are able to help someone else. There is no greater gift and no greater feeling.

Click here to continue reading the next book in the *Shattered Survival Thriller Series: **Shattered Chance***

Or turn the page for an excerpt from **Shattered Chance.**

SHATTERED CHANCE

*L*ILY GRACE CAMPANEL DISAPPEARED three weeks ago. She was an International Business major at Tulane University and the daughter of New Orleans Mayor, Philippe Campanel, and Sarah Frances Newsome.

Lily Grace was more than just the mayor's daughter. She grew up the Princess of New Orleans, in the spotlight as the daughter of a New Orleans power couple, even before her father became the Mayor. Lily Grace captured the love of her city as a beautiful and precocious child who loved the attention of the spotlight as much as the camera loved her. Her photo was a mainstay in the New Orleans society pages, and a montage included photos from dance recitals, piano recitals, theater performances and cheerleading. Since the age of three, she was frequently photographed in the most popular Jazz clubs, sitting on the piano bench and singing along with the best blues musicians New Orleans had to offer. On fall Sunday afternoons she would be on the sidelines dressed in a miniature Saints cheerleader uniform loudly supporting her favorite NFL team. She served as an honorary water girl for the team in her teens. As she grew from teenager to young adult, her childhood antics gave way to a lovely southern grace and she became New Orleans' favorite co-ed. Her disappearance stunned the entire city.

As sometimes happens in the best families to the young adults with the most promising futures, when she went to college, her brave, adventurous personality led her to try drugs. Then Lily Grace became tangled up with a drug dealer and eventually found herself owing him money, lots of money. She didn't want to involve and disappoint her parents with her uncharacteristic failure. In order to settle her debt, Rafael, her dealer forced Lily Grace to recruit some of her college friends to buy from him. When Lily Grace's friends found themselves owing money, Rafael forced them into prostitution to cover their debts. At least until the time of her disappearance, Lily Grace had escaped that particular torment.

After three weeks of captivity, Lily Grace saw her opportunity to get away from her abductors and she ran. For the first time since her abduction, she found herself left alone in the house. She fled and checked the car parked in the driveway to see if the keys might be inside. No keys, but she saw her backpack and grabbed it as she ran away. She ran as fast as she could while looking over her shoulder to see if anyone followed her. All the muscles in her body screamed and burned in pain, as she ran into an empty building, under renovations. At 3:30 on a balmy, bright, November afternoon in New Orleans, construction crews finished for the day, the site sat quietly. The building had no windows or doors, and there were few rooms, but it provided shelter nonetheless — a place to hide, catch her breath and call for help.

Lily Grace sank to the unfinished concrete floor, closed her eyes and focused on her breathing. Once she caught her breath, she checked the contents of her backpack. She only hoped her belongings were still inside. She unzipped the middle hidden compartment and found her cell phone where she always kept it. The cell phone was off. She prayed it still held a charge and pushed the power button. The screen miraculously came alive. Immediately, she dialed her mother's cell number. Her call went directly to voicemail and she left a frantic message telling her mother her location and to please come as soon as possible. She then dialed her father, who answered.

At that precise moment, Philippe Campanel, in his home office, questioned the detective assigned to Lily Grace's disappearance. He asked Detective LeBlanc how it was possible for no one to see one of the city's most recognizable people in three weeks? Who took her and why? What did they want? When he reached to answer his phone, the father was at once, suspicious, terrified and relieved to see his daughter's number on the caller ID.

"Hello, Peanut! Is that you?"

"Daddy, Daddy! Yes, it's me. Help me, I need help!"

"Where are you? I'm on my way!"

"I'm in a building under renovation on Paris Road, between Virtue Street and Law Street. There's a sign out front, it says NOLA Commercial Contractors. Please, Daddy, hurry, I don't know how much time I have."

"Stay on the line with me Peanut, I'm on my way!"

"My battery's low. I don't know how long it'll last."

"It's okay, Peanut, I'll be there in a few minutes. Is the phone's GPS locator turned on? I'm with a detective and he can track your GPS so we can find you faster. If the battery gets too low we'll disconnect, but I want to stay on the line with you. Are you okay? Are you hurt?"

"No Daddy, I'm okay. Please, please hurry!"

Michel Leblanc drove like a madman while Philippe Campanel talked to his daughter. As the Mayor of New Orleans, Philippe's primary goal was to eradicate the NOPD of corruption. He knew when his daughter disappeared, getting help from the organization he was systematically gutting, would be a challenge. Over the last three weeks, Leblanc seemed to always be one step behind whoever had Lily Grace. There were no ransom demands, no contact whatsoever from her captives, which frustrated Philippe and Sarah Frances. Even though Sarah Frances and Philippe had divorced two years ago, their daughter's disappearance forced them to work together again. Philippe thought to ask Lily Grace if she had contacted her mother yet, and she told him she had tried, the call went to voicemail and she left a message. Philippe knew they needed to contact Sarah Frances as soon as he reached Lily Grace, but at the moment, he didn't want to break the connection. They were almost there.

Leblanc pulled behind the building and Philippe jumped from the still moving car and yelled, "Peanut!" He didn't hear the gun cock, but he did hear the blast just before his vision went black, he slammed to the ground and his existence in the world came to an end. Lily Grace heard the gunshot, screamed and ran in the opposite direction. Looking over her shoulder, she recognized the man chasing her. But her father said he was with a detective. Where was the cop? In the end, however, she wasn't fast enough to get away from Leblanc. She screamed, kicked and head-butted him, trying to get away. She was too weak and tired from her long run to resist the much larger and stronger detective. He punched her hard across the face and she passed out. Once recaptured, Leblanc covered Lily Grace's mouth with duct tape, bound her wrists behind her with flex cuffs, and then did the same with her ankles. He lifted her slight frame effortlessly, put her in the trunk of his car, and quickly left the scene.

As Sarah Frances neared the location Lily Grace gave in her message, she tried to call her daughter's phone again, but it went straight to voicemail. She pulled into the site's parking lot, jumped out of her car, and ran into the building, where she found Lily Grace's backpack and phone. The phone lay in the middle of the floor, silent, dead. *How could this be? What the hell happened?* She called out to Lily Grace. Then she saw the dead form of her ex-husband. She screamed, reached for her phone and frantically dialed 911.

Sarah Frances waited only three minutes for squad cars to surround the site, following her call reporting the murder of the Mayor. As she relayed the events as she knew them, to the first officer on the scene, a detective approached and introduced himself as Jules

Pena. Pena was a tall, black man, handsome, and smooth. He was built like a former football player and spoke in a calming voice. He spoke slowly to Sarah Frances and she relaxed a bit, enough to relay the story of Lily Grace's message and what she discovered when she arrived.

The coroner arrived and Pena asked Sarah Frances if she could go with him to the station. They would be out of the way of the investigation while he recorded all the facts on paper.

"No, I can't go to the station; I have to find my daughter! She's disappeared again, and whoever took her may kill her, too."

"Okay, please come to the ambulance for them to check you out, and let's get you a bottle of water. There are squad cars out all over the area looking for Lily Grace."

When she realized she didn't have the first idea where to look or what to look for to find her daughter she agreed to go to the station.

Sarah Frances sat in an interview room for two hours. She tried to leave through the door. It was locked. She frantically looked for a window from which to escape, but there wasn't one. Finally, she screamed and pounded on the door until her fist bruised. Her throat was dry and her voice hoarse. She didn't understand the locked door. She had voluntarily come in to give a statement as a witness, not because she had committed any crime. Finally, Pena arrived with a cup of coffee and a sandwich for her. She looked at him as if she thought he must be crazy. *How could anyone eat at a time like this?*

"Why am I locked in this room like a criminal? I have to find my daughter! I can't eat, my daughter is gone, her father is dead. Why am I here, why are you here? You should be looking for whoever killed my ex-husband and maybe my daughter too!"

"Mrs. Campanel, please calm down. We are investigating and I promise every available officer in the city is working this case. I need to get some information from you for our reports. Would you mind if I looked at your phone, and listened to the message from Lily Grace?"

"My name is Newsome now. The Mayor and I are divorced, and yes, of course, you can listen to the message."

Calmer now, believing action was finally underway, Sarah Frances agreed to let the detective take her phone to the lab where he said they could enhance the call and try to get more information from it. When he returned an hour later, he found Sarah Frances frantic again, but near exhaustion, and not as feisty as earlier.

The detective ignored her frantic pleas to let her go and sat down.

"Ms. Newsome, we listened to the call from Lily Grace and we believe, she's indeed the one who left the message. According to the GPS history on both your vehicle and your phone, it appears you arrived on the scene almost an hour after the murder. We believe the time of the mayor's death is recorded on his broken watch. The watch stopped at the same time the phone call between the mayor and your daughter's phone concluded. However, we won't know for sure until we have the autopsy results. According to the Mayor's cell phone carrier, a call occurred between the mayor and your daughter for thirty-five minutes. The chief called in Detective LeBlanc since he's handling Lily Grace's disappearance. So far our investigation is leading us to wonder if Lily Grace may have lured her father to the site to kill him."

"What?! What are you talking about? There's no way Lily Grace is capable of murder. She's the ultimate daddy's girl. She wouldn't have done anything to harm him! Anyway, where would she even get a gun?" Sarah Frances felt like she was spinning on a tilt-a-whirl headed for a rabbit hole. She found the current events unbelievable and, even more so, the current discussion. *What's wrong with these people?* she wondered.

"We're still working the case. It's the early hours of investigation. What we can't explain is that there's no car at the scene. So it looks as if the Mayor drove there and someone drove away in his car. Officers are on the way to his home. If the mayor's car is there, then there will be further investigation into what might have happened, how and when."

"Well, of course, his car will be gone! How else would he have gone to her? I'm sure she called him when she didn't get me and he would've gone immediately to help her. Whoever took Lily Grace, took his car, but I assure you it wasn't my daughter. She didn't and couldn't have done this."

"Ms. Newsome, how long have you and the mayor been divorced?

"Our divorce was finally two years ago. Why do you ask?"

"Would you call your relationship amicable?"

"Well, detective, it's not common for two people who get along well to divorce. If you're asking if it was a nasty divorce, no, it wasn't. It was a mutual parting of the ways. No scorned party, no one seeking revenge."

"How did Lily Grace cope with the divorce?"

"Probably like most kids her age. She was close to us both, she was welcome in each of our homes and her father and I will both be there for the important moments in her life. She was eighteen; there was no fierce custody battle. She was going to college, she still had both her parents, it didn't affect her as much as it would a young child, and she seemed to be coping fine with it."

"Leave me your contact information, and you're free to go. Don't leave town."

"Where in the hell do you think I would go? I have to plan a funeral and try to find my daughter! I can't bury her father until we find her!"

"Yes ma'am, I'll have an officer take you back to your car. I assure you we're doing everything in our power to find your daughter and catch your husband's, umm the Mayor's killer."

Jules Pena wouldn't have been a red-blooded male if he didn't notice the beauty of the lady seated in front of him. Despite the chaos going on in her life, her face was perfect with its flawless ivory complexion, high cheekbones, deep pink lips, and strong angular chin. Her hair reminded him of a deep sable mink coat, long, smooth, sleek and shiny and matching eyes the color of strong molasses. Dressed in a watermelon sherbet pink tailored suit, an ivory silk blouse underneath and sensible ivory pumps, she was refreshing to look at. Though the suffering soulful eyes at this point in time threatened to shoot daggers at anyone in her way.

In the backseat of the squad car driving her back to her car, she pulled out her phone and pushed the speed dial number for her best friend.

"Damn, Sarah Frances are you okay? What happened? Philippe's murder is all over the news."

"I'm okay and on my way home, can you meet me at my house?"

"I'll be there in ten minutes."

"Thank you, I'm not ready to be alone yet and I have to figure out what to do next and where to go. I need your help."

"I'm your girl, and on my way."

Click here to continue reading the next book in the *Shattered Survival Thriller Series: **Shattered Chance***

ABOUT THE AUTHOR

S.J. BRADEN:

S.J. Braden is often asked if her thrillers are autobiographical. Scarlett considers this the ultimate compliment for a fiction author and usually replies, "Of course, some is autobiographical. We write what we know. And the rest is fiction." She invites you to read her stories and make up your own mind about what's real and what's fiction and to hang out with her in her Facebook readers group called Scarlett's Cozy Couch. Scarlett writes thrillers as S.J. Braden, cozy mysteries as Scarlett Moss, and poetry as Scarlett Braden.

Made in the USA
Monee, IL
23 November 2020

49090692R00157